Katharina Luther
Nun. Rebel. Wife.

Anne Boileau

Clink
Street

London | New York

Published by Clink Street Publishing 2016

Copyright © 2016

First edition.

ISBNs:
978-1-911110-61-3 paperback
978-1-911110-62-0 ebook

For Blake, Nell and Margot

Foreword

It has always struck me as astonishing that the tremendous transition from medievalism to modernism continues in Britain to revolve around the drama of a royal divorce. When Martin Luther, an intellectual monk, threw a stone into the stagnating waters of the Christianity of his day, it would have been impossible to imagine that the ripples of his action would still be flowing in our time. But they are. The Reformation was not a one-off event but a spiritual and social current which goes on disturbing the Church.

Who was Martin Luther, the scholarly though at first unprepossessing German religious who was to shake the Church and Europe to their foundations? There are countless histories to give an answer, but as in many other cases it takes an imaginative storyteller to actually reveal the man – or woman – behind some world-changing event. By choosing to reveal Luther during his courtship and marriage, fatherhood and broken vows, or rather the different vows which setting up house with Katharina required, Anne Boileau shows us the profoundly human basis of the reformed faith. She brings the aristocratic young nun and the learned early middle-aged monk together in a way which is both intimate and 'public' in the sense that, in spite of the popular anti-monastic feeling which was sweeping Europe, made marriage between a monk and a nun a sensational, even scandalous happening. And Martin and Katharina themselves had to discover the thing which each of them had been trained to live without, their sexuality.

Anne Boileau describes the Luther courtship and marriage with a delightful freshness. Here are two people in a small country town as the rulers of the world begin to take sides in the Catholic–Protestant debate. From now on Luther will be loathed or venerated. Meanwhile, and beautifully described by Anne Boileau, who is an excellent naturalist, the sixteenth century German countryside provides an enchanting reality of its own. *Katharina Luther. Nun. Rebel. Wife.* is a fine historical novel which extends our narrow view of the Reformation.

Ronald Blythe

Chapter 1
My Book

*Wo ein melancholischer Kopf ist, da ist
dem Teufel das Bad zugerichtet.*

A head filled with melancholy is like a
bathtub prepared for the devil.

Something hit me on the cheek and fell to the ground at my feet. It was a goose's foot. Someone must have thrown it from the poulterers' stall, but the women were busy plucking geese and talking amongst themselves, and seemed quite unaware of me. I was in my seventh month and beginning to feel heavy. I could deny it no longer: they were talking about me and their hostility was palpable. I knew what they were saying: "That renegade nun, she's no good. She broke her own vows and has made him break his too. A nun and a monk, marrying! It's immoral, a crime against God, a union forged in hell. Any fruit of such a union will be evil, a monster, something unnatural!"

These and other such insults were flying about the streets of Wittenberg in conversations, and spreading up and down the Elbe in pamphlets vilifying me and my marriage to Dr Martin Luther. When we first got married most of the town seemed to be in favour of our union, welcoming our marriage and cheering us as we walked to the church, applauding us when we danced with them in the evening. But the atmosphere has changed. People are jumpy, superstitious, worried, looking around for a scapegoat. Other towns have their witch hunts and vendettas, so

3

why should Wittenberg be immune from such things? But I find it hurtful, that they should turn against me; and it was me, not him, they were blaming. Simply being a woman is enough to incur their wrath, it seems. Men are drawn to women, aroused by them; but they hate them too, and despise them. But why? Are not half of our kind women? Do not all men spring from women, and as baby boys feed at their mothers' breasts? Even our Lord was not too proud to be born of woman, and Mary, the Mother of God, is universally loved and revered. Though perhaps not so much now. No, in some ways, the Blessed Virgin has been dethroned. Is that what's gone wrong?

I could bear it no longer, and made my way home along Castle Street, stumbling, and praying incoherently to the Blessed Virgin. My vision was blurred and my mouth dry. The sensation of the clammy goose's foot was still cold against my cheek. My child was kicking within me and for the first time I felt a surge of revulsion; perhaps they were right? Was it a sin, a monk and a nun, both breaking their vows? Perhaps my child is a little monster growing within me, with a tail, or scales, or what else. It might be furry, like a rat. A neighbour of the Luthers in Eisenach, when Martin was small, gave birth to a dormouse after being frightened by one in her flour bin while heavily pregnant!

I longed to return to the security and anonymity of my life in the convent. Or to my time with the Cranachs, when I was just one of the fugitive nuns, of no great import; I could go about my business without anyone taking any notice. But when I married Martin I became famous, like him; many people respected me because they knew and liked us both; but others were afraid of me, even hostile, and no longer honest. So on that Friday morning in April I felt all the doors closing upon me. I felt trapped from without by hostility and malevolence, and from within by the child growing in my belly, a child which some say is an evil thing, the Antichrist as foretold in Revelation.

Somehow I reached the Cloister gate and holding my

shopping basket against my belly I pushed open the old studded portal with my shoulder and stepped through into the darkness of the porch. Some fool, probably the goat boy Joachim, had left a wooden bucket lying in my path. Blinded by tears and the shade after the bright sunshine outside, I stumbled against it, tripped and fell to the ground. Winded and frightened, I lay on the cobbles unable to move. Was my baby hurt? Gasping for breath, I pressed my cheek against the cool stones – cabbages, fish, onions and bread lay strewn about me, and a flagon of vinegar was smashed, its acid smell and stain spreading into my sleeve. I'll just lie here, I thought, until someone comes to help me.

Tölpel the dog found me, prostrate and gasping like a netted carp. Then they all came, fussing round, Tante Lena, Dorothea, Agnes. With their sympathy and gentle hands, helping me up, dusting me down, their arms round my shoulders, my strength and pride dissolved; I broke down in wracking sobs, miserable, anxious and exhausted.

Martin was out that day, but as soon as he returned he came up to our room.

"You must stay here, dearest. Stay quiet and away from noise and commotion. You mustn't be scared or the child will be fearful too. I will not have you exposed to the calumny of those foolish, cruel people. Our baby's safety and health, your health, is too important."

I was settled in our big four-poster with the blue damask drapes and red borders, washed and brushed in my linen nightgown, my long hair loose and the pillows plumped up. It was late afternoon, and the sun was slanting in through the window. Martin sat down on the bed and touched my cheek with the back of his hand. He stroked my hair back behind my ear as if I were a child. Then he took my hand in his, and kissed it. He turned it over, and traced his forefinger along my lifeline, as if seeing it for the first time.

"It's all because of Eve."

"What's because of Eve?"

"Your pain and travail. The trouble you women have with child bearing. It's a punishment for Eve's transgressions. She took the fruit. She persuaded Adam to eat of it. It was her fault. Genesis 3 verses 16 to 22. *To the woman he said, 'I will greatly increase your pangs in childbearing; in pain you shall bring forth children, yet your desire shall be for your husband and he shall rule over you.'*"

I closed my eyes and said nothing.

"Before the Fall from Grace," he went on, stroking the soft skin of my wrist and lower arm, "women bore children with no pain, no trouble. Then Adam and Eve were cast out of the garden and life became more difficult. You women have to atone for Eve's sins. That is why I want you to stay here safe within the walls of the Cloister with plenty of rest, until our child is born. Get up late, have a long rest after lunch. Sleep. You should not go out and see ugly things or be frightened and insulted as you were today. You must keep quiet and safe, and see only those people who wish us well, our real friends."

"But what about the house, the dairy? Who will brew and manage the kitchen and the vegetable garden and make sure everything runs smoothly?"

"Your Aunt Lena is here. She knows what to do. Dorothea can manage the kitchen, and the brewing can be left to other women in the town. Stay here, my dearest. Don't worry about the household, we'll get by. You can tell us what needs doing, and keep an eye on things from up here. The captain on the bridge. Look after our baby. Forget the cruel things those people were saying. They are ignorant and foolish. Pray, rest, read and reflect. I shall visit you often, and join you every night when my work is done."

So that is why for the last three weeks I have been confined to the Cloister, in fact much of the time in my bedroom, only leaving it for necessary ablutions and short walks up and down the corridor. Never in my entire life have I been so idle, with nothing to do but pray, do a little stitch work and mending; I sleep, read and talk with friends when they visit me. So I have decided to put my time to good use; I will set down the story of my life; I may never have such a quiet time again. If I should die in childbirth then I shall leave something behind, and my child can read all about me, about his mother.

I slept and dozed for two days after my fall. Then I asked Martin to get me some paper and ink. He did more than that. He went round to the Cranachs and told Lucas and Barbara about my fall, and how he wanted me to stay in my room; and that I wanted to write down my own story. Lucas had the men in the print shop prepare and stitch a book of the finest Italian paper. Barbara had it bound in the best calfskin. It was ready three days later and Martin brought it up to me with a supply of swans' quills and a pot of best brown ink and a sand strewer. He also brought me loose sheets for letters.

Every morning I sit in bed, propped up on feather pillows and write; then after my afternoon rest I get dressed and sit at the desk by the window overlooking the garden and read, or do more writing. From the east window I watch the hens scratching in the courtyard and the washing flapping gently on the line.

Tante Lena brings me my breakfast.

"How are the goats? The hens? What about the beehives?"

"Don't worry," she says. "The goats are fine, the new kids are doing well; the hens are laying, we've got a surplus of eggs, so we're selling some in the market. The piglets are growing as you watch. The blacksmith's wife has come in to deal with the bees. As for the beer, enough other women in town are brewing, we can buy it from them. Look after your child. The Lord knows, you'll have enough to do once he's born and you're up and about again."

Dorothea comes in every morning to consult me about meals for the following day. She goes to market twice a week, and tells me how many mouths we have to feed, about the state of the larder; food supplies are unreliable, so if she sees a good bargain she pounces on it, and I trust her.

Solitude settles around me. Quietness. I sleep. And wake.

And sleep again. How tired I have been and did not realise it. Little by little my exhaustion melts away, I sit up propped against the pillows and take my calfskin book and open it at the first page.

In finest copperplate is written:

"To my darling wife Käthchen. For her story. M.L."

As I sit in my room now on my own, with no-one to talk to but myself, I begin to relish the silence. It is a vibrant silence: a kid goat bleats; a horse walks through the stable yard; a cockerel crows; the creak, creak, creak, followed by sloshing water as someone fills a pail at the pump in the yard.

Yesterday, for the first time, I heard a nightingale sing. I think of Martin, and his nickname 'The Nightingale of Wittenberg'. When he was a little boy in Eisenach, he sang in the church choir and he and his friends used to sing folk songs in the streets for pennies. Here in my room I am in a pool of quietness; it's soothing, and at the same time strengthening.

Before I married Martin and came to know him better, I took him for a giant, a rock, a fortress as impregnable as the mighty Wartburg which points a fist at the sky above the town of Eisenach. To me, as to the wider world, he was a man with the courage to defy the Church of Rome, to hold his ground at the courts of Augsburg and Worms, to state: "Here I stand, I can do no other. God help me. Amen." He was the man who pinned up the Ninety-Five Theses, spelling out one by one what was rotten in the state of the church; the theses were printed and broadcast and he became famous because of them. This was the man who wrote hymns, both words and music, which caught on as popular songs sung by urchins in the streets of cities hundreds of miles away. He was a man who, having taken on a task, would work with such concentration, diligence and speed that the printers and publishers could hardly keep up with his output. A man who could hold a crowd silent and spell-bound as he spoke, and whose books and pamphlets were sold out within days of publication.

But his strength, his impregnability, his defiance and

fearlessness are a veneer only. Inside he is vulnerable, afraid, a little boy who longs for the approval of his father and of his God. He retreats to his study and works with such concentration you can almost touch the energy in the air, hear his brain ticking like a clock's movement, as he deliberates, researches, refers, cross refers, reads, thinks, writes. It is my task to make sure he can apply himself to his work unhindered while I run the household and keep him feeling safe, reassured, and well. But for the moment, he is looking after me.

My belly is growing large and the baby is lively. It's hard to sleep with the extra weight and bulk; I've discovered a goose down pillow between my thighs makes lying on my side more comfortable. Martin is fascinated by the changes in me: he strokes my swollen stomach, and lays his ear to it in the hope of hearing his son's heartbeat. He thinks it is a boy, and I hope for his sake it is. My body seems hardly to be my own. My gums are sore and bleed a bit when I clean my teeth; the physician pulled out one of my molars. But my hair is lustrous; my breasts are larger and patterned with blue veins; my nipples have grown and are deliciously sensitive; so at night, instead of the carnal act, my husband strokes my breasts with love and tenderness and I want to purr like a contented cat. I feel at ease with myself and cannot believe that the new life growing and kicking inside me is anything other than a normal healthy baby. I anticipate my confinement with a mixture of excitement and fear. Meanwhile, I have time on my hands and blank paper to fill.

The freshly cut quill squeaks and scratches on the paper. I begin to write my story.

Chapter 2
Childhood at Lippendorf

*Man muss bisweilen durch die Finger sehen; hören
und nicht hören, sehen und nicht sehen.*

From time to time you should watch the world through
your fingers; hear and not hear, see and not see.

"Not just fleas, Greta. Head lice too!"

There must have been a wedding, but I don't remember it. I remember the screams as the three of us had our heads shaved in the courtyard, our gasps as Greta soaped us from top to toe and sloshed buckets of rain water over us. Our pale, bald heads. Then, after the water the fire.

"Bedbugs, Greta! Open the windows, throw out the bedding, we'll burn it all."

Horse hair mattresses, blankets, pillows, quilts, bedspreads, tumbling out of windows, women dragging them across the yard, hoisting them onto the flames; the fire growing in heat and fury as it was fed. The stink of burning horsehair and wool; black smoke in writhing billows, bedbugs popping.

I recall the discomfort of new, ill-fitting clothes. A sense of loss and dread as strong and heavy in my stomach as I had felt a year earlier when our mother died.

Stepmother fumigated all the rooms with baldrian.

"The whole house is infested, Greta!" She was a small woman with dark, darting eyes and quick movements and I was scared of her. Cook hated her, and so did Hildegard, our nurse, but they dared not protest. The first time I heard Cook and Stepmother arguing in the kitchen I thought, 'Oh please God, don't let Cook go away, I couldn't bear it.' And being surprised at myself, because Cook was always so gruff towards us, not warm as my mother had been, but I realised how much I loved her.

"If you can't do something useful get out of my kitchen," she would growl. So I would sit up at the table and do whatever task she gave me. I might scrub the rusty knives with a cork and sand, or shell peas or scrape scales off a fish for her. Then she would talk.

"You should have seen the banquets they used to have when I was your age, Käthchen. Minstrels in the gallery. Candles on the long tables. And so many grand guests, the great hall lit up with torches."

"Who were the guests?"

"Oh, the gentry from round about. The von Schlippenbachs, the von Bettelheims, the family from Gimborn Castle; the other von Boras, your cousins from across the valley. They rolled up in their coaches, the horses would be led off into the barn then the coachmen came into the back hall for soup, they'd spend the evening sat by the fire gossiping. No shortage of food then, you know, my parents worked in the kitchen for three days non-stop preparing; I remember once they did a roast swan wrapped in its own wings, its head and neck put back on, it looked so beautiful, the guests all clapped when it was brought to the table. Then they did a carp this big decorated with cherries on a bed of lampreys in aspic. A suckling pig glazed in honey. You wouldn't believe the banqueting table, how fine it looked, all the best silver, before they had to sell it, that was."

Stepmother wanted Cook and Elsa to leave, she said she had her own servants and they were 'surplus to requirements'. But this was one thing on which my Father stood firm.

"No, dear, Cook and Hildegard belong in this house and they will stay, they're part of our family." So stay they did.

Stepmother was a rich widow. She saved us from penury, whatever that meant. She brought with her a carriage and pair and a good draught horse. She had three brindle cows too, one of them with a calf at foot. With her came Greta her maid and a gardener-cum-coachman; they all turned up one fateful morning with a wagon full of furniture and drapes and boxes of china and pictures and things. My Father's new wife, Margarethe von Bora,, set about putting our house in order.

My mother, Katharina von Bora, had died a year before at Whitsun; it happened very quickly; one afternoon – we had been out hoeing the beet and spinach – she said she felt unwell and took to her bed. Father sent for the physician; I saw him as he came out of her room, looking grave. She lay in a white nightgown, propped up on pillows, her face pale, her voice quiet, her hand small and limp on the sheets. A week later she was dead.

We had scarcely buried her when the cattle began to die; it was the Pest. So in my child's mind the two disasters ran one into the other as if they were connected. One by one our poor cows and oxen collapsed onto their knees, keeled over onto their sides and died with horrible groans. It wasn't just our own cattle, all the beasts in the village and beyond succumbed. The corpses lay in the fields, their legs sticking out stiffly, their eyes and mouths open, their tongues swollen and black. Very soon, the stomachs swelled up and the stench was overpowering. Some of the poor people managed to salvage bits of meat which they salted and cured, but most of it went to ruin, the cadavers were left to rot in the fields; crows and birds of prey circled overhead, dropped down and tugged at the flesh; at night we heard the howling of lynx and wolves and foxes as they prowled among the corpses tearing out the entrails, squabbling over the spoils. That summer the flies were everywhere, they clustered in glistening blankets, settling on all our meagre food, torturing the horses and dogs. Of course after the Pest we had no milk or butter or junket or cheese and the price of meat shot up. The poor were reduced to eating beavers and moles.

We went to church and prayed very hard, because God must be angry with us, sending down so much difficulty and sorrow.

"I'm going to have to sell the house, Kathe. We can't afford to stay here."

"Where will we go?"

"I don't know. Lippendorf has been in our family for hundreds of years. Now it falls on me to let it go."

"It's not your fault, Father. It's just the way things are."

"You're a good girl, Kathe. Where would I be without you?"

He was fond of Irmingard and the baby too, but it was me he came to for advice or encouragement. I was older and I realise now I looked like my mother. I reminded him of his beloved wife.

So my Father set about trying to sell the family seat. But who wanted a crumbling fortified manor house with dusty attics and a silted up moat? The roof was full of holes and only twenty acres of land remained, my grandfather having sold the rest thirty years before. In the end we were saved from losing Lippendorf. Our Stepmother's wealth saw to that.

About six weeks after my mother died, after the shock of Cattle Pest had worn off, I had the most vivid dream of my life. Even now, as a grown woman, I can picture it as clear and bright as a real memory. My mother was up in the sky with two angels. The angels had white wings like swans and they wore blue flowing frocks, like the angels on the roof of our church, except they weren't blowing trumpets. My mother was between them, holding their hands and the three of them were running with slow loping steps above puffy white clouds; watching from below I realised what was happening: they were teaching her how to fly! They were picking her up and swinging her, like grown-ups sometimes do with small children, so that their legs swing up in front, and the child says "do it again!" They were laughing as they ran and my mother looked so beautiful in her long linen nightgown, her head uncovered, her long brown hair loose and flowing, her feet bare. She looked as I had seen her for the last time, but not so pale. I shouted up to her as loud as I could, cupping my mouth with my hands: "Mother!" But she didn't hear me – I think she was concentrating too hard on flying – then all of a sudden they came to a break in the cloud and I thought she would fall but just in time she found her wings. All three of them launched into the air, I heard the 'free free free' sound swans make when they fly overhead and you drop whatever you're doing to watch them go. The three of them flew up and away getting smaller and smaller so I gave up shouting. I felt sad because Mother had disappeared but happy too because I knew she was in heaven with the angels. She didn't have to worry about the poor dead cows, or Father having to sell the house. Father and I were sitting by the fire, it was late and the other children were in bed.

"Father, I dreamt about Mother. She was with the angels. She was flying above the clouds like a swan."

I waited for him to respond, but he said nothing and the silence stretched between us, the only sound being the crackling of the fire. He sat motionless, but I could tell he was weeping. Then he said:

"I killed her. It was my fault."

"What do you mean, Father? She died in her bed, surely. Was she expecting another baby, was that it?"

"Yes. But she should not have had another, the physician told us she must not have another. It was my fault."

I did not understand why it had been his fault, but I tried to comfort him. I found it difficult, after that, to speak about my mother, because he seemed to prefer not to talk about her. Grown-ups were strange, it was hard to understand the things they did and said and thought. I would have liked to talk about her more often, so she wouldn't disappear from us so fast.

I realise now that my father had simply given up, without my mother he lost heart. Three unkempt children; a small castle, with its own moat and keep, but in a crumbling state, with very few servants. Pails placed here and there to catch drips from holes in the roof. Some of the floorboards upstairs were rotten but we always knew which ones not to tread on. The windows in some of the rooms were broken and pigeons had moved in: when you opened the door the whole room exploded into a flapping frenzy as the birds clamoured to escape; the floors were thick with stinking bird-lime.

On the outside of the house, lead downpipes and guttering hung loose, and ivy tendrils crept across the windows so that if visitors called – which they seldom did after my mother died – the house appeared to them to be falling asleep.

But as it was, Father did not have to sell the Castle and we did not go hungry. Stepmother came in like a whirlwind, bringing wealth so that tradesmen could be paid, a gardener and stable boy hired, and fodder bought in. She engaged builders to mend the windows and gutters and floorboards. We were deloused and re-clothed, she cut our nails and put unguents on our sore patches; she made us drink syrup of fumitory for the tetters.

On the face of it our lives improved. But for me a shadow fell. She engaged a tutor to teach me and Irmingard, and made us wear shoes and behave in a manner befitting young ladies. I suppose I was jealous and felt displaced by her. My father now looked to her, not me, for support and company; he became removed from me, not exactly cool, but distant, as if his attention could no longer focus on me.

Stepmother warmed to the other children. Little Hans, still only a toddler, could do no wrong in her eyes, he was 'my naughty little bear cub'. She would hug him and play the game *Hier has du einen Taler,* tickling his palm. She made a fuss of Irmingard too, brushing her blond hair as it grew back, measuring her feet for new shoes, playing *pat a cake pat a cake.* Irmingard knew how to please her, calling her 'Mummy', and simpering up at her in a babyish voice. But I was sullen and aloof, lurking in the shadows, keeping out of her way as much as possible. At mealtimes she avoided addressing me directly, but spoke about me to Father in the third person as if I was not there.

"Katharina spends far too much time with that peasant boy Sebastian. I'm surprised at you, dear, for allowing it, she's becoming so uncouth in her speech and deportment." Or: "Should Katharina not be learning to play an instrument, or improve her singing and sewing, instead of loitering about in the stables? How shall we ever find her a husband if she continues to run about the farmyard like a feral cat?"

In response to these and similar remarks my father rubbed his chin, made a sort of humming sound and looked at me with a mixture of puzzlement and pity; but he seemed unable to make any suggestions on how to manage me. From time to time Stepmother and I met each other face to face; then she spoke to me directly, with tight lips and coldness in her eyes. Once I stood my ground and stuck my tongue out at her, and she slapped me on the cheek. Sebastian and I put slugs in her boots; then I was rude to the tutor and he complained to her.

"The child will have to go, Hans."

"Go? You mean, to boarding school?"

"Yes, to a convent school. And then into the convent. We'll never find her a husband, she's quite unmarriageable."

"She's only nine years old, I think we've got a bit of time yet."

"You saw how she behaved yesterday with the von Staupenfelzens. They were mustard keen to make a match, and their son's a charming boy. But it was quite plain, that when they left they'd changed their minds."

"Why was that do you think?"

"Why? My dear Hans, are you blind? Honestly, you can be so obtuse. She's like a wild cat, your 'Käthchen' as you call her. She knew we had an important visit, that she was supposed to make a good impression. Greta washed her hair the day before and braided it up. I laid out her best frock and new shoes and stockings. I told her to come down to the parlour in her best and be ready to receive our guests. But the carriage arrived and we welcomed them in, then where was the girl in question? Nowhere to be found!"

"I think she was in the stables, dear."

"Of course she was in the stables. Greta brought her in looking quite dishevelled – straw in her hair, and muck on her new shoes."

"I know, I was there, dear."

"I'm sorry, Hans, but there it is. I can't cope with her any more. I've tried, God knows; I have no trouble with the younger two, they are sweet and biddable, but try as I might I can't tame that little kitten. No-one will take her on with that wild look in her eyes."

"She's a good girl really. She misses her mother."

"She'll be a good girl if we get her to a convent and they drum a bit of discipline and godliness into her."

"Isn't she a little young to leave home?"

"You don't understand, Husband. I'm not prepared to do it. You leave it all to me, the discipline, the spiritual guidance, supervision of the tutor. You're quite happy to let your children run wild in the forest like… like little wolf-cubs. It won't do."

"So you're saying send her to school now?"

"Yes. My nieces, you know my brother's daughters, they all went away at six and they did very well. Isn't your sister the Abbess in a Cistercian house?"

"No, my sister Magdalena is a nun at Marienthron, in Nimbschen. But the Abbess of that house is a cousin of Käthchen's mother."

"In that case, she is the child's kinswoman; if you wrote to ask she would probably grant her a place there."

"You're probably right, dear. I'll miss her, though. But yes, it would be for the best. I'll write to her today. I will write to my sister too. The child has grown rather wild, and her aunt Magdalena would be kind to her, I think she teaches in the school."

"She'll be much better off there. She'll build on the lessons she's been having here, her Latin and music and Scriptures. She will become, one hopes, a bit more ladylike and devout too."

"And she'll be safer, in these uncertain times. Remember to ask what dowry they require."

"It'll be less than a marriage settlement, that's for sure."

The Abbess wrote back offering me a place to start in September. It was then July, so I still had the summer at home. The days were long and hot and Sebastian and I ran free. Stepmother, relieved at my imminent departure, became less cold and censorious. We learnt to swim in the millpond. We played in the woods. We helped with the harvest and killed rabbits as they ran out of the standing corn. We danced at harvest festival, and climbed up into the strawstacks and slid down onto heaps of straw. It seemed as if the summer days would last forever; but one morning a hint of frost was in the air and they came to an abrupt end, and so did my time at home.

My bag was packed, my hair cut short and it was time to say goodbye.

"Father, can I take my owl to school with me?"

"No, my love. Eule belongs here, he wouldn't want to live in Nimbschen. Leave him here. I'm sure Irme will give him scraps if he needs them."

It was a Thursday morning; Father brought the trap round to the front, and everyone came out to see me off: Stepmother, with Irmingard and little Hänschen, Greta, the dog Ebony; finally, Cook and Hildegard, and as I hugged them they both burst into tears. Then Irmingard and Hans started bawling too. I did not cry. As we bowled away down the drive I looked back at the crumbly old castle where I had been born, and the people standing there waving goodbye.

As we approached the gate house at the end of the avenue Sebastian saw us coming and ran out in front of us, waving at Father to stop. He climbed onto the running board and handed me something. It was a stuffed mole. I wanted to thank him but couldn't find my voice. As we drove on, he ran after us in his bare feet until he couldn't keep up any longer. Then he just stood very still in the middle of the road, getting smaller and smaller, waving. Until we rounded a corner.

Chapter 3
A Schoolgirl at Nimbschen

*Wenn das Alter stark und die Jugend klug
wäre, das wäre Geldes wert.*

If old age were strong and youth were clever
that would be worth its weight in gold.

Father stopped the trap in the market square, and we sat in it waiting for the coach to appear. My heart thumped heavily like a leaden ball and I felt sick. The church clock struck eight.

"You'll like it at school, my sweet. They'll teach you Latin, and you can learn the lute and singing. You'll meet other girls of your age and class. You've been too isolated here at Lippendorf."

"What does isolated mean?"

Of course I knew what he meant, but I just wanted to keep talking.

"It means cut off from other people."

"But I'm not cut off from you or Sebastian or the horses or Ebony or…"

"No, dear girl. It means you're not in contact with the sort of company you should be keeping, people from whom you learn and grow."

"So will I grow at school?"

"Spiritually, yes. And you'll grow tall as well."

"I'll miss you. And Conquest, and Irmingard and Hänschen and Sebastian and everyone. Will you miss me too?"

"Yes, dear girl, I'll miss you too. I'll write you long letters telling you all about the animals and the farm and your brother and sister. And when they get older they'll write to you too."

"And Eule, Father, will you tell Irmingard to feed him mice and bits of cheese when he flies into my room in the evening? Will you promise?"

I never heard his answer, because at that point the coach arrived with a great clattering of hooves and wheels and shouts and whips and jingling of harness. Ostlers hurried out from the Spread Eagle, leading a fresh team to replace the hot horses, who were unhitched, their flanks heaving, and led away to the inn stables. Some passengers alighted, the postilion handing down their bags, and other passengers, like me, were waiting to board. Father led me to the coach and looked inside. He spoke to a woman and she nodded and looked down at me.

"I'll keep an eye on the child, I'm going to Grimma myself. Don't you worry, she'll be quite all right."

And before I knew it, I was lifted up to join the other passengers, the door slammed shut and the coach was lurching away, through the town gates and onto the highway.

"My case, where's my case?" I wailed.

"It's up on the roof with the other luggage, dear. Don't you worry."

She patted my knee with a jewelled hand. I felt squashed, sitting in this confined space with eight grown-ups who I didn't know, mostly men. They smelt funny, a mixture of perfume and stale sweat and bad breath. I dug my nails into my palms until it hurt, and swallowed hard. Then I remembered the stuffed mole in my pocket, and stroked its velvety fur secretly. Trees, houses, woods, streams and bridges swept past as we rumbled along, lurching from side to side. At first I recognised the skyline but gradually the landscape became unfamiliar. When the road was very bumpy, we passengers kept being thrown back and forth against each other.

I needed to relieve myself. Would we ever stop? Should I say to the lady, please, I need to get out. But thankfully, quite soon we drew into a little town to change the horses; we had half-an-hour for a rest and refreshments at the inn, so I found the privy, what a relief! My auntie bought me a beer and a piece of sausage and a slice of bread. After that, once we were underway again, I fell asleep. I think we all slept. And so the journey went on. Driving for two hours, a short rest, more driving, then a longer stop.

At last, after what seemed like a week of being cooped up in the coach with strangers – who kept changing, with some getting off and others getting on – we clattered into Grimma. This was the last stop for the coach. The sun was setting like a red orange and a mist was rising. My escort helped me down from the coach and gave a coin to the postilion who brought down our bags from the roof.

"Now, my child, someone is meeting you here, I assume?"

"Yes, I think so."

And sure enough, there was a nun in a white habit and black veil sitting in a little donkey cart in the town square. She stepped down and walked towards us.

"Fräulein von Bora?"

"Yes"

No-one had ever called me Fräulein before, so I felt flattered. But my head was aching terribly. The nun took my bag and stowed it in the cart.

"There. Shall we go then?"

She shook hands with the lady, thanking her for minding me. I said thank you too and she patted me on the head and said,

"Well, good luck, dear girl, and may God go with you."

The journey had been exhausting. I crept into my little bed, one of twelve in two rows in a dormitory, and lay quite still, curled up tight. I thought about home and tears slid silently down my cheeks, wetting the pillow, salting my lips. Every time I nearly fell asleep I woke with a jolt, still feeling the bump and lurch of the carriage, hearing the clattering of horses' hooves, the cracking whips, the coachman cursing and encouraging the horses. I had never made such a long journey before; my head ached, and I thought it was just because I was tired and scared, but when I woke from a fitful sleep with the morning bell I felt both cold and hot and very ill.

"The child has a fever. She'll have to go to the Lazarette." I was told, not unkindly, to get up and a nun led me along a creaky passage, up some more stairs and into another dormitory which was set aside for sick girls. I crept into the new bed, and shivered and sweated and felt miserable. The next day I was covered in spots. I had caught the measles.

I was only the first of many. One of the girls died, but I never knew her. I don't know how long I was ill, but I remember being aware of this lovely person in a white habit and black headdress, sitting by my bed. I have a recollection of her cooling my hot head with a damp cloth, helping me to sit up and holding a mug of herbal tea to my lips. Of her kind hands giving me a bed-bath, her soft voice reassuring me. And gradually, as I emerged from fever, I watched her more closely, tall and graceful, gliding softly from bed to bed, nursing us. She looked like my father, spoke like my father, moved like my father. I realised then that she must be my aunt. And I loved her.

Perhaps it was because I was feeling weak and acquiescent after the measles that the imposition of a strict routine, with rules and regulations, did not seem too objectionable to me. I didn't mind the rigid timetables, the repetitive prayers, the list of petty rules. No whistling, no running in the corridors, no whispering, no jumping on the beds. Speak to grownups only when spoken to; never interrupt; at meals, begin to eat only when the nun at the head of the table has begun to eat. Say your prayers every morning, noon and evening. And so on.

We new girls adapted quickly to the daily routine: up at dawn with prayers. Breakfast, then labour (usually laundry or some other work for the convent) then lessons. Lunch. A rest on the floor in the refectory, while a nun reads to us. Exercise outside. More labour, in the kitchen or garden. Homework. Prayers. Bed.

I enjoyed the lessons. I could read already but learning to write was fascinating, comparing the shapes of the letters on our slates with the letters in the books we were allowed to look at. Our teacher Sister Plenitude told us we must master the art of fine calligraphy and painting so that when we became nuns we could copy books to a high standard and illustrate them with illuminations. To that end we learnt drawing as well, on a very small scale.

"If it were not for the great religious houses, many books would have been lost forever. Monks and nuns have kept the torch of learning, of history and the word of God alive by copying them, and teaching boys and girls how to read and write. This is why you girls must learn to write very neatly and paint very precisely, so that you can copy manuscripts and books for future generations."

We could not know then that in a few years this great industry of copying by hand would be obsolete and the monks and nuns made redundant. Printing would sweep all that away.

We learnt Latin too. Of course we knew the sounds already from church and occasionally I had heard Father talking in Latin to other learned men. But I had only learnt the rudiments. Now I loved learning the words, the declension like *dominus, domine dominum, domini domino domino*. The conjugation of verbs. *Amo amas amat, amamus amatis amant.* When we went out for play we ran about chanting Latin at each other and laughing at ourselves. The ancient language made us feel grown up, the words had an unfamiliar shape in our mouths; it was the language of knowledge and power. We had thought of it as the language of men and boys, not women and girls, so we felt proud to be learning it. Quite soon Sister Plenitude was writing up whole sentences for us to translate. To help us, she would draw little pictures of the words we couldn't guess. Life in the school was regimented and confined, but it was not boring.

From time to time we felt homesick, but gradually my old life became a distant memory. Then I lost Moly. It had been my most treasured possession when I first arrived and I was never parted from it. At night I kept him under my pillow, and by day he hung round my neck, under my tunic. Even when I was sick with measles, he stayed under my pillow. But one dreadful day, Sister Charity, a cold fish and a bully, was doing dormitory patrol before lights out. I was brushing my hair and Moly lay beside me on the bed.

"What's that?"

"It's my mole" I said, whipping him away out of sight, under my blanket.

"Give it to me, child."

"No."

"Do as I say, give it to me now. Or I shall have to call the Mother Superior."

"What will you do with him, Sister Charity?"

"That is not for you to ask. You know quite well, we should not gather possessions about us, they lead to unnatural attachments and distract us from God's love. You must relinquish all such vanities, and love only our Lord and his blessed Mother."

She spoke all this in a sing-song intonation as if it came straight out of a book of rules. I had no choice but to give him up. She held him gingerly between finger and thumb as if he were a dead rat, and glided away out of the dormitory and down the stairs. Ave tiptoed over and hugged me, trying to comfort me, but even so I cried myself to sleep that night. When I woke in the morning I thought it must have been a bad dream and felt for Moly under my pillow. But he was gone, it was true and a wave of misery washed over me. My mole had been my only connection to home; all the love that I had for my father, my sister and baby brother, for Sebastian and Magdalena, for my owl and the horses and dogs and house, all my love for them had been bottled up and held in this tiny little scrap of moleskin and sawdust. He had lost most of his fur; even the little hands and feet had fallen off, so it was scarcely recognisable as having once been a mole.

I hated doing laundry and my hands got very sore from the hot water and the soap. I showed Sister Charity my hands and asked her if I could be put on some other duty, but she was unsympathetic and said not to make such a fuss, my hands needed to get tougher and so did my spirit. But when the skin broke and the wounds became infected, Sister Plenitude overruled Charity and said I should do dry work until they healed.

The days and weeks and months went by. Prayers, lessons, labour, play, reading, prayers, bed. Festivals brought a break to the routine: Christmas, Epiphany, Lent, Easter, Ascension Day, Walpurgis night, Pentecost, Corpus Christi, Midsummer's Day, Harvest Thanksgiving, Michaelmas, All Saints and All Souls, Martinmas, Advent and back to Christmas. On some of these occasions we would meet up not only with the nuns in the convent, the ones who were not teachers, but also the village folk, some of whom used to come and do work in the school and convent. The butcher, the blacksmith, the builder, the extra farm hands, even the man who cleaned the latrines.

The nuns worked us hard but were mostly kind and fair. My childhood at Lippendorf, my time of running free, of hiding in the stables and exploring attics, riding the cob, of calling into the dusk for my pet owl, were gone. I was learning what I must learn in order to be considered for admission as a nun in the convent Marienthron.

Every year we grew taller and attained higher status, until eventually Ave and Brigitte and Elisabeth and Renate and I were the oldest and tallest; we had responsibilities; the nuns treated us with more respect; and we were beginning to look and feel like women.

Chapter 4
Life as a Novice

Grösste Knechtschaft und grösste Freiheit
– beides sind grösste Ubel

Complete slavery and complete freedom
– both are complete evil.

When I was fifteen I became a novice in Marienthron Convent. It was the natural progression and it never occurred to me that I might leave the school and return home for marriage; of course I knew that my sister Irmingard was to be married shortly, but I didn't envy her in the slightest.

My friend Ave von Schönfeld was a novice too; she and I had been friends since we were nine years old. We had shared our secrets, exchanged friendship bands, confided our doubts and fears: homesickness, dislike of Sister Charity; fear of the Abbess or the visiting priest when we were in trouble. Ave has four older brothers and she is rather boyish in her movements and sense of humour. She's tall and thin, with angular features; a prominent nose and pale blue eyes; outwardly she seems grave, but in fact she has a rebellious streak and a keen sense of the ridiculous; she and I got into trouble more times than I could count for playing practical jokes. We come from similar backgrounds; her family, like mine, is well-connected but fallen on hard times. We both love music too, and played lute together and enjoyed singing, both for fun, folk songs, and choral singing in church.

As we grew up, not only physically, but spiritually, we whispered at night about our favourite saints; about how our hearts ached when saying our prayers and coming close to Mary and Jesus: that burning sensation, the ardour we both experienced at certain times when we were praying very hard and Our Lord was listening.

So five of us, including a widow from outside who wanted to join the order, were admitted into the inner confines of the convent to begin a year on probation, learning how to be a good nun. It was a simple little ceremony, where we said good-bye to the younger schoolgirls and changed our school pinafores for a plain grey fustian tunic; we would wear this all year, so we could be distinguished from the professed nuns who wore white woollen habits and black veils. We were put under the wing of an older nun called Sister Clara, our novice mistress. On the wall of the refectory was a picture of Our Lady with the baby Jesus, holding her cloak out like a mother hen, with six little Cistercian nuns on her left and six little monks on her right; in a funny way I felt I was one of Sister Clara's little chicks. She was firm but forgiving, and smiled with her eyes if not always with her lips. If we made mistakes she looked disappointed rather than angry and when we did well she praised us and was pleased; this made us want all the more to do the right thing.

I was prone to losing my temper; it was always the same women who annoyed me. One afternoon after rest I got into a fight with another novice called Monika, she was a little older than me. She had been taunting me in silent language, implying I was snobbish. I assumed it was because her father from Erfurt had paid a handsome dowry for her, because her piggy little eyes made her unmarriageable. Apart from her pasty complexion, she had always lived in the town and had not the first idea how to milk a goat or kill and pluck a hen or catch a runaway piglet. She even refused to skin and draw a rabbit for Cook, saying it was disgusting. Our quarrel was sparked off by silent looks and little wordless insults – the very silence of it made it even more maddening – and I suddenly grew dizzy with fury; I lashed out at her and started pulling her hair and swearing at the top of my voice. I heard my own shrill cries echoing around the cloisters, and it was as if I had been possessed by a demon.

Of course the cloisters are supposed to be kept tranquil for walking up and down in prayer and meditation, and by now we were both screaming and swearing in language we scarcely knew we had. Sister Fenella came gliding out of the shadows and pulled us apart by our hair; she marched us, gripping our collars like two dogs in disgrace, across the courtyard and up the stairs to the Abbess's apartment.

On entering her study, we prostrated ourselves on the floor, as we must do when we have transgressed. Her black cat came and sat very close to my face and stared at me with his cold yellow eyes.

"You may stand up now, girls. So, Sister Fenella, tell me what has been going on.".

"Reverend Mother, I caught these two fighting like cats in the cloisters. You probably heard them. I broke it up, good Mother, but have brought them here for your correction." She stood there smugly, turning her hands around in front of her and pursing her lips primly.

The Abbess was a wise and fair woman. Although she was my mother's cousin, she never gave me preferential treatment. But I think she might have noticed the family likeness, and had a soft spot for me within her heart. Also, I am sure she understood the strain we sometimes came under, living so closely together in an all-female community, under a strict regime and with no privacy. But rules were rules, so she obliged us to wear the hated oblong hank of red felt fixed below the chin, hanging down over our chests, for a whole week; this symbolised a big ugly tongue, and was meant to shame us by exposing our use of foul language. Monika and I developed an uneasy truce after this shared humiliation. But our superior Sister Clara was sympathetic; three days into that week she and I were sitting on a seat in the sunken garden after Vespers; she knew I was miserable about the horrible tongue and she took my hand and stroked it, saying "Only three more days; look on it as a valuable lesson in self-restraint. When you feel angry – and we all do, believe me, more often than you might think – try breathing deeply and offer your anger to Our Lord. Turn your mind to something good; a brood of newly hatched chicks, for instance, or the chestnut foal which Nellie brought into the world last week; and let your anger melt away."

Dear Sister Clara. She knew how I loved horses and chickens, and I've always remembered her advice. How can you stay angry if you can watch, or even just call to mind, a hen with new chicks or a mare with a new foal? Which doesn't mean I became well-behaved and restrained overnight; but at least I became aware when anger was about to erupt within me, and learnt how to manage it. I also tried to avoid areas of confrontation. I love a good argument, but hate to get into a brawl.

I made many mistakes, though, some worse than getting into fights. I disliked being treated as an inferior and would glare, or turn my back in defiance; then we had to confess our misdemeanours in front of all the other nuns, and ask for forgiveness; "I am guilty of picking and eating eight hazelnuts on Tuesday when I knew they were not ripe. I am guilty of falling asleep in Lauds on Wednesday; I am guilty of sinful thoughts while milking; I am guilty of envy of Sister Angelica because she always gets more honey on her porridge; I beg for forgiveness of my sins." And so on.

I underwent the gamut of punishments: hair shirt for a day; sitting alone in the corner at mealtimes with only water; having to prostrate myself length by length right up the aisle of the chapel; saying *Ave Marias* non-stop for two hours on my knees instead of recreation. Another frequent but communal sin was getting the giggles in chapel – the giggles would travel like a rash along the pew, sometimes we didn't even know what we were laughing at, but it was like a volcano erupting, and the more you felt the stony glares of your superiors on you, the more you tried to stifle the laugh and the more it pushed to get out, bursting into snorts which we tried to transmute into feigned coughs or sneezes. And following on from that, the sin of accidie: not taking the offices seriously, or feeling apathy towards God or His beloved Son or Our Lady. I tried not confessing to such sins but clamming up and keeping them secret seemed to make it worse, to exacerbate my guilt about them.

Once a month we were able to make private confession to the priest, which I found much easier than telling the whole community. But despite all these transgressions Ave and I seem to have survived our probationary year; our names were put forward for election by the whole community, to be admitted as professed nuns, and three of us, including me and Ave, were voted in.

Our admission ceremony was a wonderful day. Sometimes, when I feel my faith becoming sloppy, or doubt creeping in, I try to recall, to experience again, the ardour that burnt in my heart at that time. We were given plenty of time to prepare ourselves both mentally and spiritually for what was in effect our wedding day, the day when we became a Bride of Christ. We immersed ourselves in prayer and contemplation throughout the preceding day and most of the night. When the great day dawned, 8th October 1515, we felt so special, and so sure that what we were doing was right. My father and brother and sister came to the ceremony, they stayed two nights in the guest wing. We took our vows and were robed in our new white woollen habits and black veils, and a plain gold ring was slipped onto my finger by the Bishop. Then we were made a fuss of and a special meal was prepared in our honour, for us new nuns, their families, and of course the Bishop. It was a memorable occasion, a day I remember now with unusual clarity, like a wedding day. But imagine how unbelievable it would have been, had someone predicted on that day that I would, in ten years' time, have another Wedding Day, that time to a man. And what's more, to a man renowned (or notorious!) throughout the civilised world!

Marienthron was a Cistercian house, and we lived, or endeavoured to live, by the Benedictine Rule; each day is divided by bells into separate tranches of three distinct activities: devotion, reading or study and manual labour. We must attend six offices, during which we sing through all the psalms once each week; we pray and listen to the Abbess preach or read to us; every Sunday the village priest comes in and says mass. Now and then the Bishop calls in with his entourage to make an inspection of the convent and ensure that things are running smoothly and standards are being maintained. Each one of us has the opportunity to report to him in confidence if anything is not to our liking or standards are slipping in some way.

I seem to have moved about in a sort of daze during my first few years at Marienthron, seeing my circumscribed world through a butter muslin. I was always playing the tune a beat behind: in the Chapel at Lauds I would long more than anything to be back in bed. Then at Prime, early in the morning, I felt so sleepy and knew it was a sin to yawn during the office. Before breakfast, we had to do two hours' domestic work; our duties would vary; we might be put to sweeping floors or polishing brass in the chapel; or we would help Cook in the kitchen, plucking a fowl, cleaning rabbits or fish or kneading the dough; or we might be assigned for a week to the scullery, dipping candles, boiling bones for glue or scraping pelts before they went to the tannery; at other times I worked in the dairy: milking or churning butter, or washing out the churns and cleaning the parlour. Or the hated laundry.

Our chores had to be done by breakfast, by which time we were really hungry; after Sext we had a two hour period of study in the library: reading the Bible or doing Latin to German translations or copying out religious texts in our best writing. The convent used our skills to produce fine books, copied onto best parchment; some of us, me included, had learnt the art of illuminations; this was lucrative business for the convent at that time. I never seem to have time to do such work now.

Our main meal was at midday, when one of the senior sisters sat up on a balcony overlooking the refectory and read us a chapter from Benedict's Rule. After a short rest on our beds we went outside to work in the fields or walled garden, or in inclement weather we would work in the tapestry room or the sewing room instead.

On the whole I enjoyed the farm work best. We became absorbed in whatever we were doing: singling beets or hoeing between rows of carrots or pulling out weeds; while my hands worked my mind wandered to quite other things. All too soon, the bell in the chapel tower would summon us for the next office, giving us half an hour to put away our tools, wash our hands and hurry to our allotted seats in the chapel. As I knelt and sat and stood, through the readings and chanting and praying, the Latin words flowing automatically from my lips, images of what I had just seen flickered in my mind: the freshly turned soil, a robin hopping around my hoe, pouncing on worms; a flock of doves wheeling in circles above us. As the day unfolded, each activity seemed to be coloured by the one that went before, rather like feathers on the wing of a chicken, neatly folded one upon another. More often than not I found each task ended too soon: when I was singing I wanted to continue singing, when I was studying I was reluctant to put away my books at the bell ringing: "Time for Chapel and then outside." Strange to say, though, once out of doors with my rake or hoe I was happy to stay there, and didn't want to be dragged back indoors to prayers. You might think this strict routine would be boring, but it wasn't. I think it helped us avoid small-mindedness and guarded against sloth.

After the evening meal of bread and cheese and beer we had one hour free and were allowed to talk, make music – most of us played an instrument, I play the lute and Ave plays the fiddle; we sang folk songs and played games. Also every

Saturday afternoon was set aside for recreation: we played ball or took a boat-trip on the river or went for a picnic in the park. Now and then we younger ones had a sports day, with running races and jumping competitions. Sometimes a group of us rehearsed and put on a little play for the other sisters and the Abbess was very encouraging of such things.

Because our days were so similar, following the same routine, those out of the ordinary events stand out with the greatest clarity in my mind. These memories can be triggered by particular stimuli: the baked bread aroma of ripening rye gently popping on a warm evening in July; the plash of water against the side of a rowing boat; a recorder playing a jig; the smell of blood and offal. We nuns could not do everything, not only because we were women, but because the farm was large – we must have had a hundred acres within the walls to manage. Orchards, the walled vegetable garden, strip fields, a small vineyard and water meadows for hay and pasture. So outside labour had to be called in for certain tasks. A man came every week to clean out the privies. A blacksmith fired up the forge on Thursdays to shoe horses and oxen, mend ploughshares or do other metal work.

The village butcher drove in with his tumbril on Tuesdays to slaughter a beast or a couple of goats and then in November he would bring his four sons along to fetch home the bacon: what a noise! Young pigs, knowing full well their time had come, squealing and rushing about, often escaping and having to be caught again; we had to carry endless buckets of blood and offal to the kitchen, where Cook worked frantically with her team at the range cooking up blood pudding and liver sausage and Wurst. Pork sides were soaked in brine tanks then hung in the smokery for several days. We had to scrape bristles off the fresh pig skins and they were sold to brush makers while the skins went to the tanners. Trotters, snouts, ears, lights and tripe, all had a value. We felt nauseous at slaughter time and our clothes stank of blood and death, but it had to be done. Of course for the dogs it was the most wonderful time in the year; and we all ate more meat than usual, growing nice and fat against the lean months ahead.

Harvest time in August was much more fun than the blood month. For six weeks the whole farm was buzzing like a hive – men scything, swish swish swish, working in staggered rows, one man slightly to one side behind the next, felling the standing corn. Every two minutes each mower would stop, pull a whet stone from his belt and sharpen the blade. They wiped their sweaty brows and went back to the swing and swish. Behind the mowers, women swept up the fallen corn into sheaves and bound it up with raffia. We provided them with gloves for this task. Sweep up, bind together, tie: three deft movements, which at the harvest festival, would be re-enacted in a folk dance. Younger women and children followed them, lifting the sheaves and building them into stooks while little boys dashed about with sticks, killing rabbits as they darted out of the dwindling patch of standing corn. Towards the end of the six weeks, carters came in with their own horses and carts to bring the harvest home to the stack yard. Loading the carts was a skill left to the older men: the stooks had to be packed just so, end to end, so that the load was stable. Some of the corn would be threshed straight away and the sacks of fresh grain carted down to the water mill; the rest of it was stacked to be dealt with later. How delicious it was, the first batch of bread baked with fresh flour! We had grown used to the slightly mouldy taste and smell of last year's flour; indeed, we were grateful to have any grain left at all by July. That is the leanest month of all.

Of course the peasants had to be fed and watered. It fell to the younger nuns to bring them their dinner: rabbit stew and turnips or pigeon pie; rye bread (made with fresh flour, they wouldn't stand for the stale stuff!) and goats' cheese; a basket filled with plums or nectarines. From the kitchen we loaded two panniers on a donkey, food on one side, a barrel of beer on the other. The labourers brought their own wooden plates, pewter mugs and spoon.

I picture the scene so clearly: the men sitting under one elm tree, the women and children under another. Their easy talk as they ate and drank, their voices rising and falling like the murmuring of a flock of starlings. The lazy somnolence afterwards as they dozed in the midday heat, their arms thrown across their eyes, their boots discarded beside them. Small children lay asleep against their mothers' thighs and some women fed babies at their breasts. Dogs lay panting in the heat snapping at flies. Sparrows hopping about looking for crumbs.

I remember looking at these country people before we turned home with the donkey, feeling a stab of envy and regret that I would never know this easy bonhomie, the suck of a baby at my breast, a toddler asleep on my thigh. Maybe I was affected by the strong smell of men as I handed out their food. Sweat, leather, male pungency. Some of them looked at us in a way you should not look at nuns. We lowered our gaze, but once, by mistake, I caught the eye of a handsome young man as I was offering round a basket of plums and he winked at me and drew his tongue across his lips, saying he liked plums, especially when they were soft and sweet. My face burned as I blushed up to my hair and down my neck in shame.

At the end of harvest the convent laid on a feast for all the workers. The carters who had managed not to tip over a load were presented with a harvest goose. All the men and women and boys and girls ate and drank and danced and revelled well into the night, but we sisters had to leave for Compline and were forbidden from returning to the dance. We lay awake in our little beds listening to the distant sound of their singing and pipe playing, the tramp of dancing feet, the whoops of laughter which erupted occasionally, raucous voices raised in drunken song. My heart felt heavy as, too late, I realised what I had renounced in taking my vows as a Bride of Christ. I twisted the ring on my finger in resentment; my feet twitched, longing to fall into step with the dancers; for the first time I wished, guiltily, that I could renounce my vows and join the village people in their revelling. They seemed to be more alive than we nuns, and more in touch with what it means to be human. These were the first seeds of rebellion in my heart, which would lead to nine of us escaping the confines of the convent walls.

Chapter 5
The Fragrance of Cloves

Viel tun und wohl tun schickt sich nicht zusammen.

Being very busy and doing good are
not necessarily compatible.

It was during harvest after my taking the veil that I experienced
my first monthly bleeding. It came as a shock, such red blood,
without warning; of course I knew about 'special days' and
most of the other young sisters had already begun theirs, but
still it took me by surprise. I sought out Ave for help, and she
made me some pads and showed me how to make my own
and the little backyard where we could wash them and hang
them up to dry in private. She made me an infusion of dried
gooseberry leaves to soothe my pains; Ave was learning all
about herbal remedies and making up medicines. Little did
she know how useful that skill would be when we were seeking
employment Wittenberg!

My friend Brigitte in the bed next to mine made me a
friendship band as consolation. For some reason, I was filled
with misery and wept into my pillow that night. My breasts
were tender, my abdomen ached; my heart was heavy and I felt
lonely; in my mind's eye I kept seeing the face of the young
man under the elm tree and the insolent way he looked at
me; or was it a look of longing more than insolence? I tried to
work out whether I was insulted or flattered by his look; then

I realised with regret how I would never experience the love of a man, or have babies of my own.

That night I slept fitfully and had a vivid dream. It was my wedding day. I was standing in the church waiting for my bridegroom to arrive. Then I looked round at the church door, and there he stood, in the porch, silhouetted against bright, bright light. He came into the church and walked towards me down the aisle; it was Jesus! He took his place at my side, smiling sadly at me. His mother, in a blue gown, was watching us encouragingly, her arms outstretched. But when I looked again it was not the Virgin but the Abbess. Puzzled, I turned again to my bridegroom and realised I was mistaken, that he wasn't Jesus at all, but the young peasant who had looked at me so lewdly the day before. He made as if to kiss me on the mouth and then I woke up in great confusion.

The weeks, the months, the years went by, season following season. Looking back on those days now, I tend to remember the good times and forget the petty irritations, the frustration. I miss aspects of that life, now that I am so busy and surrounded by people demanding and expecting my time and attention. More than anything else about life at the convent, I miss the silence; yet ironically, when I was a nun we had too much of it and I felt frustrated! I was always thinking about all the things I could be saying, conversations we might be having, if only we could speak. At study, we sat at our desks, studying, reading, translating a passage into German, or practising calligraphy or illumination.

On other occasions we would sit in the studio, working on the great tapestry for the Prince Bishop. At work in silence in a group of sisters, our minds were free to roam while our hands were busy. After selecting the necessary colour threads from the table in the corner, we took our accustomed places on a bench, in a row. The silence was one of concentration; if a mouse ran across the room you could hear his feet; we heard our needles pulling yarn through the canvas, our scissors snipping. We heard our steady breathing, an occasional cough or sneeze, a shoe shifting on the stone floor. The fire in the grate might crackle or a log shift and then one of us would get up and put more wood on it. You could, literally, hear a pin drop. We enjoyed a sense of warm co-operation when stitching the tapestry, of slowly, oh so slowly, bringing the picture to life. Our minds were able to wander at will, but we felt a fullness in our hearts because we were all working together, creating something beautiful.

Silence at meals was less contemplative. We longed to talk to each other at table and it was here that the imposed silence was hardest to bear. It was not quiet, like in the tapestry studio. The refectory, with its high wooden ceiling and stone floor, echoed with the thud of wooden bowls on trestle tables, of pewter mugs being filled with ale by the serving sisters. Clogs rang out on the stone floor as those nuns strode back and forth from the kitchen, their long skirts swishing. From the kitchen we heard large saucepans crashing or cupboard doors banging.

Above us, on a platform, one of the older nuns would read to us but we didn't always listen. Instead, we conversed in sign language. It's amazing, how much information you can get across by using your hands, face, eyes and body. For instance, to say: "pass the milk please" we would pretend to milk a finger with the other hand. "It's fish today" we would do a fish tail motion with one hand. "I'm so tired this evening" or "Are you hoeing again this afternoon?" or "I had a letter from my father today" or other such simple concepts were easy to get across. Sometimes our silent speech resulted in stupid giggles, which were hard to control, and one of the senior sisters would glide over from the high table to reprimand us, again, with body language.

The most powerful silence of all was when we sat in chapel. My favourite office was Tierce at 8am. Prime, at 6am was too early, I was still sleepy. We had already been up at 2am for Matins and Lauds. Tierce was after breakfast, but before the hard physical work began, so we were no longer sleepy from the night and not yet tired from the day. We sang a hymn, then recited our Latin prayers (I can still recite Tierce by heart) and sang another canon. I love singing, music was my greatest consolation when I was small and first arrived at the convent school. I enjoyed listening to the nuns singing, and I loved learning new songs in choir practice. After the plainsong we would sit in silence for twenty minutes until the great bell in the tower rang. The silence in the chapel was soft as velvet. Of course some sounds came in from outside; a wood pigeon cooing from the chapel roof; a pair of jackdaws squabbling; a gloomy little sparrow saying 'cheep cheep cheep'. If it was windy the huge elm tree beside the chapel would murmur and creek its boughs. But within the security and warmth of the chapel we could listen to the rhythm of our beating hearts and sense the flow of blood in our veins. At that time, I opened my heart to the Blessed Virgin, to Jesus, to God the Father. Most often, it was the Blessed Virgin I approached and came closest to. My heart filled with her sympathy and love. I laid my troubles at her feet, not verbally, but visually, and she took them from me. I confessed my sinful thoughts or deeds to her and she forgave me. When the great bell rang and it was time to move, to leave the chapel and disperse to our allotted tasks, I often wanted to stay longer, stay all day in such contemplation and prayer. If only all I had to do was pray, I thought, I could get even closer to Mary, to Jesus, even to God the Father. But then I would console myself with the knowledge that Sext was only four hours away and I could immerse myself again in prayer.

Although Tierce was my favourite office, my most ardent religious experiences came to me at Compline, especially in long winter evenings. The dark roof of the chapel above us, lit up by the soft light of only a few candles. The fragrance of incense. We had eaten our last meal and drunk a little wine, though we were never inebriated; but we were tired, sometimes a little homesick or despondent or lonely. The weather was cold, the food monotonous and too little of it. It was then that I experienced most strongly the burning of God's presence within me. It was like a glowing coal touching my inner being, almost painfully hot, like when the seraph, in Isaiah, took a burning coal from the altar with a pair of tongs – but in my case he touched, not my mouth, but my heart with the coal. This happened to me only three or four times, notably when I made my vows and took the veil.

If you were to ask me what, if anything, I miss most from our life in the convent, I would say the freedom to pray. Because in order to have time to pray, you need the structure and discipline, the pattern in the day's timetable to allow time for prayer. Now, I have so many things to do and so many people to see, to oversee, to negotiate with, that my soul remains hidden away, like a snail whose head is shyly withdrawn. Of course we have household prayers, in the morning and evening, and one of our number will always say grace before meals. But my head is always whirring with my responsibilities, I find it hard to lay them to one side, to recover that sense of tranquillity and closeness to God which I found in Marienthron Convent in the village of Nimbschen.

Nevertheless, little by little small seeds of restlessness began to germinate within me, within many of us younger nuns. It was as if the restlessness in the outside world was infecting us imperceptibly. Ave received a letter from her youngest brother, who is a student of Theology at Leipzig University. He was all fired up having made a trip to Wittenberg with some fellow students, and heard a sermon by Dr Luther. We read (illicitly) his sermon on Indulgences and Grace. It made us look with new eyes, even with some scepticism, at the few relics we had at the convent: a fragment of the baby Jesus' swaddling clothes; a phial of blood from Saint Bernard; a thorn from the crown of thorns. Were they forgeries, not true relics, we wondered? Another pamphlet that came in with a sack of rice was a sermon by Dr Luther on the state of marriage, and how valuable was the role of a mother. It was Sister Clara, keeper of provender, who made it possible for us to read such things; she was more modern minded than the Abbess, and had a friend in Torgau who was able to slip them in with deliveries for the convent.

One day, a delivery of oriental spices arrived. Sister Clara signed for the delivery. She invited me and Elisabeth to join her in the pantry to help her transfer the spices from sacks into earthenware pots for safe-keeping.

I love the smell of spices. Caraway, cinnamon, ginger, turmeric, nutmeg, and cloves; above all I love cloves, and I will tell you why. That day, Dr Luther's September Bible, a new and wonderfully readable translation of the New Testament, arrived hidden in a sack of cloves. Even now the smell of them reminds me of that book. We read it in secret, handing it round, taking it in turns, tucking it into the pockets under our habits. "Who's got the Bible now?" we would mime to each other, and with our eyes, point to the sister who was currently in possession of the book, the hot book, the fragrant, clovey book, so hot and powerful it might have burnt a hole in our habit. It is difficult for me to describe to you the thrill of reading the Bible stories in our own tongue. We knew them already, but they were always through a smoky glass, cloaked in the mystery and distance of a dead language, Latin. Now, these stories came alive, as if they had happened yesterday. Jesus really was at the marriage at Cana, really did change the water into wine. They spoke German to each other. They were ordinary, everyday people. The scribes and Pharisees, and the crowd who gathered wanting to stone the adulteress, according to the old law, were ordinary people, like the priest and the church elders and the peasants we met in the village at festivals. The New Testament was a book about people like us!

We shared that forbidden Bible for four weeks. We took it in turns. Sometimes, in our recreation time, we found a secluded place and one of us would read out a passage to the others, very quietly. One evening we were sitting in the tapestry studio, working on the wall hanging. We were supposed to work in silence, but Brigitte said:

"You carry on sewing, and I'll read to you, very quietly, from the September Bible. Nobody'll know."

So we stitched and drew and knotted and heard the story of Revelation, so familiar in the Latin, but so much more real and immediate in our own mother tongue: *And there appeared a great portent in heaven: a woman clothed with the sun and the moon under her feet, and on her head a crown of twelve stars. She was pregnant and crying out in birth pangs, in the agony of giving birth.*

Then another portent appeared in heaven: a great red dragon, with seven heads and ten horns, and seven diadems upon his heads. His tail swept down a third of the stars of heaven and threw them to the earth: then the dragon stood before the woman who was about to bear a child, so that he might devour her child as soon as it was born. And she gave birth to a son, a male child, who is to rule all the nations with a rod of iron. But her child was snatched away and taken to God and to his throne...

We never did hear the end of the story. The door of the tapestry room opened abruptly and in walked Sister Charity.

"What's going on here? I heard talking. Why are you not working, Sister Brigitte? What have you got under your kirtle? Let me see. Give it to me please."

"It's nothing, Sister Charity. I was just reciting some Latin prayers for my sisters' piety."

"I think you were reading something. I think you have a book on your person. What's more, I heard that it was German, not Latin. Do not lie to me, Sister Brigitte."

At that, as if as one, without prompting, we all stood up. Ave said:

"We are all complicit in this. We have a New Testament in German. We share it out. We wish to speak the Abbess."

In a rare gesture of rebellion, we refused to give her the September Bible. Instead, we all left our needles in the tapestry, our threads where they were, and walked very fast through the cloisters, up the stairs to the Abbess's apartment and knocked on her door.

"Come."

We trooped in, afraid but defiant and prostrated as we always must when coming into her presence. The Abbess bade us get to our feet. Then Sister Charity arrived, out of breath from trying to keep up with us.

"Good Mother," she said, in between her gasps for breath. "These young women have defied your authority and gone behind our backs. They are in possession of one of those books, printed books, I think it's one of that Luther's translations."

"I see." The Abbess paused, looking at all of us with her inscrutable face.

"And where is this inflammatory book?"

Brigitte stepped forward, fished under her gown and presented it to her with both hands, giving a curtsy.

"You may leave us now, Sister Charity. Thank you for your vigilance."

Silence. We stood before the great lady. She got to her feet, laid the offending book on a table and went to the window. Her black cat was sitting on the windowsill and she picked him up and turned round to face us, holding him in her arms. Her back was to the light, so it was difficult to see her expression. She said:

"You know it is forbidden, not only within these walls, but by the Church. You are exposing us all to great danger. Go now, and do not speak to anyone about this. I do not even want you to mention it at Confession, it is too dangerous. Meanwhile, you will return to your duties and repent of your disobedience. I shall summon you again in a day or two and decide what is to be done."

We left her presence in disgrace and felt very afraid. What punishment awaited us? Was she really very angry? It did not seem that she was. All the same, we were fearful and awaited her summons in trepidation. As it was, she surprised us with her leniency.

Again, we stood in a row in her room. The sun was slanting low through the lattice window. She sat at her great desk, the September Bible in front of her. Then she went to her bookshelf and brought down another, almost identical book and laid it beside our Clove Bible.

"I have thought and prayed long and hard about the matter of reading and hearing the New Testament in the vernacular. You may be surprised to hear that I have a copy of my own. This does not mean that you have not transgressed: you have been disobedient and dishonest. However, we cannot deny that times are changing.

"The Book itself? It is well done. Dr Luther is a poet as well as a scholar. I have to admit I enjoy reading it as much as you do. In fact, I have been praying and consulting with my senior sisters and the Abbot as to whether to allow it to be read out at meals. What do you think? I am always interested in the views of young people."

"It's wonderful, Good Mother," said Ave. "It brings it all to life. The parables, the Sermon on the Mount, the feeding of the Five Thousand. The people seem so real, like ordinary Germans. And Jesus is real too, as if we might meet him on a road or in an inn and talk to him as a real human being."

"I am considering allowing the German Bible to be read out loud in the Refectory instead of Latin; we may sometimes use it in Chapel too. I am taking a risk, allowing this. If the Cardinal should hear about it, we shall all be in trouble. Please be discrete and do not write home about this yet.

"So, my daughters, you have transgressed but I will not punish you. I think I know who has been bringing in these printed items. I shall not punish her either. You may go now. Repent of your dishonesty and pray for forgiveness. Times are changing, and we cannot keep floodwaters from rising. I suppose one could say it is progress. Printing and plentiful paper is changing the world more than we could have ever imagined. God be with you." She opened the door and bowed at us as we filed out.

How relieved we were, to have been found out, but not to be punished! It was almost as if a crack had appeared in the walls of the convent. The walls were high, the gates firmly shut, but they could not isolate us entirely from what was going on outside. We heard of insolent peasants defying their feudal lords and their own parents, leaving the homes where their families had lived for generations, roaming the country roads in ragged bands. They came into towns and cities, usually without permits; they were hungry and defiant and lacked all deference to those in authority.

A band of young 'pilgrims' invaded our convent one evening a few months after this. The youths came into the village banging drums and playing pipes, and demanding food and lodging for the night; the village elders came to beg our Abbess to take them in, and she agreed. Imagine, a hundred hungry youths, fired up, aggressive, defiant! They had left home and were begging their way across the country to a shrine somewhere in Thuringia where it was said that miracles happened.

The Abbess admitted them herself, showed them the barn where they could sleep on straw, and instructed the kitchen staff to kill six capons; some of us helped chop up vegetables and we made three cauldrons of stew for them, which they devoured, and washed it down with plenty of beer. They had their own bowls and spoons and mugs; then they fell asleep on straw in the barn. Some of them were no more than ten years old. But seeing these defiant children and young men unsettled us. We wondered why they were roaming the land like this, and how they dared to kick over the traces, leaving their parents, their landlords, their homes and travelling without papers. We were, I think, a little envious of their boldness.

Another group were also questioning the old order. Intellectuals like Dr Luther and Philip Melanchthon and Erasmus of Rotterdam were defying the authority of the church. The atmosphere of change blew in like cold draughts through the cracks in the walls and affected us young nuns profoundly. Turbulence in the streets, dissent in the church. The older sisters tried to keep these things from us, tried to stop up the cracks, but we heard about them in letters from home, in pamphlets smuggled in by complicit tradesmen, simply by listening to lay people who came and went. We exchanged news and opinions in bed at night, whispering in the dark, or in our recreation hour if we were alone.

One particular day stands out in my mind as being the point when my acquiescence was swept away for good. It was my twentieth birthday, 29th January 1520. I was sitting on a high stool in the library with three others, engrossed in my task of copying out a Latin script. We all had head colds, it was a bleak time of year. Sister Clara came in quietly and touched me on the sleeve, whispering "Sister Katharina, you have a visitor." I left my work and followed her to the entrance gate, to a little meeting room where we are allowed to receive visitors. Sister Clara indicated before we entered that she would sit quietly in the corner reading, as was the rule. As she pushed open the heavy door I saw a young man waiting for me. He got to his feet as we entered.

Who was it? He stood there awkwardly, his eyes sliding away from my gaze. His hands were large and red like a peasant's, the sleeves of his leather jerkin were too short. His leather breeches were worn and patched up and his boots old and scuffed. For all that, he was tall, strong and good-looking; I stared at him in confusion as Sister Clara looked at me as if to say: do you know him? The stranger made a tentative step towards me and said:

"Don't you remember me, Käthchen?"

I knew at once who it was.

"Sebastian! Of course I do, how could I forget?"

He was my milk brother. I had not seen him since I was nine, since I had left home to come to the convent school. His voice was a man's but the intonation, the way he moved, took me straight back to our childhood, when we had played together. I took both his hands in mine, and we laughed and cried; I wanted to throw my arms round him, but held back. We are not supposed to touch, beyond the initial handshake. My milk brother, the son of my wet nurse, Magdalena Blankenagel.

"What brings you here, Sebastian, tell me everything,"

I said eventually, drying my tears and blowing my nose. I indicated a chair, and sat down opposite him on the other side of the little wooden table. Sister Clara took up a seat in the corner and began to read. I did not mind her being present. It was windy and through the high lattice window I could see the bare branches of elms shifting against a grey sky. Sebastian sat down and laid a package wrapped in grey linen on the table, pushing it towards me.

"It's your birthday ain't it? So I've come to see you. I took a ride in a wagon, then I walked, then I had another ride on a mule cart, and then I walked. So here I am. And they gave me soup when I got here. They say I can spend a night. And I brought you this, from Miss Irmingard."

My little sister had married three years before and already had two babies.

"It's so good to see you," I said, looking at his chiselled face, slightly unshaven, and tried to reconcile the man before me now with the ten-year-old boy I had known. I longed to open the parcel, but decided to leave it so as not to waste my precious time with Sebastian.

"And I brought you something else, a present from me," he said, wiping his nose on a foul rag. He leant back and fished out something from his trouser pocket and laid it on the table in front of us: a small parcel wrapped in green cloth. What I unwrapped and held in my hands took me back fifteen years. It was a stuffed mole. I took one look at it and burst into tears.

"Oh Käthchen, don't cry, I never wanted to make you cry. I just wanted to make you another one, that's all, like the one I made for you when you went away to school, do you recall? I missed you so much when you left, things weren't the same after that, and Mother, she missed you too."

"Thank you, Seb, it's a lovely present." I laughed through my tears and wiped my runny nose and tearful eyes.

"And thank you for bringing the parcel from my sister. How is she? How are the children, and her husband?"

We talked of home. My brother, now old enough to assume

some of the responsibilities of the estate. Of my father and his wife, and their difficulties keeping up standards. So many young people had left the village, seeking a new life in towns and cities. Sebastian wanted to leave too.

"Could you ask your Mother Superior if she needs a handyman? I can do most things. I could work here, for the convent, be useful around the estate."

"I can ask, but I think it's unlikely. Where will you go otherwise? You might be able to find employment at the docks in Leipzig. But don't you want to go back home?"

"No. I've finished with that place. My father's killing himself with drink, my mother's killing herself with work, and for what? Don't you worry, I'll make my own way now."

The Abbey Bell tolled the hour and Sister Clara stood up, indicating that our meeting time was up. I asked her if she thought Sebastian might be able to find work here, and she told him to come with her and she would introduce him to the Mother. I clasped his hand and we said goodbye. As our eyes met, we were both thinking the same thing: shall we ever meet again? I picked up the package from my sister and left the meeting room.

We had no real privacy in the convent, but the nearest we came to having our own personal place were our beds, two rows of four simple cots in a long, high ceilinged room. The windows were too high to look out of and the floor was bare boards. They wouldn't miss me in the library, I had been given time off for my visitor. So I took the parcel up to our dormitory, sat on my bed and laid it down beside me. A gift from my sister. What would it be? Something to eat probably, and perhaps a new inner bodice to keep me warm, or a pair of stockings. The packet was quite light. I undid the knot carefully, and folded up the string. The linen cloth fell away to reveal a shoe box. I prized off the lid which had no hinge or fastening, and inside, wrapped in fine paper, lay a pair of brand new dark brown leather shoes; the rich smell of high quality rawhide leather rose from the box and I lifted them out with joy. They were elegant but not too fancy, with a slightly raised heel and two goats horn buttons.

"Dear Kathe, I very much hope this packet will reach you in time for your birthday. I had these shoes made by our cobbler Focher, he used my last – I know our feet are almost the same size, because we've sent you shoes before, but I told him to make them a bit wider for you. So I do hope they fit and that you like them. You may need to <u>adjust the soles</u>. Fancy, you will be twenty years old very soon! I am sending this gift with Sebastian and pray he may have a safe journey. Christian sends his love, as do our two little ones, who are growing so fast, I sometimes look at them in amazement and think, are they really my daughters?

With all my love, your sister Irmingard.

I was thrilled with the shoes and tried them on straight away. They fitted perfectly, I walked up and down the dormitory, testing them for comfort, and being careful because the soles were slippery. I saw how worn my old shoes had become. But I longed for more news from my sister. I read her note again, and noticed the underlining when she mentioned the sole. So I slipped the shoes off, and peered inside each one; sure enough, as I lifted away the inner sole in the left shoe, I found a letter, neatly folded and tucked beneath it. A long letter on fine paper, in her best handwriting.

Dear Kathe,

I hid this letter in the shoe for fear of censors at your gate. I'm sure you will have had the sense to find it. Of course it all depends on Sebastian getting there and not being robbed on the way. The roads are so dangerous, we're warned not to travel after dark. But it's not always possible to reach a safe billet before nightfall when the days are so short so I am praying for him. I have a sort of feeling Sebastian is leaving home, though he did not say as much. Father and Stepmother will miss him, he's been such a help to them since old Blankenagel took to drink and poor Magde is getting old and worn out.

But I don't really blame him. The peasants are fed up. Pay is so low now, and rents high. They hear the older people complaining about how much better it used to be. They want to work for decent money, to learn a trade, to have a home of their own. They don't want to pull their forelocks to the Squire and all his family, with the constant threat of eviction from their cottages.

Christian says it's a recipe for civil war, the peasant classes becoming so unruly and disrespectful. I'm glad we live in a town – our servants are well paid and well fed, so I don't think there's any danger of them leaving or becoming unpleasant.

But that's not the half of it. All this trouble with the church, you wouldn't believe the commotion! It's largely because of a man called Dr Luther in Wittenberg. I'm sure you will have heard about him. He got into trouble with the papal authorities because he nailed a piece of paper on the church door saying what was wrong with the church. It was a long list of complaints; they were called theses. Anyway, they sent him for trial in Worms, and on his way home he disappeared and everyone thought he must have been murdered; so then of course a lot of people were sad and said what a pity, such a great man, a priest and theologian, cut down in his prime because he dared to speak his mind. But a year later, lo and behold, he popped up again, apparently he'd been in hiding all that time, and some people forgot how they had been sad at his death and started complaining about him all over again. I'm just telling you this, though you probably know it already, because I have the opportunity of getting a letter to you without (I hope) its being confiscated by your Abbess.

The latest scandal is unbelievable: we heard a fresh eye-witness account from a friend of Christian's called Heinrich. He's studying theology at Wittenberg. He stopped with us for a night on his way home to Görlitz for Christmas and he was boiling over with the excitement of it, of what happened there, and this is what he told us:

The church in Rome ordered Dr Luther to stop preaching and lecturing and recant all his previous declarations against the Church such as his Ninety-Five Theses and all the other books and things he had preached and written. All his books containing such material must be burnt. If he did not recant within sixty days he would suffer excommunication and many of his colleagues and accomplices too. That time expired on December 10th. At nine o'clock on Sunday morning, December 10th, he posted a notice on the door of the lecture building in Wittenberg inviting all students to come and witness a burning of the godless papal constitutions and writings. A huge fire was prepared just outside the Elster Gate behind the hospital. A great throng of students gathered there and the master kindled the heap of wood. Then Dr Martin Luther threw the anti-Christian decretals, together with the recent bull of Leo X, into the fire. He said as he threw them onto the fire: "Because you have grieved the saints of the Lord, may eternal fire grieve you." Then the doctor walked back to the city, followed by a great many doctors, masters and students. But that was only the beginning of a whole day of burning and riotous behaviour. Bonfires were lit all over the town, in the school yard, on a farmer's wagon, on street corners. The crowds sang bawdy songs and played trumpets and waved papal bulls about; some men stood up on wagons and read them out in silly voices and everyone laughed in scorn, then they were shredded with swords and flung on the fires with ribald singing and cheering, along with heaps of other papist books and pamphlets and decrees. It seemed unthinkable that people should dare to treat papal documents with such disrespect.

The next day Dr Luther stood up on a dais in the town square and declaimed in his booming voice, so that it echoed about the houses: "These bonfires are nothing but child's play. We should not stop at burning the writings of Rome, we should burn the Pope himself, that is, the Roman papacy, together with his teaching and cruelty. Unless you contradict with your whole heart the ridiculous rule of the Pope, you shall not be saved. For the kingdom of the Pope is so contrary to the kingdom of Christ and to Christian life that it would be better and safer to live all alone in a desert than to live in the kingdom of the Antichrist." What happened in Wittenberg on December 10th, and the following days, has caused an uproar all over the country, it's almost as if a fire is spreading, a fire of dissent, all over Germany. As you can imagine, Father and Mother were horrified when I told them this story, they said everything is going to rack and ruin.

In telling you this I am taking a risk. But I feel sure you would want to know, if you have not heard about it already.

Dear Sister, be careful and stay where you are, Christian feels it is the safest place for nuns, to stay behind walls in these turbulent times.

With all our love and best wishes,

I sat very still after reading this. Some people say it won't be long before the end of the world. Apocalypse. The signs are there, the portents. But how will the world end? Will it be consumed by flames or be inundated beneath another flood? Or maybe it will become very cold and freeze and be covered with ice so that all creatures die. Which would be preferable? Drowning, freezing or burning? On the whole, I could most easily imagine the world being consumed by flames, in raging fires, spreading uncontrollably, the wrath of God at us, poor sinners. Dante's *Inferno*.

I thought of all the bonfires I had enjoyed as a child. Fires on Easter Saturday, the return of light; on that day, every single fire in the village would be extinguished. Then, on Easter morning every family, every household, would go with a taper to fetch a flame from the fire in front of the church and take it home to rekindle their own home fires. It meant that we all burnt the same fire from the same source, to symbolise a sense of unity. We used to light fires on Walpurgisnacht, the night before May Day, for scaring away witches; we felt joyful at the coming summer but afraid too, of pestilence and hunger. Then there were the Midsummer fires, when everybody marched round the fields carrying torches, and bones were flung on the fire to drive away dragons; when boys would set a wheel alight and roll it down a hill. In November we had the bone fires after slaughter. These festivals were part of our childhood, and in a more muted way we celebrated them here in the convent. They were fires of celebration, cheerful occasions of laughter and conviviality.

This was different. We now heard about horrible fires where the Church was burning books as seditious, where people were burnt for heresy or witchcraft. And now this: fires of defiance, the burning of papal decrees, the people up in arms defying the Church! My feelings were confused. On one hand I was scared, shocked, appalled. But also, in a sort of way I felt excited and wanted to be out there too, sharing in this restlessness and commotion!

Chapter 6
Ascension Day

Wenn Gott wollte, dass wir traurig wären, würde er uns nicht Sonne, Mond und die Früchte der Erde schenken.

If God wanted us to be sad, he would not give us the sun, the moon and the fruits of the earth.

A particular event pushed me to that point where I knew I had to leave. It was Ascension Day, 1522. I had been a professed nun for six and a half years. We were setting off, as was tradition for Ascension Day, on a boat trip upstream to a beautiful water meadow known as Bernard's Island; it isn't really an island, more of a peninsula, because the river curves round it in an oxbow. Crack willows and huge elms grow on the banks, trailing their leaves to touch the surface of the water; the meadow itself is full of flowers; we fish and paddle and play catch the bean bag, and generally relax. Ascension Day was just one of several holy days when we had a complete break from silence and routine, and were allowed to enjoy some sort of trip or day of amusement to lighten our spirits.

But this Ascension Day was different: the skipper had cast off and the brown sails were filling in the breeze, the old black barge horse plodding along the tow path, when we heard a sudden splash at the stern followed by the screams of women. We hurried aft to see what the commotion was and there, in the river, lay a nun, face down, her white habit billowing around her,

her black veil spread out on the like bats' wings on the water's surface. Sister Clara jumped in after her; (she knows how to swim, as I do) followed by the skipper's mate; they turned her on her back, lifting her face out of the water, and swam with her to the bank, dragging her up onto the grass. The skipper hauled down the sail allowing the boat to float on the current, back to the jetty. It was Sister Ruth, one of the older nuns; she had tried to take her own life, but had survived. A cart was brought down to carry her back to the sanatorium.

This incident shook us up. I had worked with Sister Ruth in the dairy, but did not know her well; she had seemed to be content and devout. Suicide, even the attempt at it, is a mortal sin, they say your soul goes straight to hell. We spent the rest of the day sitting on the river bank, plucking at the grass and whispering about Ruth, wondering why she had fallen into such despair. Our picnic of cold roast duck and wild garlic stuck in my throat.

That same Thursday evening after Compline I sought out my aunt Lena, as I do in times of crisis. We strolled up and down the orchard as dusk fell, beneath rows of cherry trees in blossom, and she told me Sister Ruth's story.

"I knew she was suffering from melancholia; I prescribed white poppy and valerian to allay the symptoms. I thought she was getting better. I am very fond of Sister Ruth. When I first arrived here she was my novice mistress. She was a lively, funny woman in those days; she made us laugh. If we were to come close to Jesus, to Our Lady and to God the Father, she told us, we must be able to love one another, and love life itself. We young novices were sitting with her by the river, just there where she jumped off the boat. It may have even been Ascension Day. She said to us: 'Look at the river, girls. See, it has pools, they're dark and cool, and that's where the big fish swim. But there are shallows too, gravel beds and riffles, where the small fish are safe from big ones, marshy stretches with reeds and rushes where dragonflies and mayflies breed, and where bitterns and reed warblers nest. Beavers build their dams too, which alter a river's course. If a river were nothing but one deep channel it would be boring wouldn't it? Contrast is necessary for diversity.

'In the same way, in our devotional life, we need the riffles and gravel beds of fun and laughter: they provide a place in our hearts for inspiration and devotion. Let those little fish swim in the shallows of recreation and they will grow into bigger fish in the deep pools of prayer.' She spoke to us like that, in images which were fun to listen to and easy to remember. We all loved and admired her. But recently she has become withdrawn, and we assumed she was suffering from rheumatism and toothache as so many of the older nuns do. But I was unaware of the extent of her wanhope."

"What's wanhope?"

"It's when your hope fades away, it's like despair."

"Have you ever had it, aunt?"

"Yes I have, but only now and then, usually in February when the days are short and cold. When the days get longer I feel better. Anyway, we gave her a hot bath and put her to bed in the sanatorium, and she ate some chicken soup. I sat by her bed for a while, and she told me what was wrong. For the last three visitations of the Bishop she confessed to him that her heart was no longer in her prayers, that she was bored during the offices and unable to pray deeply. The only thing that lifted her spirits now, she told him, was working in the dairy. The cows seem to soothe her, she says. The Bishop was displeased, and on the third such confession he grew impatient and said:

'Sister Ruth, if you cannot rise above your accidie you will forego the privilege of burial in hallowed ground. I shall have no alternative but to have you buried, when your time comes, in a field outside the convent walls.'

"So Ruth thought, 'then I'll make sure I die in the river and go to a watery grave among fish; I'll be washed down to sea and rest with mermaids. The Bishop wants me to rot in unhallowed ground like a dog trampled beneath grazing cattle."

"I thought she liked cows."

"Don't be facetious, Kathe. It's the unhallowed ground, the insult, the torment in Hell she is afraid of."

"I think that was very cruel of the Bishop."

"So do I, Kathe, in confidence, and the Abbess was furious when he told her. But the fact is that accidie is a sin and must be punished.

"Supposing you just can't help feeling miserable; how can you dispel doubt if it creeps in? Jesus forgave Thomas, didn't he?"

"He did. And sometimes I feel the rules are a bit too rigid, but on the other hand if things are allowed to become lax, there lies perdition."

"Tante – I mean, Sister Magdalena…"

"Yes, Sister Katharina?"

"Can I ask you something, very confidentially?"

"You may, but I can't promise to be able to give you an answer."

"You won't tell on me?"

"I won't tell on you."

I peered about us to make sure no one was listening, as we strolled slowly up towards the abbey, our habits swishing through the dewy grass. It was almost dark and crickets were rasping and bats were swooping among the trees above our heads. I heard their high piping cry which older people cannot hear.

"Do you ever want to escape from here? I mean, to go out into the world and not be a nun?"

"No, I don't. I am content here. I'd be terrified if I had to leave, I know nothing about the secular world. No, I'll stay here until I die, among other sisters, in the routine of the Rule. But you, dear girl, you're feeling restless, I can tell."

"Yes I am restless. I feel left behind. So much is happening outside. Things are changing. It's happening out there! Bonfires of books, defiance of Rome, of even the Pope himself. We're stuck here, left out of all the excitement; we whisper about it at night, in the dormitory. We want to leave, Tante. The thought of growing old here is driving us mad! Aren't we allowed to change our minds, and leave?"

"You've taken solemn vows, Kathe. Unless your parents asked for your release, it's well nigh impossible. And what would you do in the outside world, how would you survive without a male sponsor? It's a dangerous and mean world out there!"

"But don't you see, we want danger, we want excitement, we want to be part of the new way of worshipping; children are being taught to read, so everyone can understand the Bible in German. We can work as teachers, we could teach older women to read. But it's not just that. The peasants here, they have such fun, they're full of life! They laugh and dance and tease each other. And another thing: we never meet any men! I want to marry, Tante Lena, I want to know what it feels like to be loved by a man; I want to have babies, to hold a baby to my breast as Mary did Jesus, to give suck. And wouldn't we be more useful out in the world, with all the troubles and upheavals, and angry peasants roving about; we could do more outside than we ever could here, shut up within these walls. But please don't tell anyone!"

"Of course I won't Kathe! You're my brother's child, how could I betray you? Am I right in thinking that a certain Doctor of Divinity is behind these seditious thoughts?" We had come to a stone bench set into a yew hedge, and sat down together. The stone was still warm from the sun though the air was cool; a full moon was rising behind the tall elm and stars were beginning to appear.

My aunt was right. Dr Luther's writings had unsettled us, made us hanker for more. For some reason, though, I was unwilling to admit that it was he who had made us question our future as nuns. But in my pocket I had a well-worn sheet of paper. I had carried it round, and referred to it, for so long that it had grown polished and soft, like cloth. On it I had copied out in my best hand extracts from Dr Luther's writings:

essays, sermons and pamphlets which had been smuggled into the convent; we nuns fell on them as hungrily as pigs at the trough in the morning; we read them, and copied down from them in secret, then passed them on one to another, furtively; we passed them while kneeling in the choir stalls at Prime or sitting on the bench stitching in the tapestry room, or bent over a tall desk in the library copying manuscripts. Hot printed material, exposure of injustice, out-dated restrictions, sclerotic laws, the dead hand of the Church in Rome. We passed them on while out weeding in the walled garden, or after washing out the stilling pans and pails in the dairy. I drew the paper from my pocket and peered at it, realising that it was now too dark for me to read. Never mind, I knew most of the quotes by heart.

"Tante, I don't know whether you've read much of Dr Luther's work, but can I quote you some of the things he has written – things which have made us question what we're doing here?

"Please do, Kathe."

"Priests, monks, and nuns are duty-bound to forsake their vows whenever they find that God's ordinance to produce seed and to multiply is powerful and strong within them. The church has no power by any authority, law, command, or vow to hinder this which God has created within them."

"And you do you feel this ordinance strongly?"

"We all do. And this one's from an open letter he wrote this year: *'A woman is not created to be a virgin, but to bear children. In Genesis 1 God was not speaking just to Adam, but also to Eve when he said 'be fruitful and multiply' as the female sex organs of a woman's body, which God has created for this reason, prove. God establishes chastity not through our oaths or our free will but through His own powerful means and will. Whenever He has not done this, a woman should remain a woman and bear children, for God has created her for that; she should not make herself to be better than God has made her.'"*

"So is it just that? You want to marry and have children, is that it?"

"No, it's not only that. Times are changing, don't you sense that too? The old ways are going out, it's new and exciting and it should be open for us young ones to go out there and be part of the new way. Even Reverend Mother talks about it, about the reforms: she thinks it's because of printing, ideas spread so fast. Don't you feel restless too, and excited, Tante? Don't you feel confined, restricted, frustrated? I know we took our vows but we no longer feel it's what God wants of us. It seems a waste of our lives, to be locked up inside these walls. Holy Mary, we could scream sometimes with frustration!"

"I can see that. But it's different for me. I'm older than you. This is my home, my way of life. I can't imagine anything else. And as for babies, well, I've missed the boat on that." She laughed and began to hum a song about a dove: 'Too late, too late, it's too late for you.'

"So, my rebellious niece, what plans are you and your friends hatching?"

"Nothing definite as yet. But we're thinking about it. Whispering. Planning our escape."

"Kathe, do you realise how dangerous it is to run away from a convent? Any lay person caught helping you to escape could be hanged. Think about it. It's a mean bad world out there! Men are violent and lewd, you don't realise what dreadful things they can do to women. I'm worried about you, and fearful for you."

"Oh Tante, you mustn't worry. Whatever we do, we'll be careful. Ave has written to her family, they might help. Or else we might even write to Dr Luther. If I had to stay here for the rest of my life I would end up like Sister Ruth, I'd go down with wanhope! Or I'd throw myself out of the tower room window and land splat on the ground, ready for an unsanctified burial!" We both laughed.

"You're a dreadful girl. But I love you, and want the best for you. I'm not saying I'll help you, but if you need advice, you know I'm here. Have you written to your father?"

"No. He wouldn't understand and anyway he never answers

my letters. He and Stepmother are dead set against Dr Luther and his reforms as I'm sure you know. Dear Tante, thank you for being so understanding."

We got up from the bench and turned towards the Abbey, its towers and roofs silhouetted against the darkening sky, a few lights appearing in windows. I gave her a big hug as we parted. I knew in my heart that she would help us escape if need be. And that evening I became resolved to escape, even if it killed me.

Chapter 7
Escape to Wittenberg

Ihr habt einen gnädigen Gott, der will euch nicht würgen.
Ein Christ soll und muss ein fröhlicher Mensch sein.

You have a merciful God who does not wish to throttle you.
A Christian should, indeed has a duty to be, a happy person.

Ave and I began to hatch our plans. We drew in accomplices one by one, other young nuns who we knew were also feeling like caged birds, longing to stretch their wings and fly. We knew it was risky, that if we were caught we could be punished or even sentenced to death, but by now we simply didn't care. Eventually nine of us were secretly plotting our escape; we never passed notes, but conveyed our latest plans in whispers when we were alone, or made signs at meal times to arrange secret assignations. These were the names of the plotting sisters: Magdalena, Elisabeth, Leneta, Brigitte, Veronika, Margret, Anna, Ave and me.

Imagine it! To travel, to see market towns and different landscapes: mountains, forests. Famous cities, such as Dresden, Meissen, Torgau; Eisenach with its famous castle, the Wartburg, where we heard the great Martin Luther had spent eighteen months; the Elbe sandstone mountains, the enormous hill fort called Königstein. Such names had a magic ring, I could see them in my mind's eye, from what I had heard or read, and wondered whether I would ever visit such places.

We imagined the joy of conversation, the excitement of argument; to meet men of our own age and class, who were well travelled and educated, to listen to their discussions and learn from them. Above all, I have to admit, we wanted to experience love, sex and marriage, to be mothers. Martin Luther said that this was the best thing a woman could do, that it was our destiny to bear and raise children, there was no nobler activity. We were all now in our mid-twenties. We knew that if we left it much longer our sands would run out, and we would die barren spinsters.

Ave sent a secret message home to her favourite brother, pleading with him to help her, but he refused, as did her widowed mother. They would not sanction her plans for escape, saying the convent was the safest place. So, several months later, Ave wrote a letter to the great Dr Luther himself. She showed it to me before sending it.

Dear Dr Luther

We are nine nuns in need of help. You have written that nuns should not be kept within convent walls by force. You say that if nuns wish to discard the veil and lead a godly life in the outside world they should be free to do so. You also write that chastity is not for everyone, and that God created women to be with men and bear children. For these two reasons we want to leave the convent, but our families will not help us. We are writing to ask for your help, so that we can leave this convent and start a new life.

We waited in trepidation. Had the letter got there safely, to Wittenberg? Post was so unreliable, even though Sister Clara had sent it with a sympathetic tradesman.

"I cannot help you directly," she had said to Ave and me.

"But I can help you send letters in secret if you like. I know a traveller who frequently drives to Wittenberg. He will take a letter to Dr Luther for you."

He did not reply directly. But six weeks later a note came

in with a pot of ointment for my sore hands. They get cracked and infected in the cold weather, and this cream came from a special pharmacy in Torgau. So I opened the pot of ointment, and under the lid, folded very small, and separated from the ointment by waxed paper, was a note, in a neat hand.

"Herrings to be delivered on Good Friday. Be ready to leave shortly after nightfall. Wear black cloaks, no luggage. Empty barrels on wagon, get into them. ML."

Oh dear Mary, Mother of God, what had we let ourselves in for? Was it too late to back out?

Palm Sunday broke clear, cool and bright. It was one of the Sundays when the villagers came to us, a young man dressed as Jesus riding on a donkey, followed by other villagers waving rushes. We all lined the road and cheered him as he passed, strewing his way with the rushes – which represent palms – and sang hymns. But in our hearts we were full of dread for the coming Friday.

The whole of that week we could not sleep. We were sick with terror at what we were about to do. Anna was physically sick at supper and had to go to her bed, and Sister Clara thought she must have influenza.

Yes, we had longed for freedom, as caged birds do; but we were safe in our cage, and knew so little about the world outside. How would they receive us? Would we know how to behave? I knew hardly any men, except the garden boy, the plumber and blacksmith and butchers who came in occasionally; the priest and now and then the bishop.

"I can't do it, Kathe. I'm going to stay here." This was Veronika. She was very pale and drawn. "I've got a headache and I feel sick. You go. I'll stay here. I shan't tell."

"Have you asked Sister Lena for some powders?"

"No, she might guess something's up."

"Roni, she knows already, she alone knows, and she's my aunt. Come on, we'll go and find her together, maybe she can prescribe you something and you'll feel better by Friday. We've still got three days to go."

My aunt was sympathetic. She made up a strong herbal tincture, put it in two bottles and told us all to take a teaspoon three times a day, diluted with beer. It did indeed cure Veronika's headaches and helped to calm us all down.

Herr Koppe wrote to the Abbess saying that because of the unruly mobs and danger on the roads, he would deliver the usual nine barrels of salt herring himself (he usually employed drivers) on Good Friday when the roads would be safer. The convent always provides salt herrings for the village poor at Eastertide as a gesture of thanks and celebration.

From our dormitory window we saw the wagon roll in through the convent gates; we watched with dry mouths as the full barrels were rolled down the ramp into the cellar and twelve empty barrels loaded up onto the wagon. The two horses were led away to the stable to feed and rest while Herr Koppe was invited into the Abbess's private rooms to take fish broth and bread (but no wine seeing as it was Good Friday). All was quiet as dusk fell. The moon rose, full and bright, and stars began to twinkle. It was cold. But for the first time that week all nine of us felt well. We were excited, frightened, but feeling fired up and ready.

Ave gave a sign. We wrapped the black cloaks about us, and tip-toed down the stone staircase and out into the yard, cursing the moon for shining so bright; praying that no one would look out of a window or walk into the yard, we climbed up onto the wagon and picked a barrel each; I clambered into mine and squatted down, lowering the lid over me. It stank of fish and vinegar and mustiness; my heart thumped like a bell's clapper and my palms were sweaty. We crouched in our little prisons, very still, no doubt all of us telling our rosaries as hard as we could, saying the Lord's Prayer, the *Nunc Dimitis*, anything to ward off the terror, asking God for His protection and mercy. In Latin, of course. It seemed more powerful in Latin. And waited. The door opened, voices in the courtyard, a man, and the Abbess, and another sister. The horses were being led out of the stables, backed into the shafts, hitched up. Restless hooves chafing on the cobbles.

"That's it, then, Mother. Thank you for the soup. I wish you all a Happy Easter, and enjoy the herrings, they're the very best, from Lübeck."

"Fare thee well, Herr Koppe, and thank you for bringing the fish. And a Happy Easter to you and your family too."

The wagon lurched into motion. Hooves scraped and clattered across the cobbled courtyard; the horses snorted as they got going; we heard the heavy wooden gates swinging open, the night porter's good wishes, the driver's farewells. Little did they know, the Abbess, the sisters, the porter, what cargo Herr Koppe was taking away in his wagon. Empty barrels? No. Tonight there would be nine empty seats at supper and nine empty beds in the dormitories. The horses settled into a steady trot and we swung along the road. The driver whistled. Our hearts slowed down, the worst was over.

After what seemed like an age, but was probably no more than twenty minutes in our stifling barrels, Herr Koppe stopped the wagon.

"Out you get, young ladies, stretch your legs, dust yourselves down." We clambered out of our barrels, climbed down off the wagon and gratefully hid behind some bushes to relieve ourselves. We pulled off our veils and stowed them in a sack and hid them in the ditch. It felt strange having a naked head, because of course as nuns our hair was cropped short.

"We'd better get going now, we've a long way to go. Here, you can sit on these sacks in the middle. If we get stopped, they'll see nothing but barrels. But keep quiet, mind, no laughing or sneezing!"

So the nine of us huddled together, back to back, on a heap of hessian sacks, surrounded by empty barrels, wrapped in our black cloaks. We smelt of fish. But we were free!

It was past midnight by the time we reached the Elbe, and our wagon boarded the ferry to take us across to Torgau. I had never seen such a wide river, and the current seemed so strong, but the ferry was on a chain, and quite safe. Herr Koppe's kind old mother took us in.

"Look at the poor children, they're cold and tired and frightened. They'll be hungry, I'll be bound."

She gave us fish broth, seeing as it was Good Friday, which blended in with the fishy smell of our clothes.

"Now you'll want to sleep. There, you can lay yourselves down on the floor by the stove, I've put blankets out for you. Don't worry about a thing. Tomorrow my son will take you on to Wittenberg. I've gathered together some clothes for you, and we'll cut those habits into rags for the paper mill. Now go to sleep, children and don't worry about a thing. Sufficient unto the day is the evil thereof."

So we slept. Deeper than we'd slept for over a week. The sleep of relief and alleviated tension. The most dangerous part of our adventure was over.

The next morning, that sombre Saturday when Jesus lies in his tomb, we dressed in clean plain clothes and head dresses – how strange it felt to be in secular clothes! I found it quite unsettling, seeing my sisters looking like peasants really, not like themselves at all. Frau Koppe gave us a pair of shears and we cut our habits up into little pieces so they would not be recognised as such. I felt a twinge of regret, my habit was like an old friend.

Magdalena von Staupitz went straight back to her family in Torgau; her parents hadn't wanted her to leave the convent, but when they heard that she had got out and was already in Torgau her mother came rushing over and embraced her with laughter and joy. Anna and Margret were also taken back, by brothers or parents. Leneta was offered shelter by an old uncle and aunt. But five of us, Elisabeth, Brigitte, Veronika, Ave and I, whose parents would not or could not take us back, travelled on in a smaller vehicle with Herr Koppe to Wittenberg, a two-day drive. We were to be taken to Dr Luther; it was he after all who had incited us to leave, to rebel, and he felt responsible for us. He had told Herr Koppe that his house could be our first refuge.

It was almost dark as our wagon approached the Elster Gate. For the very first time I saw the three towers and the sturdy walls of the little town I would come to know so well. Our wagon rumbled through the gate but came to an abrupt halt, at a barrier across the road. A gatekeeper in uniform sauntered out from a watchman's hut, with a piece of paper on a board in his hand, and looked up at Herr Koppe.

"Name?"

"Leonard Koppe."

"Your business in Wittenberg?"

"To deliver my cargo, nothing but five young lady passengers; Dr Luther expects them."

"And their names, Sir?"

We gave our names, one after another, like roll call. Elisabeth von Canitz, Brigitte Büttelheim, Veronika Lauder, Ave von Schönfeld, Katharina von Bora. The gatekeeper held his list up to a lamp hanging by his booth, and peered at it closely. "Which of you is Fräulein Büttelheim?" Each time he called out the name, he held the lamp over us to peer at the relevant face, then ticked the name off laboriously, oh so slowly. The horses shifted restlessly, tossing their heads and jingling the harness; behind us the big gates were rolled shut by two more uniformed guards. We had arrived just in time.

"And they'll be staying at the Black Cloister, you say?"

"Yes, as guests of the Doctor."

"For how long?"

"For the time being, I cannot say further."

"They'll have to register with the Council for a permit of residence. Single women aren't..."

"Yes, yes, we know the regulations regarding single women. Now for pity's sake, man, let us be going on, my horses are getting cold and my passengers are tired."

With a shrug he raised the barrier and we drove on past the castle and the church and down the main street. We entered a large market square with fine houses and a town hall. The clopping of hooves on the cobbles rang out in the darkening streets and a few people stood still to watch us pass; there was little traffic at this late hour.

Herr Koppe stopped the carriage at a studded gate set into in a high stone wall. This must be it, the Black Cloister, the home of the great Doctor himself. He got down from the driver's seat and, lifting the heavy knocker, hammered loudly on the gate. A dog barked. Footsteps. Slowly, the gates swung open and the horses pulled through the archway into a courtyard.

Behind us, the gates banged shut, and out of the dark arch walked a monk with a cowl, holding a lamp, a dog running before him.

"Herr Koppe? Is that you? Is it the fish? Have you brought me my salt herrings?"

"I have indeed, Herr Doktor, five fine herrings, all the way from Nimbschen bei Grimma, alive and well."

The two men laughed and embraced.

"You're a brave man, and a good one. The Lord will thank you. The boy will see to your horses, come in, you must be more than ready for a beer. A fine Sauerbraten[1] awaits you."

We clambered down from the wagon, Herr Koppe helping us. We were stiff in the joints, tired and cold. And nervous too. The great man peered at us through the darkness, holding up his lamp.

"And you, young ladies, welcome to the Black Cloister. Come on in, warm yourselves by the range. Dorothea will serve you your supper in the kitchen."

The great man himself, the doctor who was known all over Germany, who burnt papal bulls, whose own books were burnt – who had set Germany on fire with his defiance and boldness. Here he was, dressed in a monk's habit and cowl, talking about herrings and Sauerbraten.

We followed him into the huge monastery, and found ourselves in the kitchen; it was a cavernous, ill-lit room with a high ceiling and a large open fire. Metal hooks hung from the beams, cauldrons hanging from some of them; a spit with a ratchet and handle was on the left of the fire; clumps of herbs

---

[1] Pickled beef

hung from the beams and jars of spices stood in rows on a high shelf. Dorothea, who I supposed was his housekeeper, came forward and greeted us, her huge roughened hands clasping ours one by one; this gesture, more even than her voice, a strong Saxon dialect, was filled with warmth. She was a large woman in her forties, dressed in a plain grey frock with a white apron.

Dr Luther stood watching us, the faintest smile on his face.

"You have had quite an adventure. I can see you're hungry and tired. I'll leave you now, in Dorothea's good hands; sit down and eat, her Sauerbraten is next to none. Then she'll show you where you are to sleep. Tomorrow we'll decide what to do next. Meanwhile, have a good rest. Come, Herr Koppe, we'll break bread together through here."

The two men left the room, the Doctor's arm on our coachman's shoulder. That was the last we saw of our 'abductor', so we weren't able to thank him for risking his life on our behalf. He drove away at dawn the next day, while we still lay in our beds. And of course we couldn't write as it might have incriminated him.

We were allocated a cell each, monks' cells they were, unchanged from when the Monastery was closed a few years before. Plain, whitewashed walls, one little pallet bed, a chair and a small shelf fixed to the wall, which could be raised and used as a desk or table.

The five of us woke as the clock in the tower rang seven. Elizabeth knocked on our cell doors and we pulled on our makeshift new clothes and met in the dark corridor, whispering and giggling. We wanted to go down to the kitchen, but it wasn't so easy to find. Dorothea had led us up to our cells by candlelight. The passages and corridors were narrow, with odd steps, corners, blind alleys and locked doors. It was like a labyrinth. Eventually we found our way downstairs to a side door leading out to a back yard. Empty pigsties, a few hens scratching about, a cow byre and two stables. One horse, and the freshly vacated stables of Herr Koppe's team, but no other animals. From there we found a gate through a high wall into the courtyard where we had alighted yesterday, with a large elm tree and a well in the middle. From there, we went shyly into the kitchen.

Dorothea greeted us with a grunt, not unfriendly, but as if to say: "Don't think I'm going to be waiting on you forever." But she set down five bowls of steaming porridge, a jug of milk and a tub of runny honey. She made us a large pot of verbena infusion and as we tucked in, very hungry all over again, she stood over us, her arms folded, with her white apron and white head dress.

"You've spent Easter on the road, then."

"Yes, it was a long journey."

"You missed the goose I cooked for Easter Day. It was a fine fat goose. I stuffed it with chestnuts and currants. And cabbage, we had, and turnips too."

We ate in silence as we were used to doing; then the dog we had seen the night before trotted into the kitchen, wagging his tail and greeting us one by one with his nose. He was followed by his master, the great man himself. We got to our feet as he entered.

"Sit down, dear ladies, sit down and finish your breakfast. We need to talk about your future. Dorothea, be so kind as to show them through to the refectory when they're ready."

"Yes, Herr Doktor."

We filed through into the refectory where the monks would have eaten when this was a busy monastery. Now it was a quiet, forlorn place, the monks having left three years before. A long trestle table, with benches either side, stood in the middle of a narrow, high-ceilinged room. On one wall was a large painting, divided into ten, depicting the Ten Commandments. The room was unheated and smelt a bit dusty.

He was waiting at the table, with papers spread out before him, but when we entered he stood up and invited us to sit down on the benches. Try as I might I found it hard to reconcile the two Martin Luthers. One was the image I had already formed in my head: a younger, good-looking, rebellious man with blond curly hair and modern clothes; the other was the real Dr Luther: a corpulent, middle-aged monk with a tonsure, a shabby old habit, a frayed rope round his middle and leather sandals. I couldn't help noticing his toenails were dirty and his clothes were a bit smelly. But as he spoke, he moved his large hands with grace and expression, and his eyes sparkled with a sort of wild energy, a fierce intensity. So very soon, the false image I had had of him receded. This was the real Dr Martin Luther, and we were in his presence, in his own home. It seemed quite impossible, like a dream. Any moment, I would surely wake up and find myself still in my narrow little bed in the convent, dreaming about our escape, dreaming of being in the presence of the famous Dr Luther.

Chapter 8
The Cranach House

Ein gutes Werk ist, was andern wohltut

A good deed is that which benefits someone else.

"Are you rested now, and well fed?"

We nodded, tongue-tied in this man's presence. We were unused to men of any sort, and this was no ordinary man.

"My children," when we were settled at the table, "You have left the convent. There is no going back, you realise that don't you?" Again, we nodded.

"I feel responsible for you. I must admit, I did think most of you would be welcomed back into your parental homes, but no matter. I suspect it was partly because of me that you decided to break free. It therefore falls on me to find you each a position, either here in Wittenberg or in some other evangelical town. I am going to make enquiries about the town; I hope some families will come forward who are willing to take you in as house daughters, at least for the time being. You can help with the household, with children, with livestock. Of course this is only a temporary expedient. Some of you will undoubtedly marry; and if not, you might consider teaching. My colleague Philip Melanchthon is shortly opening two schools in the town, one for boys and one for girls. He will be looking for good, sensible teachers.

"Apart from that, you need to register at the Town Hall.

Can you do that this morning? And find your way about, explore a little, go and see the church. Settle in. Are you happy with that plan?"

We nodded, still tongue-tied. Speech did not come naturally to us after living in silence for so long. We were overawed to be in Dr Luther's presence. While sitting listening to his deep resonant voice, I thought, suppose Mother Superior could see us now, dressed in secular clothes, in the presence of the man who had dared to defy the Church! What would she say, what would she think? Was she angry with us for leaving? Or sad?

Already I missed the nuns I had loved: Sister Clara, my novice mistress, Sister Magdalena, my aunt; the Abbess, who is my cousin on my mother's side; and other friends from the kitchen, the dairy, the garden, the library. I even missed, in a stupid moment, the cows in the byre and the old donkeys in the stable. But this was not the time to dwell on the past and what we had left behind.

"My dear young women, you're going to have to learn how to speak, or they'll make mincemeat of you."

Then chuckling at his own joke he got up and left the room; we were on our own. What a lot we had to learn! Freedom can have a bitter taste. We were not prepared for the raw reality, the brutal unloveliness of life in a town, outside the confines of Marienthron. The convent had been our home since we were eight or nine years old. The walls had kept us safe. Life was run according to rules and routine; nuns in authority over us made all the decisions and everything followed a strict pattern; we knew that meals would be provided and work would be demanded of us. We prayed and sang, studied and laboured, whispered and grumbled, and slept; and the days rolled into weeks, the weeks into months, the cycle of seasons and festivals turning around year by year; nothing ever changed very much, except that we grew up and older with every new year.

To be a Cistercian nun was to have a position in society, a certain status. Now we had no status, we were simply spinsters. We had also lost a bond between us, the bond of imposed silence, which had given us an inner strength. All that security was swept away when we broke free; as fugitive nuns we were nobody; no longer very young, we realised this: we were unmarried, unloved, unknown in the town, invisible, even risible; at best, an embarrassment to those men who had encouraged us to run away. However, most people were kind to us, especially the Herr Doctor who felt responsibility for finding us somewhere to live.

On our third day in Wittenberg, Ave and I ventured out to the market. Acch! We were quite overpowered by all the smells: sewage and sweat, manure and garbage, general putrefaction.

"Watch where you put your feet, Kathe! Look, mind that heap of offal!"

Sure enough, a heap of cow's entrails lay slopped on the cobbles; four mangy kittens were fighting over them, among the clustered flies.

"Here, put this to your nose." I gave Ave a lavender bag and kept one for me; we both held them close to our noses as we picked our way along the streets. We'd never seen such crowds: men, women, children, heaving and jostling, stinking of sweat and dirty clothes, their breath foul, their hair greasy. They shouted and called, swore and sang bawdy songs. And the traffic! Oxcarts, horse carts, cattle going to market, gentlemen on horseback, women leading donkeys with panniers; small boys driving pigs in twos and threes along the street with sticks. Squealing pigs, lowing cattle, bleating goats, cackling fowls, cats, rats, mice, dogs, and everywhere, people, people.

In a narrow side street, a farm cart had got stuck; its team were impatient, tossing their heads, but their passage was blocked by an oxcart full of beer barrels; this in turn was obstructed by a donkey cart which had tipped over and shed its load of turnips; the donkey lay pinned to the ground by the shafts and was braying in distress, waving its legs and trying to stand up. Passers-by were watching with arms folded, shouting suggestions and laughing. The coachman and drivers were swearing at each other, cracking whips and goading the oxen, their voices rising above the braying and lowing and clattering hooves.

We slipped away and reached the market square by a narrow alley. Women stood behind their stalls in village costumes. They must have travelled in from the country, their produce laid out before them on cloths or in baskets. I clasped Ave's hand, and we explored down the aisles between stalls. Hanging from awnings were rolls of cloth, leather goods, hanks of wool, baskets, clogs and ropes, lace and fine cloths, herbs and spices, barrels of sauerkraut, hams and cheeses, birds and rabbits and ducks in cages. It was a jumble, and yet there was order in it. We gazed about us in wonder, taking it all in and wishing we had some money. I wanted to buy a length of blue worsted to make myself a nicer dress.

We were engrossed in looking at the merchandise, when we heard a man shouting:

"I smell fish."

"So do I. Salt herrings to be precise."

Two young men, one a butcher in a blue apron, the other selling baskets.

Ribald laughter. Eyes turn on us. Some hostile, some just curious, watching how we might react. We blush and turn on our heels, wanting to leave the way we came, but then we hear more voices, women among them:

"You can tell 'em a mile off. Fugitive nuns them! Cropped hair, tight lips."

"Not just the lips is tight!"

"Anyone fancy unbuttoning them?"

At that the young butcher leapt over his stall and stood in front of us, belligerent, aggressive; his hands were bloodstained, his breath foul. He did a little dance in front of us, someone started to play a jig on a pipe, they were goading us to dance; now we were surrounded by a hostile audience, clapping and jeering. I was dizzy, felt my feet slipping away from me. The ground came up to hit me, and I lay there winded.

"Help! Oh please God, help me!"

"Leave her alone, you young scoundrels. What do you think you're at? Them women is the good Doctor's, you just leave them be or you'll be in hot water right enough! Shame on you! Shoo!"

An elderly woman helped me to my feet and flicked a cloth in the direction of the youths, who slunk away like whipped dogs. She dusted me down:

"There there, don't you worry, them youths is just uncouth and unschooled. They won't worry you no more." Ave hugged me and we stifled our sobs. The onlookers were muttering, then someone broke wind very loudly amid a fresh gale of laughter, but by now they were turning away, having lost interest in the rumpus.

My heart was pounding, my breath short. We walked as fast as we could without losing our dignity, back to the haven of the Black Cloister. We reached the portal in the big door and pushed it open; once inside, the sweet stillness of the courtyard enveloped us like velvet and we burst into tears. We sat down on a stone bench by the well and wept deep wracking sobs. Around us now, the soothing trickle of the water, a rustling breeze in the elm; all the bustle and jumble and chaos of street life seemed to melt away like a bad dream, leaving us drained and exhausted. Tölpel came and licked our ankles. Would we ever dare to venture out again?

We needed help, so Dr Luther sent a message to a neighbour and supporter called Elsa Reichenbach to give the five of us advice on how to survive in the wicked world and teach us how to disguise our fugitive status. She called at the Cloister the following day. A well-built lady in her forties, she was woman of substance; her maid followed her, carrying baskets of merchandise. The maid went to the kitchen and Dr Luther showed the grand lady, with us following like chickens, into the refectory; Dorothea brought us all a tray with beer, bread and gherkins and the Doctor left us women alone.

Frau Reichenbach sat in a chair at the end of the refectory table and stared at the five of us one by one with an unblinking, open appraisal. It was as if she was assessing what each of us might make of our lives, where we might find a role in the unforgiving secular world.

"Well, my children, tell me all about it."

The five of us looked at each other, none of us wanting to speak first. In our almost imperceptible silent speech the exchange was like this: "You tell," "No, you." Eventually the other four persuaded me to talk.

"Well, ma'am, you see, it's not how we imagined it, being out. Being in the secular world."

"I don't suppose it is. But what did you expect?"

"I don't know; I suppose we thought it wouldn't be so different; we wanted to be free, to be allowed to speak, we wanted to live normal lives as women, to help with Dr Luther's reforms in the church."

"And you're finding it noisy? Crowded? Even frightening, perhaps?"

"Yes. It's very noisy. And we didn't realise about the violence, about how people get attacked at night. We're scared to go out now, since we were insulted in the market."

"Yes, we heard about that, it's all over the town, and do you know who's getting the blame for it? The Doctor, for encouraging you to escape from the Convent."

"I wish we hadn't!" cried out Elisabeth and burst into tears.

"Elisabeth wants to go back to Marienthron, but they probably wouldn't let her back in now." I said.

"You're right, they wouldn't. You've got to make the best of it now."

Elisabeth was still snivelling, so I kicked her ankle under the table.

Frau Reichenbach sat back in her chair, her legs stretched out in front of her, her knees apart, eating her gherkins and staring at us. She was wearing a fine brown silk dress with a gold brocade bodice and the headdress of a married woman. Her face was of a high colour, with brown eyes and strong eyebrows.

"My dear girls," she said eventually. "Never having had a daughter of my own – we were blessed with only one son, and he has boarded a ship for the new world – would you allow me to give you some motherly advice? Woman to woman, so to speak?"

We nodded dumbly.

"So tell me, what don't you like about life in Wittenberg?"

"It's the commotion, ma'am, the noise, the crowds, and the traffic.

"Yes, and they don't like us," said Ave.

"And another thing" said Elisabeth. "It's money; we never needed it in the convent, but now you need money for everything, you have to pay to sneeze out here; we feel so beholden to Dr Luther, he's given us somewhere to sleep, and meals too, but we need to earn our living." She wiped her nose on a kerchief.

"Please don't think we're begging for money, we just want your advice on how to earn it; we want to find an occupation, to do something worthwhile." said Ave.

"The trouble is, we're not really qualified for any work," I said. "I mean, we trained to be Brides of Christ, so we know how to pray and sing and read and write and copy the Latin; we can work in the garden and do the livestock. But we haven't learnt a trade as such; so what can we do except get married?"

"If you were ex-monks you could become pastors but as ex-nuns that option is not open to you." said Frau Reichenbach.

"The people seem to resent us. They know we're fugitive nuns."

"It's a small town, dear girls. New faces, you know, and gossip. It gets about."

Brigitte said, "Dorothea overheard Herr Cruciger telling the Doctor that the Council are worried we'll be a burden on the parish, and what was he planning to do about us? And of course he can't keep us here, so he says he is going to ask around for families to take us in as house daughters."

"A good idea, but of course only a temporary measure."

Frau Reichenbach leant forward and took another gherkin, cut it in half and laid it on a piece of bread, and began to eat it, slowly, looking at us. Silence fell as we waited nervously for our new friend to offer a solution to our predicament.

"Well, dear girls, you have various options. You can, as you said, get married. That would seem to me to be the most straightforward solution. There's no shortage of eligible young men in Wittenberg. The other would be to return to your own families; I assume you've all asked them for help? Disapprove, do they?"

We nodded again.

"I see. So your other option is to become teachers. You can teach reading and writing and Latin and the catechism. Perhaps you can teach music too? I'm told Dr Melanchthon is starting up a school for girls here in Wittenberg. So that's another option."

We agreed, but felt a bit disappointed, as this advice was nothing new.

"But meanwhile, you need to learn how to survive, how to blend in, be less conspicuous in town."

"But how?"

"Well, let's take a look at you. Stand up."

We all got to our feet and stood in a row in front of her.

"You're all quite thin, aren't you? And your clothes are dreadful, so let's get that sorted out for a start. I'll arrange a visit to my dressmaker, but in the meantime I'll have my maid bring over five old frocks, I have two to spare myself, and I'll ask my friend too, she's recently had some new garments made. Then at the dressmaker you can choose your fabric and he'll make you each a nice new outfit, which you can use for Sundays and best. In lightweight cloth for the summer months."

"But Frau Reichenbach, we have no money, how can we pay the dressmaker?"

"Don't worry about that now. We can sort out bills later. But my dear children, you can help yourselves by simply changing the way you behave. Let's start with deportment. You move like nuns, I've seen you, creeping along the street, eyes on the ground, hands clasped, staying close to the walls, as if someone was going to eat you. Get rid of the frightened rabbit in you! I tell you, if you think someone is about to eat you, they probably will. It's quite understandable to feel afraid, but you must never show it. Walk straight and tall. Hold your head up boldly. Look straight ahead. Don't catch men's eyes, but don't studiously avoid them either. Let's think about your gait. Have you noticed how the women in the town move? I don't mean women of the night, just normal lay women? They move their hips, their limbs are loose and so are their arms. Look, I'll show you."

She got up from her chair and demonstrated what I thought was rather a louche way of walking, but of course she was exaggerating. She stuck her feet out sideways and swung her hips as she walked, her arms loose, her head held high.

"I don't really walk like this, I am a respectable matron, but young women nowadays tend to move in a bolder way than when I was your age. Women with babies on their backs move with a swing too. Look about you; imitate other women. Laugh, relax. And as soon as your hair has grown long enough, roll it up on your head and discard your headdresses, we want to show that you're unmarried. You mustn't hide your light under a bushel."

"I can't imagine anyone would ever want to marry me," said Veronika, who is a mousy little thing with freckles, but everyone loves her.

"Why ever not, what nonsense! Once Herr Löffler has fitted you out and we've sorted out your hair you'll look like a princess, you'll be quite irresistible!"

We all laughed at the idea of Veronika, or any of us for that matter, looking irresistible. We talked more generally then, and were able to ask her where to get things inexpensively, when the post left for the north or the south, the name of various people who might help us, such as the apothecary and his wife, and where the dressmaker had his shop. She gave us confidence, and chased away some of our misgivings and regrets at escaping from the convent.

She stood up to leave. "You're fine young women, I'm sure a lot of families will be falling over each other to take you in as house daughters. I might even take one of you myself!" she laughed.

After showing her out the five of us strolled into the vegetable garden and sat down on the grass under the apple trees; they were just coming into blossom, fragrant in the April sunshine.

How we talked! For years we had communicated with sign language, only having an hour each day for real speech. And yet we knew one another like sisters, as indeed we were, in a sense, with all the tensions and irritations and love that relationship brings. But as we sat beneath that tree with the blossom petals falling down like confetti, I let their talk wash over me, and retreated into my own thoughts. I thought about the word freedom, tested the sound of it in Latin and German and French. I thought about my pet owl. How, when he was fully grown I let him fly free. He flew away into the night, into the dark forests; he must have learnt to hunt and look after himself. But even in his freedom he chose to come back, almost every evening, to see me. He adapted, so why couldn't we?

The weeks went by and we learnt to adapt. We heard from some of the other nuns, the ones who had gone back home. Magdalena wrote to say that already a young man was paying her court. The others were safely settled back in their homes, either with their parents or their brothers' families.

Elisabeth took up a place at the new girls' school, teaching Latin and the catechism and reading and writing. Brigitte was paid court by an older man, an ex-monk who was appointed as pastor in a nearby village, so she left. Then Veronika was offered a place with a family, tutoring their children. Which left just Ave and me at the Cloister, still looking for a position.

Our high birth was against us. If we had not come from patrician backgrounds, if we had learnt a trade from our parents such as saddlery or shoemaking or dressmaking, we could have found work easily enough; times were difficult, but work was available for those with skills and many people had money to pay for such services. But these were the occupations of the artisan class, not open to young gentlewomen. What did the future hold for us?

We acquired new dresses and learnt how to move and behave in a more appropriate manner. Frau Reichenbach continued to give us advice and encouragement. She invited me to stay with her but I couldn't have left Ave alone at the Cloister and she could not take us both.

Men looked at us both as we walked around the town and as our confidence grew, so did our power to attract them. Men displayed, unwittingly, a vulnerable hunger, a longing. What a discovery! We women have power over men, because they desire us! When I was alone in the parlour I gazed at my face in the mirror, turning this way and that, getting used to my looks in secular clothes. I longed for my cropped hair to grow so that I could leave my head uncovered, as befits unmarried women.

It was May when at last someone came to our rescue. One morning Philip Melanchthon came round to the Cloister. He teaches Theology and Greek at the University and is a great scholar. He's not much older than us, but works all the time with Dr Luther, writing about Theology, translating the Scriptures. He has red hair and a funny face. I like him; a pity he's already married! He and Catherine live next door to the Cloister, so he drops in quite a lot.

This morning he greeted me and Ave after prayers and said:

"Fräulein Katharina and Fräulein Ave, Herr Cranach and his wife told me yesterday they would like to meet you. Shall I take you round to their house now, and introduce you?" We already knew about Herr Cranach: he is a painter, one of the most prosperous men in the town. He has an apothecary's shop and a printworks. He publishes books. He and his wife Barbara live in a fine house only five minutes down the street from the Black Cloister. They have three children.

We said yes please. The three of us walked down Castle Street. I already knew the Apothecary's shop but had not ventured into the other premises. We went through the archway into a cobbled yard behind the shop. A large linden tree stands in the middle, its green leaves still tender. On the right, looking west, there is a wooden barn and stables, then across the south side a brick building with a pan tiled roof and dormer windows. Herr Cranach has his studio here, on the first floor; the ground floor provides accommodation for the apprentices. On the left is the print workshop; this was where Philip led us; he knocked on the door and we walked in.

The atmosphere of industry was palpable; the long low room smelt of ink and paper and machine oil from the presses; and the sour odour of young men in leather. A blond youth was occupied in measuring and cutting paper, another was sitting on a high stool at a desk wearing an eye glass and selecting metal letters with a pair of tweezers, slotting them into frames; two others were bent over panels of wood, chipping and incising them with sharp tools. At the far end of the room, an older man (I later learnt his name was Melchior Lotther) was operating a printing press.

Philip had gone in search of Herr Cranach, so Ave and I waited by the door of the workshop, uncertain what to do next. Two of the apprentices looked up and we lowered our eyes; then a hush fell as the men paused in their work to stare at us. We turned our backs on them and stared out of the window in embarrassment, feeling the heat of their gaze. Gradually the sound of their work resumed.

To our relief Philip soon reappeared.

"Herr Cranach is busy with a sitter, but Frau Cranach is in the dairy, and would be glad to meet you."

We followed him through the door at the bottom of the courtyard into a small farmyard. The Cranachs keep two cows and Barbara was in the dairy churning butter. I saw a tall, slim woman with brown hair under a linen snood, dressed in a simple grey dress. When she saw us she came out of the dairy, stooping under the low beam, and approached us, drying her hands on her apron.

"You must be Ave and Katharina. How good to meet you both. Are you settled in at the Black Cloister? Is it dreadfully uncomfortable? Are you getting enough to eat?" She laughed as we shook hands, and we assured her that we were perfectly comfortable.

"Shall I show you round? I expect you've seen the workshop already. We'd better not go into the studio now, but I can show you the livestock and garden. These are our two cows. This one is fifteen, my mother gave her to us as a wedding present, a wonderful cow, she's never missed a year. The brindle is her daughter and she had her first calf just last week, a bull unfortunately. I expect you both milk?"

"Oh yes, we both took turns in the dairy at the convent," said Ave. "I enjoy milking".

"So do I," said Barbara and laughed. "Milking soothes away your worries. Of course I'm lucky, I don't have to do it every day. But I try to do the milking at least once a week to keep in touch with our cows."

Barbara showed us two sows lying on clean straw in adjacent sties. One of them was suckling eight new mottled piglets. Next to the sties was the goat stall, with two kids; the nannies spend the day outside the city walls with the town goatherd. A number of hens were scratching around in the yard, one of them with a family of chicks. Barbara led us through a doorway into a walled vegetable plot, recently tilled, with rows of seedlings, a pile of beanstalks lying at the edge waiting to be put in. The soil was black and fertile, full of promise with the growing season just beginning.

"You really have a lot to do here," I said.

"Yes we have. My husband takes on too much, he thinks he can do everything. We have the chemist's shop to manage and medicine receipts to make up. The publishing business needs supervising, though Melchior does much of that. Then of course Lucas has his painting studio, with three apprentices learning the trade and our two sons. Hans shows great promise, and I think little Lucas does too. But of course when important people call, they don't want to be painted by understudies, so my husband has to do most of it. Then all the workers expect a hearty midday meal and what appetites young men have! I'm lucky, though, I have Elsa to help with the children and the dairy, and Cook manages the kitchen.

"And the garden, who helps you with that?"

She laughed. "Anyone I can find! I requisition the printing lads when I can. Then there's Elsa, and the boys; you, if you like."

"I would love to help you," I said and Ave offered her help too. "We both did gardening in the convent, didn't we?"

"What other experience have you got? What do you know about herbs and medicines?"

"I worked with Sister Magdalena in the dispensary in the convent. I know a certain amount about prescriptions, and how to make them up," said Ave.

"That's good. Then would you consider helping the Apothecary?"

Ave nodded vigorously.

"And you Katharina, would you give me a hand in the house, and with the boys' education?"

Yes, yes and yes.

"In that case my husband and I are prepared to offer you both a room and work in the Cranach House. We can't pay you much, but you can live with us as house daughters, and join in with everything. How does that seem to you?"

We were almost speechless with pleasure and relief, and simply nodded our assent.

So that was how my friend Ave and I came to live in the Cranach household. They gave us a room each and we lived and worked as part of their family.

Chapter 9
Ave in Love

*Der Mann soll so mit der Frau leben, dass sie ihn nicht gern
wegziehen sieht und fröhlich wird, wenn er heimkommt.*

The husband should live with his wife in such a way that she
is sad to see him leave and happy when he comes back home.

My hair grew, and my confidence grew with it. The children
liked me. Herr Cranach became less forbidding and treated me
like a daughter, teasing me, making fun of me in a harmless
way at meal times. Barbara noticed what I did well and what
I was not so good at, and made appropriate use of my skills.
I helped her in the dairy, in the vegetable garden, and in the
busy summer months we four women, Cook, Elsa, Barbara
and I, worked together, picking, shelling, drying, pickling,
preserving fruit and putting by.

Barbara Cranach, of all the people who have helped and
encouraged me over the last two years, is the person I love and
respect most. She is fifteen years older than me, and I have
learnt a great deal from her. I don't mean just the practical
matters of running a large household: how to keep order
among the servants, how to get the best out of all the workers,
from the apothecary or engraver to the lowliest swineherd. I
have also learnt from her the virtues of calmness in the face of
any crisis, major or minor. Of warmth, gentleness, the art of
listening; the importance of firmness combined with affection

when dealing with children or subordinates. I observed, in the course of our daily life together, her wisdom, fairness and humour. And yet she never dispenses advice without being asked for it, and when you do need it she always qualifies what she says with something like: "That's what I feel, but you might not agree."

Barbara is respectful to her husband and defers to his authority while never actually being subservient. As a house daughter with the Cranachs I grew by simply being with the whole family, observing how they led their lives. I had not lived in a family since I had left my own home when I was eight. I told myself, 'If ever I should marry and have a household of my own, I want to preside over it with the same strength and consequence; I want to command respect from those working for me, and love from my husband, and recognition from his colleagues and friends, as Barbara does.'

I look back now on those eighteen months with the Cranachs as a kind of apprenticeship. My skills at planning and running the provender in a large household, of bookkeeping, of managing domestic staff, of dealing with children and their ever changing demands, were developed there, not only by working for Barbara and Lucas, but by observing how they worked and lived together. Ave says the same thing, though she had less to do with Barbara than I did. Our skills for the secular world were honed at No. 1 Castle Street, and I am eternally grateful to the Cranachs for that.

Ave and I soon fell into the routine of the house, slipping into our role of 'house daughter'. They made us welcome and appreciated us for who we were, and seemed to feel no prejudice at our status as fugitive nuns.

Meal times were noisy and cheerful. The main meal at midday was a gathering of all the hands, from the printworks and the studio and the pharmacy. Cook would make a large cauldron of stew, or dumplings with milk soup, or sausage and sauerkraut, or Kassler Ripperl with beans, depending on what was available. Herr Cranach said Grace and then we all sat down together in the long dining hall next to the kitchen. The room rang with the clattering of pewter mugs, knives and forks on plates, talk and laughter. I enjoy the company of women, but I do think that the presence of men lightens the mood; more laughter and jollity comes into play when both sexes are present.

It was a strange sensation, eating with such a cheerful lack of restraint: joking, laughing, telling stories, when from the age of thirteen we had been required to eat in silence. What I noticed, as I looked around the table, was how much people use their hands while talking. As much communication goes on with the hands as with the face and voice. Even when people are allowed to speak, they still use their hands and faces to augment what they are saying. We had communicated in very much the same way at the convent, but without speech, and still managed to say a great deal.

After the midday meal came the Midday Rest. Everyone retired to their own rooms or the workshops for one hour of quiet. Even the animals observed this ritual, the lame crane, the hens, the cows and pigs, the kid goats and the pair of storks on the roof; everyone would gratefully shut their eyes and snooze.

More industry followed in the afternoon, then by five o'clock all the workers went home and a sense of peace descended as the family and household servants reclaimed the house for ourselves.

The best conversations took place at supper. The staff ate in the kitchen and the family, including Ave and me, sat in the more intimate Stube with its tile oven, eating a light evening meal. House guests would normally eat with us in there, while their servants ate in the kitchen. How everyone talked! Ave and I listened and learnt. After the dishes were cleared away we would sometimes make music and sing.

The summer rolled on. Ave worked in the pharmacy and before long I noticed a change in her. She began to glow. It was a Sunday in August and we were getting ready for church.

I had put on my best dress, the one made for me by Frau Reichenbach's tailor – fine green woollen cloth from England, with black satin trim and a black bodice. I knocked on Ave's door, her room was in the front of the house overlooking the market square.

"It's me."

"Come in."

Ave was pinning up her hair, now just long enough to tie in a knot. She looked wonderful in her dress, which was like mine only grey with bright blue trim.

"Ave, you look lovely. What's happened?"

"Oh Kathe, I think I'm in love."

"Am I allowed to guess who?"

"Go on, then, guess."

"Is it Herr Axt?"

"Right first time! Look what he gave me."

She pointed at a vase of flowers on her bedside table. They were delicate and fragrant.

Basilius Axt was the son of Dr Axt, the Chief Apothecary. He was in his fourth year of apprenticeship to his father. Ave helped him in the shop; Basilius would look up remedies in a the newly published Apothecaries' Guide; sometimes he would consult his father; then he copied down the ingredients and the proportions, and he and Ave worked together, making up medicines, ointments, unguents, potions and pills. The two of them pounded, ground to fine dust, pressed into pill makers; they shredded herbs and boiled and distilled and strained and poured infusions into bottles; they melted fats and herbs in pans to make unguents; they counted out tiny white pills and put them into little waxed paper boxes and labelled them with long names. Unguents and ointments were packed up too in waxed paper cartons; they wrote and stuck on labels. Two apprentices worked in the shop with them; whenever I went in there they would be busy with their hands, reading, filling up phials, assembling boxes, writing labels; their work was never done. The pharmacy was a pleasant place to work, with its wide north-facing window, its broad wooden work tops, the drawers and shelves, bottles and phials and burners and pans. And it smelt lovely too, depending of course on what herbs or remedies they were working with on that day.

Customers came in with prescriptions from one of the town's physicians, and others came in with their ailments, seeking advice. Ave loved the work, and knew she was learning a valuable craft and doing something useful.

"He says I'm beautiful."

"Well, you are," I said. But I felt a stab of envy. No one had approached me in this way. Men looked at me with desire, but they did not approach me. On the other hand, I had not yet met a man who aroused my interest.

"Oh Ave? Has he kissed you yet?"

"No, but we touched hands yesterday. We were filling up a row of bottles with some sticky cough syrup and I knocked over one of them. We were wiping it up together and our hands touched. He looked into my eyes, Kathe, and then he said, 'Ave, you are so beautiful.' I didn't know what to say. So I just looked away and giggled."

"Oh, you shouldn't giggle, Ave, he might feel hurt."

"No he wasn't hurt, he disappeared behind the counter and came back with a bunch of flowers. He gave it to me with a gallant flourish, as if I were a princess. Look, smell, aren't they pretty?"

They were. A posy of wild roses, white and pink; and meadow sweet and irises and dog daisies, all mixed up with delicate grasses and sedges. I smelt them but my heart felt heavy at my friend's good news.

I gave Ave a big hug. She had a glow in her face. It reminded me of certain times of extreme devotion in the convent, when I saw such a glow in the faces of my fellow nuns; at such times I was aware that my own face must be glowing with a fervour, as it were a manifestation of the fire burning within my soul. Was being in love with a man rather like being touched by the Holy Spirit? I thought of what Dr Luther had said, that women are created to be loved by a man, to bring children into the world. So maybe it was a similar thing, to be in love with Jesus, with God, and to be in love with a man. Then I thought, no, you're being profane, Kathe, it's not like that at all.

We walked to Church on Sunday with the Cranachs.

"Good morning Herr Cranach, Frau Cranach. Good day to you. And good day to you. How is your mother? Yes, we may see some rain later on." Touching hats, occasionally pausing to shake hands. The whole town were making their leisurely way to St Mary's Church for the morning service, to hear Dr Bugenhagen or Dr Luther preach. It was strange and seemed almost profane, but exciting, to be praying in our mother tongue; to hear the word of God in German. And we sang Dr Luther's hymns and his setting of the Psalms in German. And every week, as we attended Church with Frau Barbara and Herr Lucas, we began to feel more accepted in the wider community of Wittenberg.

Pews have just been installed, at great expense, so people can sit comfortably to listen to the sermons. I sit next to Ave and think about her and her apothecary lover, Basilius. I like him and want to be pleased for her, but selfishly don't want her to marry. I feel a gall of jealousy rising up inside me; but who am I jealous of? Basilius, for taking Ave away from me? Or Ave, for finding a man to love her? How stupid and shallow I am, to have such base feelings, when I ought to be glad for her!

A few weeks later I had another reason to feel jealous of my best friend.

It was a Sunday afternoon in September, a time when everyone is very quiet. Ave tip-toed over to my room and we were sitting together on my windowsill enjoying the afternoon sun, resting our bare feet on the roof tiles. She seemed strangely excited, but said very little.

"Go on, Ave, spill it out. What's happened? Have you got betrothed, is that it?"

We were whispering so as not to disturb the household.

"No, Kathe, his parents say he's too young, he must get his

qualifications first. So we'll have to wait. But oh Käthchen, something else has happened, I need your advice."

"Tell me."

She fished in her pocket and brought out a letter. It was written in a fine hand on good paper. As soon as I saw it I knew the signature, a famous signature. She handed it to me to read.

Black Cloister. Thursday.

My dear Fräulein Ave

I hope you do not think me too bold in writing. I wish to tell you of my feelings towards you.

I admire you greatly. You are a fine, talented woman. I am impressed by the dignity and courage with which you have adapted to secular life. I see you as being a woman of steadiness and good sense. Above all, I see you as living with the Lord Jesus.

I write to you to ask you, in all humility, if you would consider being my wife. I cannot offer you a life of luxury or wealth in this world. But I can offer what I have, which is my wit and intellect; and my calling to Christ.

I am sending this letter to you via my friend Lucas Cranach. He knows about my feelings and supports my suit. Should you wish, after due consideration, to reply to this letter, he will be happy to convey it to me in all confidentiality.

I remain your humble servant,

M Luther

So that was it. Over the last few weeks the Doctor had been calling in more and more frequently to eat with the Cranachs. He had discarded his frayed old habit and rope sandals and one of his wealthy admirers had paid for him to have some decent modern clothes made. He no longer looked like a shabby old monk. His tonsure had disappeared and his hair was growing thick and wavy. One evening he joined us for the evening meal; it was a Wednesday, because I remember we had been to the market that day. Dr Luther and Herr Cranach were discussing the creation of a large altar piece, a triptych, which the Council had agreed to pay for and Herr Cranach was planning to paint. The children were in bed, the candles were lit and we sang some songs; Dr Luther kept looking across the table at Ave.

"You have a beautiful voice, Ave."

"Thank you, Herr Doktor."

He continued to stare at her, until he gave a little cough, his hand to his mouth, and looked away, embarrassed. Ave blushed, and I pretended not to have noticed. It was clear that my friend had made another conquest. Somehow, though, I had put this out of my mind and only now did I recall that little scene.

Why was I so envious of Ave and her two suitors? I did not love Dr Luther, though I found him awe-inspiring and powerful. I didn't love Basilius either. But I was envious of the way Ave was able to attract men, to gain their admiration. Men did not approach me like that. Am I ugly, unattractive? Or am I, as some of the senior nuns used to tell me, too outspoken and opinionated? Perhaps that puts them off. Whatever it is, I do not have what Ave has, the ability to draw men to her as a foxglove attracts bees.

"What should I do, Kathe? It's such a compliment, I can't really believe it, that the greatest man in Germany wants to marry me. Tell me what to do. Should I say yes?"

I felt torn. I loved Ave, we were like sisters. But I resented her too for apparently adapting so much better than me to secular life. What sort of advice was I supposed to give her? What did I know about such things? I scraped my foot up and down on the roof tile until my sole hurt, and wondered what to say. Eventually I twisted round and jumped back through the window into my room. I barked at her, rather more sharply than I meant to:

"Don't ask me, Ave. Ask Barbara. Or Frau Reichenbach. Sorry. I really can't help you."

Chapter 10
Hieronymous

*Wenn es keine Vergebung der Sünden bei
Gott gäbe, so wollte ich Gott gern durchs
Fenster hinauswerfen.*

If God did not forgive us our sins, then I would
happily throw God out of the window.

Ave was twisting her skirt anxiously in her hands, looking at
me with wide eyes, as if I could make her mind up for her. She
glowed with excitement and indecision. So when I told her
she should go to Barbara or Frau Reichenbach for advice she
looked hurt. I was sitting on my bed now, and she was sitting
on the window ledge, her back to the light.

"But I want to know what you think, Kathe. You're my best
friend. Please. Help me."

"Do you love the Doctor?"

"No, I'm rather scared of him, to tell the truth. I love
Basilius and I'd like to live with him. But isn't it an amazing
chance, to marry someone so important, Dr Luther I mean?"

"Not if you don't love him, Ave. I would have thought it
could be very trying, living with a man like that; he's always
the centre of attention, he's so important but people hate him
too. And then he might get arrested and executed, and you'd
find yourself a widow. And what about Basilius? If you love
him, can you just turn your back on him?"

"He would probably marry someone else; oh heavens, I couldn't bear that!"

"So that's it: with your heart you want Basilius, but with your head you like the idea of being Frau Dr. Luther, am I right?"

"Are you angry with me, Kathe?"

"No, not angry. I think that I'm sad at the thought of losing you."

At that she put her arms round me and whispered in my ear "you'll always be my very best friend."

We sat quite still on my little bed, embracing, but I knew that my friend was slipping away from me.

After a pause Ave slapped her knees and said:

"Dear Kathe, you've helped me make up my mind. I can't turn my back on Basilius, even for the Doctor. I'll write back to him, explaining that my heart is already pledged to another. He'll understand. In fact, I think I might tell Basilius first. Maybe his parents would let us get married sooner after all, if they knew that another man was courting me? What do you think?"

"Yes, good idea, tell Basilius. As you say, his parents may reconsider, they wouldn't want to lose you. After all, you're not just a pretty face, you're useful to them in the shop too, aren't you?"

"You're teasing me now. I do believe you're jealous!"

"Yes, I probably am!"

So she told Basilius. He was dismayed at the thought of losing her to Dr Luther and persuaded his father to allow him to marry Ave the following month. And so Ave was able to write back to Herr Doktor telling him that unfortunately her hand was already given to another.

I feel bad about it. I did not attend their wedding. I had planned to go, of course, and I helped her choose the stuff, and the design for her wedding dress; we spent the previous day together preparing the breakfast and arranging the flowers. But on the morning of the wedding I woke with a terrible sick headache and could do nothing but stay in my room with the curtains drawn. Ave was hurt and wrote a curt little note saying I had let her down. But I really couldn't help it.

They moved to Weimar six months later. Herr Cranach has opened an apothecary in the main square and Ave and Basilius manage the shop and live above it. What a wonderful opening it is for them both! They say Weimar is an elegant town, with a castle and park and a great many fine houses. But I do miss my friend; what a lot we had been through together! Of course we write letters to each other as often as we can.

In due course it was my turn to have an admirer. We had been living with the Cranachs for nine months when I met the student Hieronymous Baumgartner. He had pale blue eyes which looked at you bold and straight; he was tall and fair, with curly hair and his limbs were strong from riding and fencing. I had never set eyes on anyone so handsome. My first impression was that he knew it, and was consumed with self-love. Nevertheless, I fell under his spell. He treated me with respect, not the suspicion or barely cloaked disdain with which so many men treat women. He listened to me, and seemed interested in my story, my life in the convent, my escape; he did not judge me, or dismiss me as just another ex-nun. We talked and talked; about Rome and the evangelist movement, our neighbour Philip Melanchthon, who had been his tutor three years before; the teachings of Erasmus of Rotterdam; his prosperous mercantile family and their home in Nürnberg, his hopes and plans.

He told me about a famous painter called Albrecht Dürer, who lives in his city and is a friend of his parents; it was this connection which led him to come to University here and why he knew the Cranachs; the two great artists had never met but admired each other's work and often wrote to each other about their art, their trade.

To begin with the two of us were seldom alone; at mealtimes our eyes would meet. I became aware of him watching me, and he was aware of my interest in him. Whatever he said at table to the wider company, I knew he was saying it partly for me.

He had returned to Wittenberg to learn about printing, which meant that he came to the Cranach House every day. After his stint at the press or the typesetting frame he took to coming through to the house. He enjoyed the company of the boys, Hans, aged ten and Lucas aged eight, and sometimes he joined us for the end of our lessons. I was teaching them Scripture, Music and Latin and would have taught them calligraphy and illumination, had they not both been far more accomplished than me, even at that age, in all things to do with art. So at the end of our sessions, towards lunchtime, we would finish off with some music and singing.

Hieronymous must have heard us one day and knocked on the schoolroom door. We were singing a song about a raven and his mate and he joined in. Then he said "Do you know the one about a swan?" "Yes, of course we do!" said Lucas, so we all sang the madrigal 'The Silver Swan' several times. Then he sang us an English song, called 'My Dame Hath a Lame Tame Crane', which we did not know. The children wanted to learn this one, because first of all the name Cranach was like crane, *Kranich*, and secondly because the family have a pet crane; she's like an elegant old lady and limps about the yard with the poultry; now and then she ventures through the scullery into the kitchen and Cook shoos her out. Elsa's father found her on the roadside with a broken leg which meant she could no longer fly; these long legged birds have to run fast before they can take off. So he brought the wounded thing to Hans, and his mother let him keep her. In the autumn they have to shut her in the hen house to stop her trying to fly away as the flocks gather in the sky for their migration south. So when we learnt the song about a crane it seemed very apt; the boys enjoyed getting their tongues round the English and sang it with Hieronymous at lunch until the whole company learnt the song and joined in: family, guests, apprentices and servants, all singing about a lame crane in a foreign language. How we all laughed, because as we sang the bird herself poked her head through the window, holding it on one side as if she knew the song was about her!

After that Hieronymous took to visiting the schoolroom regularly at midday, and the boys looked forward to his visits. Sometimes he took them fishing in the afternoon, or they invited him upstairs to their father's studio. At other times he stole time off to be with me.

I remember one particular afternoon in April. The boys had finished their lessons and the morning chores were done; we had eaten lunch and the whole household was quiet for the midday rest. Hieronymous took my arm and we walked down the street, through the Elster Gate, past the fairground and over the causeway into the water meadows.

It was probably risky for my reputation, going out alone with a young man, but I wasn't worried. The sun shone, the Elbe flowed past, smooth, powerful and eddying. I have never seen the sea, but this river is so wide and so deep, I sometimes pretend it is the sea, especially when it's misty and you can't see the far bank. A few horses were plodding upstream, pulling barges, their brown sails furled; other barges were gliding north with the current, a breeze in their sales; their horses accompanied them on the tow-path, occasionally trotting to keep up.

Life was thrumming after the long dormant season. Frogs and toads were croaking in the marsh and we breathed in the fragrance of wild flowers: speedwell, forget-me-nots, Pasque flowers, buttercups. The air was buzzing with insects: dragonflies, lacewings, butterflies, mayflies. Larks hung suspended above us, spilling out their strings of notes. We stood still to watch a great sea eagle circling above the river; without warning it dropped vertically into the water, then emerged beating its enormous wings in spray and floundered awkwardly back into the air, clutching a writhing fish in its talons. We held hands and laughed, and played 'hit the cockchafer'; we felt alive and the air was heavy with love.

Suddenly, he stopped fooling around, stood still in front of me and cupped my cheeks in his hands, his expression grave.

"Kathe," he said. He kissed my hands: my knuckles first,

then, turning them over, he kissed my palms; he kissed my wrists, and the soft skin inside my arm; then he embraced me, kissed my eyes, my cheeks, my lips. And overhead, a skein of cranes are flying, their long necks stretched out in front, their long legs behind, calling, calling. My knees are weak, and I am filled with desire for him.

There are those who like to imply that my husband was not the first man to know me. They can say what they like. If I were to refute their allegations they would not believe me. I have to admit I wanted him. I felt his lips on my lips, his tongue on mine; his warm breath on my neck, the ache within me. As our intellects entwined in sweet conversation and our spirits entwined with affection and humour, so it followed, as night follows day, that our bodies should entwine and want to become one as well.

While I was in the convent, I used to dream of life outside those high walls, free from the constraints of routine, silence, temperance, abstinence, self-effacement. I dreamt, as any young woman would, of running barefoot in spring grass, of playing silly games of hide and seek, of laughter and conversation. My longing for the embrace of a man had been more nebulous, I could not really imagine how it might be. But now, I knew what I wanted yet it was forbidden fruit.

That evening I lay in my little bed above the printworks and relived our afternoon together. The hum of insects, the homing cranes and tumbling eagle, the warmth of sun on our skin; the Elbe flowing clear and strong; our desire for each other as strong as that river, flowing north. My secret place, up to then dormant, was awakened. With my hand, in the darkness of the night, I discovered my petals, open like a foxglove welcoming a bumble bee: moist, warm, aching. For Hieronymous I lay awake and ached.

After that we met when and where we could: in the dairy, the cow shed, the cellar, behind the beehives in the orchard, in the hay meadows by the river. Our passion grew. Intellectually, emotionally, physically, we belonged together; life without him seemed unimaginable. Then, one day towards the end of May, I came home from the market carrying a goose and a basket full of fat white asparagus. Hieronymous was waiting for me in the entrance hall, dressed for a journey.

"Käthchen, my sweet, I'm going home for Whitsun. I want to tell my parents about you, about us. But I'll write, my dearest, and I'll be back, and we shall be betrothed. Be patient. Wait for me. I love you."

He held me close, and I smelt his male pungency. At that point young Lucas and Hans and little Ursula all ran into the hall to say goodbye to him, so we drew apart; he tousled each child on the head, pulled on his gauntlets, and strode out into the courtyard where his man was holding their two horses under the linden tree. He swung up into the saddle, touched his hat, and with scarcely a backward glance, the two horsemen clattered away, sparks flying, through the archway, out into the square, turned left for the town gate and were gone.

The afternoon before, Hieronymous had been unusually ardent and now I understood his sense of urgency. The day had been hot and still. It was the midday rest and he whistled up to me quietly like an owl; I was sitting on my bedroom window ledge, my feet bare on the tiles. Hearing his call, I swung back into my room and crept down the stairs, holding my shoes; we met in the courtyard. He took my hand and led me into the farm yard behind the house; he drew me into the cool darkness of the hay shed and embraced me; then he spread out his cloak on the sweet new hay and we lay down together. We kissed with a sort of desperation; he unlaced my bodice and slid his hand beneath it, touching my breasts; but when he tried to pull up my skirt, I resisted. So instead, gently, he guided my hand to his member. Touching him down there, for the first time, I was startled, almost scared, at its hardness. It was as warm and hard and smooth as a cow's horn and, as you can with a cow's horn, I could feel blood pulsing in it.

I did not let him enter me. But after he had left, I would

sometimes wake in the night with my whole being crying out for him. Deep within me I felt a movement like the fluttering of a linnet's wings, a linnet trapped in a cage; its wings beating with a sweet, rhythmic ache of longing. I lay still, savouring the sweet pain until it abated, then I shifted a little in my bed, and the fluttering resumed. But in the morning, I would feel ashamed of such sinful feelings. As part of our vows the priest had told us "You should promise when evil thoughts come into your heart to dash them. Promise: Daily in your prayers with tears and sighs to confess your past sins to God. Promise: Not to fulfil the desires of the flesh. Promise: To hate your own will."

So I did my best to banish wicked thoughts of lust, of envy, of hunger; I should focus fiercely on our Lord, and on the Blessed Virgin. If we are cold or hungry or thirsty or in pain we should accept it as a privilege, because suffering, even of such a mild sort, is sent to strengthen our souls. I told my rosary, emptied my mind of temporal things and begged the Lord to forgive me.

How young we were when we took our vows of Poverty, Obedience and Chastity and became brides of Christ! I had no concept of what I was renouncing; now it seemed to me that the hardest of all the abstentions was Chastity. The vow of obedience I had already broken by escaping from the convent, and I witnessed disobedience all around me, especially in the peasants' rebellion against their fiefs. The vow of poverty was not difficult to keep at that time, because I had no money of my own, and had been living on the charity of Dr Luther and his friends, and now the Cranachs; my fortune was my youth, my wit and my ability to work. But chastity, it now seemed to me, was the worst of all. I had renounced the chance to marry and have children.

I remembered my talk with Tante Lena, on that Ascension Day when poor Sister Ruth tried to drown herself; I told her how I wanted to meet a man and to be a mother. Only a year ago, and I was still so naïve! I realised what a lot I had learned in the thirteen months since we escaped from the convent. I was not a nun now, I was a grown woman, with fleshly desires. I would marry Hieronymous, and we would know each other and delight in our flesh and I would bear his children.

For the first week after my lover left Wittenberg I felt buoyed up, optimistic. I imagined him being reunited with his parents; he would tell them about me and ask their permission to marry me; and I did not think they were likely to object; I may not come with a dowry but I am of noble birth. So I went about my duties with vigour. I would be up with the town crier at 6am to say Prime on my own: I find it hard to dispense with this routine, so thoroughly imbued in us at Nimbschen. At the Cranach House we said Grace before and after meals, and ended the day with family prayers, but apart from that devotions were not an important part of the household routine. The Cranachs are hardworking Christians, devout, certainly, but in a measured way. And they agree with Dr Luther's criticism of the Church, and his exposure of the corruption and the selling of indulgences.

My first duty before breakfast was to milk the two nanny goats and allow the kids to strip suckle them. Then I let the nannies out of the yard gate as soon as Gert the goatherd arrived. I would milk them again after they came home shortly before dusk. I enjoy milking – the gentle squirt squirt into the pail, the rhythm of my hands on the teats, the warm goaty smell of her flank, the importunate bleating of the hungry kids.

After breakfast I spent three hours in the schoolroom with the boys, teaching them and supervising their work. As I went about my tasks I thought of Hieronymous. Where was he now, what was he doing? Another week passed. The boys missed him and so did I. Each Friday – the day for mail from the west – I longed for a letter and each Friday I was disappointed. When no letter came, I would find reasons to justify his silence. He is busy seeing all his relatives. The turbulence and unrest in the land means messengers are hard to find, the postal service unreliable. He is waiting to write to me until after he has spoken to his father about our betrothal. Maybe even now he's on his way back from Nürnberg! So I decided to write to him, even though I had heard nothing from him. I would keep it cheerful and light-hearted and refrain from expressions of passion or emotion.

Dear Hieronymous,   *July 15ᵗʰ 1524*

It's one o'clock and I am sitting on the roof in the sun; the household is quiet. After lunch I lay down to sleep as we've been so busy and I was tired but then I thought of you and wanted to write you a letter. I miss you. Writing to you is the closest I can come to being with you. I hope you will write back to me. Perhaps a letter is already on its way?

Hans and Lucas miss you too. They asked me to go fishing with them, but of course I couldn't. So Hans invited me up to the studio to show me what he and young Lucas had been doing. I hadn't been up to Herr Cranach's studio before. I didn't realise how big it is with the two rooms; the workshop with the various assistants and then through that his own private studio where people come to sit to him. The rooms are so spacious and light, even though the windows face north. I like the smell of parchment and oil and putty and paper; and such an atmosphere of industry! When I went in, two of the apprentices were busy making ultramarine blue. One of them was pounding a lump of lapis lazuli in a bronze mortar, and the other was taking the fragments and grinding them into a fine dust. The lapis came in a large block all the way from Afghanistan, and was very costly; Herr Cranach says there's no better blue for the Virgin's gown and a very clear sky. He was so pleased when it arrived on a cart, wrapped up in old oriental carpets and bound together with rope. It took a crane to lift it off the cart, then they had to break it in four before carrying it up to the studio.

Another apprentice was making tracing paper with fish glue. It seemed to be a very elaborate process, but Herr Cranach likes to plan his pictures first on tracing paper.

The boys are learning a great deal by spending time in the workshop. They showed me some charcoal pens they had made only the evening before; it's so easy, you just lay a bundle of sharpened willow twigs in a sealed casserole and leave it overnight in the ashes of the fire; and Hans gave me a lesson on how to sharpen my quills – apparently I was doing it quite wrong! Do you like my writing? This quill was fashioned by Hans. Lucas has done a creditable drawing of the crane, he did her feet separately, then her head and beak and finally the whole bird, in charcoal and wash. And Hans has been working on a study of the pigs. The spotted sow farrowed shortly after you left, so they are a fine sight, eight of them, lying asleep in a row beside their dam. He goes down to the sty with his chalk and slate and watches them and makes sketches. Then he comes up to the studio and draws them again on paper and finishes it with ink and a tinted wash. I'm impressed by how much they both know already, not just the drawing but also about preparing paper and parchment, the names of the colours and how they are made and so on.

Herr Cranach thinks Hans is the more promising of the two, but Barbara thinks that Lucas, though still young, has more application; you will have seen yourself how engrossed little Lucas is when watching the older men working. Sometimes Herr Cranach allows them to sit in the studio and watch him paint, but they have to sit very still and not talk.

I am still teaching them Scripture and Latin. They sometimes ask for my help with music as well. And we're still singing!

Some hens have taken to laying eggs up on the roof, not far from my bedroom window, I think we should fetch the eggs down, or one of them will start sitting on them and we'll have a family of chicks stranded up on the roof! What would the hen do then, they would have to tumble down from a great height!

Anyway, that's enough about us. I wonder how you are and what it's like being back home in Nürnberg? Our times together, our afternoons by the river, our conversations, the laughter you brought to the house – they seem to be slipping away into memory. We all miss your singing too. Shall you come back soon?

Please give my kindest regards to your parents and sisters.
I send you my love,
Käthchen.

I did not want the Cranachs to know I had written to him – they would think I was being forward – but I took it round to Frau Reichenbach and she agreed to arrange for it to be sent. I think she understands my point of view, and thinks we are well matched.

I wrote him another, different letter, saying all the things I really wanted to tell him. How I desired him, his lips, his hands, his eyes, his body. How I missed his conversation, his wit and intelligence, our arguments about religion and our shared love of music and poetry. Did he long for me in the same way? Do you love me as I love you? Miss me as I miss you? I wrote it, but refrained from sending it. Instead, I put it into an envelope and posted it under my pillow. How I longed for a letter back from him!

Do you suppose he has been attacked by highwaymen? Is that the reason for his silence, his prolonged absence?

Still we heard nothing, no good news, no bad, and the weeks rolled by. I had to admit it: each succeeding day that passed with no news meant I was less likely to hear from him again. A heaviness began to pull on my heart. Had he really forgotten me? Surely he must still love me as I loved him? My energy drained away. I gave up my early prayers, lacking the will to rise at dawn. One morning I failed to milk the goats in time for Gert, so they were let out with their udders tight and full. Barbara was annoyed with me.

"Kathe, what's the matter? Are you ill?"

She was expecting again and her body and face were thickening. She looked tired and worried. These were uncertain times to bring another baby into the world. She had already gone through three confinements, and was anticipating her next one with a mixture of dread and resignation. The three children were a joy, but they must be fed and clothed and cared for, and so many dangers await the very young. An unwritten law: refrain from loving your infant child too much. Keep a certain aloofness between the child and yourself. Be practical. Care for him as best you can, keep him warm and clean, feed him, show him appropriate affection, teach him the word of the Lord. But protect yourself from grief – for every parent knows the probability of that infant dying before it reaches its fifth birthday. Each child is only lent to you by God.

She had shadows under her eyes, her step was heavy, she held her back when rising from her chair or walking upstairs. When Ursula climbed onto her lap and stroked her cheeks with her dimpled little hands she would lean her head against the wall and shut her eyes. Where once she and I would laugh and sing together while we worked, now she seemed to have little time for me. I wanted to stretch sheets with her, something we both enjoyed and laughed over, but she turned away and told me to get Elsa to help. Her aloofness made me even more miserable. I could not confide in her about Hieronymous.

I am single and twenty-six, and the man I love has disappeared and does not write: shall I ever have a husband, a family, a house of my own? If I stop being useful to Lucas and Barbara, will they ask me to leave, and if so, where else can I go? So I apply myself all the harder to teaching the boys and helping in the dairy and the garden. There's always so much to do in the summer; the days are long and it's tiring. I can forget the pain when I work and then I sleep because I'm exhausted. The University closed for the summer recess and Wittenberg became rather quiet like the birds do in the hot late summer.

Then, one evening we were sitting round the table in the family Stube. Herr Holzschuher, a cloth merchant from Nürnberg, and his wife were staying with us on their way to Carlsbad for the waters. He happened to mention the Baumgartner family, who trade in furs and fabrics.

"We know their son Hieronymous, he's been learning the publishing trade with us," said Lucas. "He studied Theology under Philip Melanchthon a couple of years ago."

"Yes, that'll be their younger son. He's just become betrothed, a suitable match, it seems. Though we were surprised at the haste, and the bride is only fifteen. Yes, a handsome fellow, that young Hieronymous."

This news struck my heart like a rapier, and I felt my cheeks beginning to burn. Then young Hans perked up and spoke without leave: "Hieronymous? He used to come here all the time, we went fishing with him, didn't we, Mother? He came up to the studio, to see what we were doing."

Then Lucas joined in: "Yes, and he liked Katharina a lot. They played games together in the dairy didn't you Katharina?"

An awkward silence ensued, and my cheeks burned like coals. I had to get up from the table, and as I left the room, Herr Cranach tactfully turned the conversation to other matters. So Hieronymous has discarded me. Was I not worthy of him? Did his parents disapprove? And yet my family has a coat of arms and a family tree going back centuries. The Baumgartners are only bourgeois merchants. From something Philip Melanchthon said, I know now what the real problem is: runaway nuns, even those of noble birth, are considered suspect, unreliable, soiled goods. The cruelty of his rejection is like a sword piercing my heart.

I go about my work with a dry mouth and heavy heart. Lessons in the morning, clean out the goat stall, wash down the dairy, feed the hens, collect the eggs. The ones on the roof, though, are inaccessible, so I ask one of the typesetters, Caspar, if he can help me fetch them down. He clambers up the drainpipe and puts all the eggs in his hat, then slithers back down the steep tiled roof on his bottom and hands the hat down to me, laughing. Fifteen fine brown eggs. Jumping to the ground, he loses his balance and clasps onto my arm for support, then apologises, blushes and looks away, confused. I know he desires me, as so many of them do; a nice enough lad, but his leather jerkin is ill-smelling and his fingers stained with ink. I give him four of the eggs to take home to his mother, by way of reward for his trouble.

The next evening at supper I told Herr Cranach and Barbara about the rogue hens, and their secret nest on the roof.

"We must clip their wings," said Herr Cranach. "This evening, after supper when it's dark. We'll do them all, for good measure."

So after the meal Herr Cranach and I went out to the hen house with a lantern and a pair of scissors. The hens were perched for the night, already drowsy and stupid in the dark. He took each hen and held her firmly by the thighs and fanned out one wing. I took the scissors and cut off the primaries, about eight of the long strong feathers. Clipping just one wing has the effect of de-stabilising the hen when she tries to fly, so she loses her balance and gives up trying.

"We'll leave the cockerel, he won't disappear."

We were nearly finished, just one more speckly hen, a beautiful glossy pullet just at point of lay; he splayed out her wing but I made a mistake: I snipped too close and cut the tip of her wing, the fleshy part – she squawked and flapped in pain and indignation, and in the light of the lantern I saw little spurts of blood, four or five times, spray out from the wound. Blood was on my hand and on my sleeve. I cried out in dismay. But Herr Cranach told me not to make a fuss, the pullet was fine, and they were all done now. We returned to the house and Lucas put the lantern on the kitchen table. I handed him the scissors and looked in shame at my white apron spotted with crimson. Barbara said: "You'd better go and wash, and change your apron."

I lit my candle, said goodnight and went first to the washroom to rinse out my apron and wash my hands. Then with a heavy heart and a dry mouth I climbed the stairs to my room and crept into bed. I clipped her flesh, her poor finger-tips, not just her feathers. I lay bunched up in a tight ball, the feather bed enveloping me; I smelled my body; my sweaty armpits, my slightly fishy feminine moisture, my pungent feet like ripe goats' cheese. Barbara was aloof and cool towards me. I sensed that in some way I was displeasing her. Then I thought about my faithless lover and tears slid down my cheeks onto my pillow. I was a linnet once, singing from the top of a tree. Now I was caged and mute. My inner voice said: 'Accept it, Kathe, he's not coming back. He's forgotten you.'

Chapter 11
A Debate

Wir sind besser geschickt zu verzweifeln denn zu hoffen. Denn Hoffen ist aus dem Geist Gottes, aber Verzweifeln ist aus unserm eigenen Geist.

We are better at being anxious than being hopeful. Because hope comes from the spirit of God but anxiety comes from our own spirit.

The kitchen was hot and dark, reeking of blood and beasts' innards. It was the eve of Saint Martin's and two pigs had been slaughtered. The carcasses were hanging from their hocks in the meat larder. I kept looking at their pale eyelashes, so perfect, like everything else about them. Now we were dealing with the 'fifth quarter': hearts, tongues, bladders and lights must all be put to use, nothing goes to waste. The skins to the tanner, the trotters, tails, snouts and ears to the renderer, the rest we process ourselves. Every part of a pig has value except the squeal, they say, and it's true, the pig is one of man's best friends.

Chopping up offal, frying onions, making breadcrumbs, mixing, stuffing skins and bladders. Boiling up oats in the blood, black pudding, blood sausage, liver cheese; I'd had enough. My gorge was rising at the smell of death; I kept seeing the pigs as they had been the day before, greedy, curious, sociable. We had raised them from new-born piglets, each one with its own character. But in the blood month such thoughts are not helpful.

I needed fresh air; it was one of those sublime autumn days, when the light is crystal clear, the sky bright blue like the lapis lazuli Herr Cranach uses for the Virgin's cloak; the few remaining linden leaves glowed like the gold leaf he uses for halos and the borders of the angels' gowns.

"Barbara, I can I take a break?"

"Of course, Käthe, we can manage now. Go out and enjoy the sunshine."

I washed my hands and removed my bloodstained apron; I took my woollen cloak from the hook by the back door, picked up the mending basket and escaped through the scullery into the cobbled yard; it was mild for November, the warmth of the low sun especially delicious because you know it cannot last. I was going to sit on the bench against the southern wall but was surprised to see four figures already there, deep in conversation.

It was Philip Melanchthon with three house guests; Herr and Frau Holzschuher who stopped by on their way home from Carlsbad, and an older woman who I hadn't seen before. Not wanting to disturb them, I walked towards the walled garden, but Philip saw me and stood up.

"Good day, Fräulein von Bora. Please come and join us. We are trying to sort out the world and its many problems." So saying, he offered me his seat.

"I don't wish to intrude."

I hoped I did not smell too strongly of blood and slaughter.

"You're not intruding," said Philip. "We could do with some light relief couldn't we? Allow me to introduce Herr and Frau Holzschuher, from Nürnberg."

"Good day to you. Yes indeed, we have met before."

It was he who had told us at table, to my confusion, about the betrothal of Hieronymous, when young Lucas had been indiscreet and I had left the room in a hurry. I hoped the couple had forgotten the incident.

"And Fräulein Biber. May I present Fräulein von Bora, who lives here with the Cranachs."

We shook hands all round and I took Philip's place while he fetched another chair from across the yard.

The usual pleasantries were exchanged about the fine day and the arduous business of butchering; I observed Philip's companions. Herr Jakob Holzschuher was a heavy-set man, I guessed in his early forties, with a well-trimmed brown beard and thick curly hair; he had a broad belly, piercing brown eyes and was wearing costly coat of beaver and brocade; his knee high boots were made of the best calfskin. His wife was a well-built woman, and wore a green velvet dress with black satin trim and a fur lined worsted cloak; her hair was dressed in elaborate plaits and ribbons, an exotic style for Saxony. She smiled warmly and laid a heavily jewelled hand on mine, in a gesture which meant, 'we women, we understand the burdens of running a house.'

"Ah, the fifth quarter, it's quite a task, but satisfying too, especially if the beasts have done well."

The other woman sat quite still. She was older, about fifty, I would guess. Her head was covered with a white linen cap; her plain grey dress had been carefully darned in several places. Her face was angular and pale; had it not been for her hazel eyes, which had a twinkle in them, she could have seemed quite stern. Our eyes met and in a flash of recognition we both knew: we were – or had been – Brides of Christ. There was an affinity, a sense of sisterhood, between us.

"Have you travelled far, ma'am?" I asked of her.

"I have come from Arlsdorf convent. Herr and Frau Melanchthon have kindly taken me in for the time being."

"We heard that your house had been dissolved. Was it a shock for you?"

Fräulein Biber hesitated.

"Not really. I think we had been expecting it, but all the same it was, shall we say, disruptive." She gave a rueful chuckle.

"But if it was God's will that the convent be closed, we have to accept that. All our community are scattered to the four winds, and we have to find some other way of being useful in the modern world. Jesus taught us not to worry, what shall I eat tomorrow, what shall I wear. I am confident the Lord will provide." Silence fell.

"Forgive me," I said. "I've interrupted your conversation. Please carry on."

I took up my sewing.

"Well, as I was saying," said Herr Holzschuher, clearing his throat and slapping his knees, "However painful it may be for some, nothing should be allowed to halt the progress of the new reforms. We can no longer tolerate the superstitions of the Roman Church and the nonsense doled out to the masses, nor Rome's corruption and autocracy. Who is Pope Leo to decide how we are to worship and what we may read?"

"But my dear," said his wife gently: "so much has been destroyed, so many beautiful images, pictures, statues. I think it's very sad. In fact, I find it quite blasphemous."

"'Thou shalt have no graven images'," said Melanchthon in his deep voice. "All these statues and pictures of saints are little better than idolatry. And don't forget, many of the so-called saints never even existed. Some of them were pagan gods that the Church of Rome simply turned into saints so that heathens would feel more at home with Christianity. We want to return to the simplicity of the Christian movement at its very roots; a plain table and a cross, the Word of God read out from the Holy Book, in the vernacular; thorough instruction of the young in the catechism and the Scriptures; clear doctrine from our pastors."

"Quite right," said Herr Holzschuher. "Out with all the flummery. Never mind all the money Rome has extorted from the gullible folk. That corrupt prince of the church has done nothing but build monuments to his own glory with the pennies of the poor. In Nürnberg, the general view is that we can worship God best through work, in the fields and mills, in caring for the deserving poor. Mysteries and fantasy, old rituals and magic, they've have had their day."

I watched the nun as the two men exchanged their roughly similar opinions. She sat still, her hands in her lap, with the faintest smile on her lips. I wondered what she felt about it all; she still had to learn (as I had when I first escaped) that men tend to ignore the opinions of women, especially when it comes to theological debates. I admired the merchant's wife; she was not afraid to have her say.

"But so much that is precious to the common people is being swept away. The festivals and holidays mean a lot to them, lighten their burden, give them respite from their labours." "Respite you call it, dear wife? Far too many holidays, that's one of the reasons so little work gets done. The people expect to celebrate every saint's day, any excuse for a party, almost once a week some sort of a feast, I despair sometimes, at the idleness of our workers in the fur industry. How can you run a business like ours if the workers are constantly downing tools; how can the harvest be brought in, or fealty be paid, if the peasants are spending so much time and energy preparing for a feast or enjoying a feast or recovering from a feast?"

The men laughed at this, and Philip asked the visitors if they would like some form of refreshment. He does this sometimes, coming over to the Cranach House and entertaining guests; I think he spends more time here or at the Black Cloister than in his own house. We all declined the offer.

Frau Holzschuher continued:

"On our journey here from Carlsbad the coach was held up by a gang of angry young men with pitchforks and poles, but the coachman managed to see them off with his matchlock. But further on, between Leipzig and Torgau, we came across a group of elderly peasant women, on their knees at a crossroads; we told the coachman to stop and Jakob asked them what the trouble was. They got to their feet and told us that the shrine where they had always stopped at each morning on their way to the fields had been smashed and desecrated. We saw it, the shattered remnants of our Blessed Lady, in a heap on the road, the wooden shelter in splinters.

"Well, you know, the simple people need to understand," said Melanchthon, "that this worship of wood and plaster is misguided – Truth lies in the Scripture – '*sola scriptura*', unmediated by the heresies and obfuscation of the priests. If the common people are confused and have doubts, their pastor will clarify it. Strewing flowers in the streets, bringing offerings to shrines, burning incense or carrying statues around the town, all these things have nothing to do with the true God."

"How can you be so sure?" asked Frau Biber, quietly.

"Because, good lady, I have read and studied the Scriptures and discussed these matters with other learned men who understand such things. Where in Scripture will you find references to processions and holy relics and shrines? It is enough to lead godly lives, as Herr Holzschuher says, to live in communion with one another and to celebrate the Lord's Supper every Sunday. Nowhere do you see it written that we must build vast churches, appoint bishops and deacons and cardinals and monks and nuns and all the pomp and panoply of the Roman Church."

"Certainly there are abuses but these can be remedied. Are we in danger, when trying to find a new way, of sweeping too much out, of obliterating the essence of spirituality from the simple people?" Frau Biber looked across at Philip with her clear grey eyes, a steady, bold stare, the stare of a woman who has been in authority over others.

Herr Holzschuher twisted round in his chair to face the woman in grey: "Excuse me, ma'am, with the greatest respect for your calling, I have to disagree. We need, to use a womanly metaphor, to sweep the room clean, clear out the clutter in the cupboard, start afresh. Pomp, ritual, mystery, keeping the poor in ignorance and superstition, all this has grown out of all proportion since the Church in Rome became so overblown with its temporal powers. A clean sweep is what we need."

"But are we sweeping the room with love or with anger? I perceive a lot of anger in your Movement. Where does that lead us? Our Lord asks us to be forgiving, to love our enemies as ourselves. Women and children are fleeing their homes, sleeping rough on the roadside; young men leaving home to fight, housemaids are squabbling at the village wells. It seems as if civilisation is breaking down. We see brawls on the streets, hijacks on the country roads, women afraid to venture out alone. Is this what it takes to reform the church? Anarchy, in the name of Christ?"

"Not anarchy, but truth," said Herr Holzschuher. "To see the truth the people must change; change is always painful; but each man must be true to his own conscience. The Pope has no right to look into men's souls, nor to tell us what to think or where to enquire. The Church in Rome fears progress and hates new ideas. And why should we in Saxony be told how to worship by people living in Rome?"

"But if we had no Pope how would disputes be settled? Would not the whole of Christendom be like a fleet of little boats, all sailing towards rocks?"

"The Pope does not settle disagreements," said Philip. "He does not listen to argument or act as judge between two parties. Remember how he and his Cardinals reacted to Doctor Luther's criticisms; they summoned him before a court and then had him excommunicated. It was only thanks to the intervention of The Elector Frederick, and God's protecting hand, that he was not sentenced to death by burning."

"Yes, the Pope is a sinner too, as we all are," continued Fräulein Biber. "Possibly he is fallible. But in the end these matters over which we disagree are trivial, superficial, compared to the love of God and to the salvation purchased for us by Jesus on the Cross. Remember our Lord's words: unless we are as little children, we shall not enter the Kingdom."

"I agree with the Fräulein," said Frau Holzschuher. "All this intellectual excitement and ferment, this questioning of ancient traditions and customs – it's the men, being rebellious – they should listen to the women." (Thigh slapping laughter from the men at this suggestion.) "Oh, you can laugh. If women were given a chance, we would find a way of reforming and modernising without sweeping all the old traditions away."

I made a small grunt of assent at this and she turned to me:

"Tomorrow, for instance, Fräulein von Bora, what's happening tomorrow for Martinmas, here in Wittenberg? Is there to be a procession?"

"Yes, there is. It's all arranged, with a donkey, and the usual sweet biscuits."

This is an ancient custom, much loved by the people: one small boy is chosen to ride on a donkey, followed by all the other children holding candles and singing hymns, re-enacting the story of Saint Martin giving half his cloak to a beggar.

"Pastor Bugenhagen doesn't want to disappoint the children."

"I'm glad to hear that. To my mind, the reformers need a bit more humility, more consideration of the old people who love these traditions, and want to hand them down to their children and grandchildren; women in particular rely on rituals, and believe in the powers of certain objects and places; and why shouldn't they believe in miracles? Miracles happened in the Bible, why shouldn't they happen now? The Good Lord knows, we need more than a miracle to bring back some sort of order and peace to this world."

"You have said quite enough now, Wife."

"Forgive me, Herr Holzschuher, but I have to agree with your good wife; women do have wisdom and understand more than you might think. Apart from that I would remind you about all the good work the Mother Church has done, much of that work undertaken by women: convents and abbeys take in the poor and hungry, if you like they tear their cloaks in half for the less fortunate; they educate peasant children and look after the sick in their hospices. Where will the poor go now?

"Not only that, the convents have kept alive higher learning, reading and writing; and they pray; we should not underestimate the power of prayer, and the good it spreads throughout the world. But now the monastic houses are being gradually disbanded. Where will the traveller find shelter, the hungry find soup, the sick and dying some care and dignity? Who will pray for the world in her hour of need? And what is to replace them?"

A brief silence followed the ex-nun's speech. I began to think that this lady must have been a high-ranking nun, an Abbess, perhaps, or a Mother Superior?

"It's true," said Philip after a pause. "You're quite right, the monastic houses have always contributed a great deal – in fact as you all know, Dr Luther was himself an Augustinian monk – and Katharina here was a Cistercian nun at Nimbschen. I do agree with you, provision will have to be made to fill that gap. And it is being done already. Town councils are raising taxes so that they can build poor houses, schools, hostels. Here in Wittenberg, for instance, the old Franciscan Friary is being converted into a poor house at the Town's expense. And we're building two new schools, one for boys and one for girls, on the site of the old candle factory. Some of the candle women will get work there. Our children will benefit, they'll learn to read and write and grow up knowing their catechism. And as for higher learning, well, Wittenberg University is a good example: new universities are the best place for learning now. And of course the copying of books by hand, one of those houses' main sources of income, is likely to become redundant before too long."

"Yes, and another thing," said Herr Holzschuher, "forgive me for saying so, present company excluded I'm sure, but some monks and nuns have been living in luxury and idleness, on the donations of the rich. Do you recall those monks last year in Nürnberg, Hildegard, when they were chased out of their monastery and driven through the streets? The people hated them; they harnessed six monks up to a wagon like oxen and whipped them and made them pull it through the streets, the crowd were falling over each other, for laughing. They were fat and unfit, they went quite red in the face at the effort.

The council broke it up in the end, because one of them fell down with a heart attack – it was getting a bit ugly – and in the end, most of the monks made their escape; I'll bet they're living on a fat pension even now. Frankly, their order was idle and corrupt, most of us thought they got no more than they deserved."

We at Nimbschen had certainly not lived in luxury, far from it. We had worked hard and eaten frugally; and when indigents and beggars came to the convent door they were fed and given shelter. And we prayed and sang to Our Lord, which surely helps the whole of humanity. I was about to speak my mind, but Fräulein Biber spoke for me, her voice low but firm.

"Herr Holzschuher, I have lived in a convent since I was twelve, and it was no life of ease for us. Of course there have been lazy, opulent houses, throughout the history of the Church, and from time to time good men came to put right the abuses. Look at St Francis of Assisi – he gave away everything he owned and for centuries his followers owned nothing. It is in the nature of human affairs that things will start off well, then gradually standards slip; but I feel that you in Nürnberg – or indeed in any of the cities that have espoused the new ways – are in danger of destroying too much. In your zeal for a fresh start, you will find you have swept away not only the corrupt and rotten, but something much more important: holiness."

"Holiness? It's not a word I use a lot."

"The church is like a body – diseased and sinful, as we all are sinful, but within it there is a beating heart of love. I fear that the new rationalism has no heart in it. The incantation of familiar words, the celebration of mass in Latin, the singing of psalms and plainchant, with mystery and incense, these communal acts speak to men's souls. Processions around the town, the festivals, repeated year after year: these are what make sense of people's lives. For the simplest and the poorest peasant, a holy mass or benediction is more powerful than a thousand wordy sermons, however clever the preacher. When I see an old woman kneeling before the altar, or lighting a candle in front of a much-loved saint, or stopping on the road by a sacred shrine, as you saw, Ma'am, I see the purest love of God, not superstition and ignorance."

"So what do you think about all the relics that people pay so much to acquire, to see?' asked Philip. "Most of them are fakes. Don't you think it's mere exploitation of the poor and gullible, playing on their superstition and ignorance?"

"Yes, it is a form of exploitation and a way of raising money to rebuild churches. But I don't think it matters. If the poor believe in the divinity of such things, then it helps them in their faith and devotion. It's the same when we make a pilgrimage; for us it is the journey, the commitment, the struggle to reach the sacred place, rather than the place itself which is significant."

"Hocus pocus. They believe if they touch this or that relic they'll be cured of some malady or their crops will grow or their sick child will recover. They are not 'praying,' they are being duped with the promise of miracles, if you like."

"But they are like children, they don't know any better. If you take these things away from them, they'll seek out some wise woman in the forest and get her to cast spells, or prepare noxious infusions. If the Church denies them a little magic, they'll look for it elsewhere. That is what I fear and I am not alone."

"Well, I think we must agree to differ," said Philip, with some condescension. "A new world is dawning, and these old customs and ways of thinking must be set aside to make room for the new."

"It may be a new world," said Frau Holzschuher, "but it is a frightening and unstable one. You forget, Herr Melanchthon, things are in ferment out there in the countryside, in villages, on the roads, people don't know who they can trust, they're scared of their village being pillaged and ransacked by angry peasants; often the priest has run away leaving a void, even the landed gentry are on the move, or barricading themselves into their castles. You are in a cocoon of relative tranquillity here in

Wittenberg. The checkpoints at all the entry gates, the guards keeping troublemakers out. It's not the real world."

"It's the real world all right, madam. You could say we're in the eye of the storm here, with Dr Luther in our midst. We are at the very hub of the Reform movement. It may seem like peace, but refugees are pouring in from other towns. Which is why Wittenberg is so crowded, so full of refugees, mostly supporters of our cause."

"Well, I can only say what I've seen. Wittenberg's like a haven of peace here by comparison. We've seen angry hordes roving on the country roads, defying their feudal lords, abandoning their families, their villages, chanting slogans like: 'the last shall be first' and 'blessed are the poor, for they shall inherit the kingdom.' The old order is gone forever, but what has replaced it? And I agree with Frau Biber. People need a little magic in their wretched, brutish lives."

How right she was. But Wittenberg wasn't really so insulated against the troubles. Witchcraft was on the increase. Two women had been burnt in the town square only the week before, accused of having liaisons with the devil in the woods on the other side of the river. One of them was an aunt of Elsa's; Elsa's mother had come to Herr Cranach, asking him to plead with them for clemency for her sister; she protested that she was a good woman, that she was only helping bereaved folk to get in touch with their dead relatives; she was a barren widow so had no children to care for her. The neighbours had noticed the comings and goings in her little hovel by the river and reported their suspicions to the authorities. Herr Cranach listened to his maid's mother with sympathy but said he was sorry, but he had no power to overrule the courts. So the poor woman was burnt at the stake, along with another old nursery maid accused of casting spells on some children in her care. It was a grizzly spectacle and a large crowd turned out to watch. For my part it made me quite sick and I'm sure it's not good for children to see such things. Poor little Uschi witnessed the horror, knowing it was Elsa's auntie, and suffered bad dreams for several nights after it.

"Christ told us to judge not, lest we ourselves be judged," said Fräulein Biber. "'Let him who is without sin cast the first stone'. What is more important? That the Church should mete out punishments and spread fear, or show our Lord's love and infinite mercy? Should they condemn old women to the stake, or try to reform them? If men of the world insist on punishments and cruelties, let them do so in the name of the world and not of Christ."

"Dear Fräulein Biber, you should not take these sayings literally," said Melanchthon.

"But is that not what you and your fellow scholars are doing – drawing us back to the Scriptures, relying on them alone for truth and guidance?" I said, no longer able to hold my tongue.

Philip looked a little taken aback at this, but he said "Have a care what you say, Fräulein. We are not yet living in the Kingdom. If we do not act decisively to root out a small evil, cruel though our actions may appear, a far greater evil may occur. As we punish the wicked, we must be careful not to do so in such a way as to take some wicked pleasure in their suffering – we do it only for the glory of God and out of love for him and his creatures."

"Well said, Herr Melanchthon," applauded Herr Holzschuher, and cast a condescending look in my direction. I looked down at my darning and saw that in my anger I had driven a needle into my palm without even feeling it. I held my tongue. I was furious with Melanchthon, and offended by the wealthy merchant from Nürnberg. Men can be so obstinate sometimes, so intractable.

Without our noticing, the sun had moved round and it had grown chilly. We all got up without more ado, shook hands and went our separate ways: I went back into the dark kitchen. My armpits were sweaty, though I had been sitting quite still for some time.

Chapter 12
Two Proposals

Ich fliehe mit aller Kraft die Einsamkeit,
wenn ich unlustig bin.

I avoid solitude with all my might when I am without joy.

Time is a great healer. I found out at last what had been alienating Barbara from me: it was all to do with the ringworm that had taken hold in the household, affecting the children in particular. She thought I had infected the children with it, whereas in fact I had caught it from them. We were all dosed with syrup of fumitory and ointment of samphire and field scabious. Anyway, we recovered from that, and partly through a desperate desire to regain Barbara's affection I threw myself into my work and was as helpful as I could be. After Christmas Barbara was delivered of a fine baby girl, whom they named Barbara. She says she's at her best when she has a baby to nurse. How on earth could my own mother have handed me over to a wet-nurse, instead of feeding me herself?

Another man was paying me court, and although I didn't like him, his advances did improve my bruised self-esteem. He's a humourless man, a pastor almost twice my age. He smells of old books and dusty cupboards; he clasps his hands in front of him, in a kind of supplication and walks a bit lopsided, close to the wall and on the shady side of the street, as if bright sunlight might catch him out.

His name is Dr Kaspar Glatz. He took to dropping in on the Cranachs for supper; he must have been watching me. However, I was taken by surprise when, one evening during Lent, he asked for my hand in marriage. We were sitting on our own in the parlour and without warning he lunged at my hand with both of his, clasping it clumsily, and in a thick voice said:

"Fräulein. I've been wanting to ask you for several weeks: would you consider becoming my wife?"

I had to stifle a laugh. Had I encouraged him? I am naïve in such matters. I did quite enjoy intellectual discussions with him, so maybe he misconstrued my interest as something more; but he held no attraction for me; his skin is pale, his eyes lacklustre. He is lost in books and antiquity, in religious theory, in Greek and Latin and Hebrew texts.

Subsequently, I discovered that he had been encouraged in his suit by my sponsors. Once it became clear that Hieronymous was not coming back for me, the Professor Herr von Amsdorf and Dr Luther felt responsible for the last 'herring' left unclaimed and they were keen to find me a husband.

Herr von Amsdorf called by and asked me:

"Have you thought about Herr Glatz's proposal, Fräulein von Bora?"

"Herr von Amsdorf, the answer is no."

"Well, tell me, my dear, is there any man of your acquaintance who you would consider as a spouse, if he were free and willing?"

"If he were free and willing, I can think of two men: the first one is you!" (I said this with a laugh and a sparkle, so he need not take it as a serious suggestion, though I would have gladly married him.) "Or, failing that, I can think of one other."

As I said this I looked at him defiantly, knowing that what I was about to say was bold.

"And might I know who that is?"

"Dr Luther."

Von Amsdorf made a sort of puffing sound as if to say, this woman has a nerve. He stood up and took his leave courteously enough, but left the room shaking his head. He must then have gone straight to the Black Cloister and told the Doctor about my rejection of Dr Glatz. Much later, I learnt that on hearing this Dr Luther had sworn in fury and said "Who the devil *will* she have then?" Whereupon von Amsdorf told him what I had said to him.

After von Amsdorf had gone I sat in a daze staring at my hands. The skin was cracked and my fingernails were dirty – I'd been thinning radish seedlings. Why, when he asked me who I would be happy to take as a husband, had I heard myself say the Doctor, almost before I knew it myself? What had made me say that? I smiled at my own audacity and then laughed out loud. Where had I got that idea? Of course I admired the Doctor, respected his intellect and courage, was grateful to him for helping me and the others to break out of the convent, and for looking after me since. But marriage? And yet, was it such a foolish idea? I needed a husband, and the Doctor certainly needed a wife. Indeed, he wanted a wife, or he would not have proposed to Ave. Perhaps that little stab of jealousy I had felt when he proposed to my friend had sown a seed in my heart, imagining I could be his wife just as well as Ave, who had turned him down.

What was the attraction? You could say Dr Luther was even more absorbed and lost in the world of ancient Hebrew, the Greek language and life in Palestine fifteen hundred years ago than was the worthy Dr Glatz. But in every other way he is incomparable to Glatz. Dr Luther is brimming with energy and humour. He laughs, jokes about down-to-earth things like farting and bowel movements. He sings with his lute and writes songs and hymns; he loves small children; he walks through the town greeting people cheerily; he rides out of town, to and from the villages, noticing when birds arrive, where they nest, when they gather for their autumn migration; he rejoices in wild flowers in their season, in the greening in spring of the great oaks and elms along the river bank. He loves his dog, his hens, his horse, the goats and pigs. I caught him once, leaning over the Cranachs' sty door watching a sow feeding her litter.

"I'd like to think she'll go to heaven, the old sow, when her time comes. She has the blessedness of any mother, look at how she feeds and cares for them; and yet all her piglets must die, just to feed us, to hang by the hocks in the larder, then in the bacon room, to see us humans through the winter."

Above all, Martin rejoices in being alive, whereas Kaspar Glatz seems lost in a world of dusty books. As Julian of Norwich once said, he sees God in everything.

I cannot say I love the Doctor. But how many people marry for love? Usually it's an economic union, a union of mutual benefit to the couple in question and the families involved. I began to weigh up the reasons why a marriage between him and me might not be such a bad idea. Here I am, a single woman no longer in the first flush of youth, of noble birth but with no dowry, and few prospects of a good marriage; I have cast myself out into a dangerous world, hostile to women. And here he is – a monk nearly all his adult life, still in fear for his life, with too much work and very little money despite his fame, (or notoriety). Everyone agrees, Barbara, Frau Reichenbach, even Catharina Melanchthon: he needs a wife to manage his affairs. And poor Dorothea his housekeeper – she's a good cook, but she's not very bright and goes mad trying to run his kitchen and his household and feed all the hangers-on and droppers-in. I could be that person. I know from my years at the convent how to run an estate and mind the pennies; I have learnt from Barbara how to run a home and give a husband support and encouragement.

Added to that, I am well educated; unlike most secular women, I read, write and speak Latin, I am well versed in the Scriptures, and schooled in theology. I enjoy music and singing, and can hold my own with him in a conversation or a song. I would be more than a helpmeet and wife, I would be a soul mate, a companion to him, someone to exchange ideas with, someone to encourage him in his intellectual endeavours, someone to confide in. Above all, Dr Luther and I have this in common: we have both experienced the monastic life, with all the intellectual, spiritual and ascetic rigours that entails.

So I sat there wondering what his reaction might be. He is not handsome. In matters of personal appearance and hygiene there is room for improvement. His skin is pale and he is overweight; but his hair is thick and curly, his chin determined, his nose prominent; his hands are broad and strong, if often stained with ink. He neglects to cut his nails or shave as often as he should. His clothes of plain wool are shabby and not always clean. And heaven only knows when he last took a bath.

To some he is notorious – he has overthrown everything they hold dear. But he has a magnetic power. His eyes sparkle with a dangerous energy. If your eyes meet his it's almost as if he can see into your soul. His gaze has a different power from my suitor Hieronymous; when he looked at me he touched me in my inner core, aroused my womanhood. When Dr Luther looks at me he sees into my mind, my soul; and that is exciting in a different way. He has a presence. A room might be full of people talking, moving about, greeting one another – but when the Doctor walks in a hush falls and all eyes turn to him.

His power is not of the sword but of the word. What he says or writes today can be read next week in Paris, Lucca, Seville or Cambridge. This power fascinates me. And yet for all this fame he seems a lonely figure.

One evening a few weeks ago the Doctor came into the Stube as supper was about to be served; Barbara invited him to join us. He said grace. After the meal he stayed on, drinking wine, telling stories, anecdotes; little Uschi sat on his knee as he told her, told all of us really, the story of Rumpelstiltskin; we all joined in the incantation: "Straw into Gold, Straw into Gold! Rumpelstiltskin is my name!" Then we fetched our various pipes and lutes and fiddles and made music – Lucas had recently bought some printed sheet music; then we sang songs in parts, folk songs, plainsong, and one of Luther's hymns, 'Praise be to you, Lord Jesus Christ'.

It was bed time for the children and Dr Luther raised his glass in a toast: "If Theology is to have the first place, I would give music second, and the very highest honour. Singing is such a good way to pray, the melody lingers in your head and plays back to you, again and again. To sing is to pray twice."

The candles burned low, and still we sat and talked and sang. Eventually he got to his feet and said: "Well, good people, I must leave you." Before he left we all joined in the beautiful canon which comes from Psalm 115: *non nobis domine non nobis, sed nomini tuo da gloriam, sed nomini tuo da gloriam, non nobis domine non nobis.* Then Lucas showed him out of the warm cosiness of the Cranach's parlour.

I thought of him walking home on his own to the Black Cloister, to its cold dark rooms, its shabbiness and discomfort. Nothing has been done to the building since the monks left five years ago. They haven't even installed a tile oven, only a huge open grate which smokes when the wind is in the wrong direction. The walls have no hangings, the floors at ground level are bare cold flagstones, and upstairs there are only plain wooden boards, with no rugs or rushes. And though he is not usually on his own, the household is a loosely knit collection of men; students who share his roof as paying guests; visiting ministers or one-time monks; various travelling scholars who call on him and whom he then invites to stay. It is not, as a monastery is, a united community with all the warmth and inner politics and tensions and gossip you inevitably get in a community. People come and go. Dorothea is the only woman in the place, apart from a couple of day time maids; and she has her hands full just managing the kitchen. I know how uncomfortable it is, because I lived there for three months; it's badly heated, inconvenient and grubby. Did he feel lonely?

He has a boil on his chin – I want to draw out the pus with a bran poultice and smear it with honey and clary sage. He complains of gallstones and Barbara has prepared infusions of of blackthorn leaves for him, but I am sure that with his mind on higher things, writing sermons and doing translation, he'll just forget to prepare them when he gets home. Dorothea is not the mothering type, so she doesn't look after him as he needs to be looked after, as I would. As I want to. Gradually it dawns on me how much I admire his intelligence, his humour, his earthiness.

He has courage. When he published the Ninety-Five Theses he knew full well the risk he was taking. He knows full well what happened to earlier rebels like Jan Hus and Jerome of Prague a hundred years ago. They were burnt at the stake as heretics. That could have happened to the Doctor after the Diet of Worms; it could still happen. There are those even today who would gladly see him dead. Herr Cranach thinks that if the Emperor Charles had not been waging war in France he would have hunted Martin down when he emerged from hiding in the Wartburg. But Hus said this before they killed him in Konstanz: "Today you kill a goose (which is Hus in the Czech language) but later will come a swan, which you will not be able to kill!"

Over the next few days I spent a lot of time in quiet prayer to our Lord and to the Blessed Virgin, but being very careful not to ask for anything. I just prayed that His will be done, in this as in all things. I had been taught never to ask for selfish things in my prayers. To hope for what I want may be to hope for the wrong thing. Yet I am filled with a deep conviction, that it was not wrong to say what I did say to von Amsdorf, whatever the consequences. All the same and just in case, I offer up prayers to St Jude, the patron saint of lost causes, for this most unlikely of outcomes.

I was in the kitchen garden with Elsa thinning beetroot seedlings when young Lucas came out to find me.

"Tante Katharina, my Father wants to speak to you. Up in his studio. He says, can you come up?"

"Thank you, Lucas, I'll be with him shortly."

I wondered what he could want with me. He had never invited me up to his studio before; it was a male preserve, women went there only to sit to him. I hurried indoors, washed my hands, took off my apron and straightened my hair. I walked up the stairs and through the first studio, where five assistants were at work. They looked at me curiously as I greeted them; I knocked on Herr Cranach's door.

"Enter."

He was sitting at his enormous desk, with papers spread out upon it. He is an imposing man with a long white beard and stern appraising eyes. He has a way of looking at you up and down as if assessing your proportions, planning to paint you. He is old enough to be my father, and quite a bit older than his wife. His voice is quiet but full of authority and I have never heard him raise it in anger. He is a stern but fair master; his apprentices are lucky and they know it. All the same, I am cautious in his presence.

He bade me sit down. In the corner was an easel, and the room smelt of linseed oil and turpentine. He was wearing his painter's smock and had obviously stopped work for a few minutes.

"The Doctor came to see me this morning."

"Oh yes?"

"Yes. It was about you."

I felt myself blushing and lowered my eyes. My fingernails, I can't get them clean, all that weeding and thinning. And the skin is dry, I must get some more hand cream.

"I have something important to tell you. When I tell you, you must take your time before making a decision."

He cleared his throat and stood up, as if what he was about to say was awkward and he was thinking how he should put it. I thought I knew what was coming. He stood with his back to the window, stroking his beard and staring at me. His eyes are so piercing!

"Dr Luther has asked me to put a proposal to you on his behalf. He asked me to ask you, with the greatest respect and honour, if you would consider becoming his wife. I must say, I have never been asked to make a proposal by proxy before, but it seems that he cannot bring himself to do it. I am, so to speak, his agent in this matter. So, Katharina, there it is. As I said, I would advise you to take your time, not to rush into anything. Ponder on it, say your prayers; discuss it with my wife; I cannot offer you advice. Ultimately, it must be your decision and yours alone."

"Holy Mary, Mother of God! He is proposing marriage to me?"

"He is asking you to be his wife, Kathe, yes. To be Frau Dr Luther."

"Herr Cranach. I must confess, I am speechless."

"I'll say it again. Take your time. No need to hurry. I will tell him I have passed on the message. When you have considered it carefully, you can give him an answer. I will not presume to offer you advice."

"Thank you, Herr Cranach."

"Goodbye then, dear girl. I'll see you this evening. Better not tell the boys. Keep it to yourself until you've come to a decision."

I got up to leave the studio, but before I reached the door he said, "And Käthchen, my dear, you are like a daughter to Barbara and me. We wish you the very best. Do not feel in any way pressured. You are welcome to stay with us as long as you like, as a member of our family. I want to tell you this so that you can consider your options before deciding what to say to him."

When he said this I felt close to tears, and went over to him and gave him a big hug. I love him, almost like a father, because I suppose he has filled the absence of my own father.

I left the studio in a daze. I remember nothing about leaving it, or what I did after seeing Herr Cranach. I think I must have gone to my room but somehow I was in a state of shock. It was one thing daydreaming about possibly marrying the Doctor. But now that he had proposed, I felt excited, but frightened too. Was

I capable of managing a man of this stature and importance? Could I do it? On the other hand, why shouldn't I be up to the task? I want to do something with my life, to be useful, to channel my energies into some worthwhile work. Here is a man who needs the help and support of a capable woman. But on the other hand, it may be dangerous, to live with a man who is hated by the powerful, whom some would gladly see dead.

That afternoon I went up to Barbara's bedroom. She was sitting on a nursing chair beside the bed feeding the baby. I sat on the window seat and watched her. The baby looked up when I came in, then went back to her mother's breast and sucked and grunted and wriggled her arms and legs. How fast babies grow, she seems almost too big now to be at the breast.

"What's happened, Kathe?"

"Barbara, Lucas has talked to me. He made me a proposal of marriage by proxy!"

"Yes, I heard about that. You've made a conquest, Kathe!"

"You knew about it already? You know who it is?"

"Yes, Lucas did tell me. I don't want to say anything, Kathe, because I think you must make your own mind up on this. You know I love the Doctor, we all do. But we love you too, and we want you to make the right decision. Don't rush into anything. Take your time and be absolutely sure before you say yes or no."

I hugged Barbara too, awkwardly over the little Barbara, now asleep in her mother's arms, smelling milky and cosy.

That night I couldn't sleep. I was faced with the most momentous decision of my life. The world spun round with images of what might be: me as the lady of the Black Cloister, being hostess to his important guests from far away; landlady of his resident students. Me, walking arm in arm with the great man down the streets of Wittenberg, exchanging greetings; "Good Day Doktor, Good Day Frau Doktor." Me, having to go into his house and sort it out, clean it up, modernise it; having to assert myself over Dorothea. Then I fell to thinking about the more intimate side of marriage. Sharing a bed with him. His large peasant's hands exploring my body. His kisses. Congress. Such thoughts about Hieronymous had set me on fire, but with him? I was not exactly repelled, but nor was I drawn to the idea.

But then I think about his power over other people. The hush when he walks into a room, or stands in the pulpit before a crowded congregation. His presence at meal times, the way people listen when he tells a story or sings a song. The Cranach children gather round him and plead with him to play his lute and sing. His nimble fingers on the strings, his deep, melodious voice.

Yet for all his fame throughout the world, for all his power, knowledge and intellect, he seems vulnerable and rather lonely. Of course women always think men on their own are in need of a good woman. But I can't help feeling pity when I imagine him alone in that great Black Cloister, with only a housekeeper and a maid and a string of itinerant guests and students; a man eating alone, praying alone, sleeping alone.

I had to give him an answer, yes or no. Then I knew what I would do. I rose before dawn and milked the goats. Then, as the sky began to brighten, and the stars retreated, I let myself out of the house and set off to walk across the town. Market day, and the stalls were being put up. Women were setting out their produce: great mounds of asparagus, both white and green; pink and red rhubarb with large umbrella leaves; carrots and turnips, early spinach, onions and garlic. There were fowls in cages and freshwater clams in boxes of damp moss; rabbits hanging in clumps, heads down. But I wasn't shopping, I was on another mission. I passed the Old Friary, now encased in scaffolding, being converted into a school for boys. I ignore the ribald remarks of the builders, who are already hoisting up buckets of mortar and bricks on pulleys. The sun has burst up behind the church towers, throwing brightness and shadows onto the highest roofs. Swifts swoop screeching in the shade between the houses and in the sky above swallows are dipping and flirting in circles. It's a crisp, cool May morning.

I reach the house with its studded oak door and pull on the bell rope. Inside, the hollow clanging followed by footsteps. Two eyes peer at me through the peephole, then the maid recognises me, unbolts the door and lets me in.

"Good morning, Fräulein von Bora. Do come in. Would you kindly wait a minute while I tell Madam you're here."

"I hope it's not too early for her."

I stand in the grand hall, staring round at the carved furniture, the Turkish rugs on the walls, a lantern clock ticking from its high shelf; in the empty fireplace are five madonna lilies in a tall blue and white Chinese vase. This is the wealth of a successful merchant. How different it is from the spare furnishings in Luther's Cloister, or the restrained prosperity of the Cranach House.

"Katharina my dear girl, what a pleasant surprise. I don't usually get visitors so early – I'm barely out of bed and as you see my hair is not yet dressed."

"I'm so sorry, Frau Reichenbach, but I really had to talk to you."

"My child, are you in trouble? No, I can see you're not. In fact, you're glowing with health. Don't tell me, is it love? I can't wait to hear, come, let's go into the parlour and you can tell me everything."

We went through into the smaller room, the tile oven warm and the room smelling of wood smoke. We sat down facing each other at the round table draped in a sumptuous oriental carpet.

"Frau Reichenbach, I want your advice. I have to make a decision. An important decision.."

"You've had a proposal, am I right?"

I blushed and looked down at the pattern of red and blue and white of the rug from Turkey.

"Yes."

"And am I allowed to know the identity of this courageous suitor?"

Frau Reichenbach always makes me laugh. But my laughter dissolved with no warning into tears; I had had a sleepless night and the strain was telling on me.

"Go on, dear girl, go ahead and cry." She fished a hanky out of her pocket and I wiped my eyes and blew my nose.

"It's Dr Luther. He wants to marry me."

She became suddenly grave.

"Well now. The good Doctor himself. Well, well, well. Did this come out of the blue or were you sort of expecting it? Has he been courting you?"

"No, he hasn't. No flowers or poems or declarations, nothing like that. In fact, he got Lucas Cranach to make the proposal, he didn't actually ask me in person."

"What did you say? He got Lucas to propose to you on his behalf?"

"Yes. Yesterday, it was. So last night, I couldn't sleep a wink."

"I'll bet you couldn't. My goodness, Kathe, this has taken me by surprise, I must say. Have you asked Barbara and Lucas? What do they think about it?"

"They won't advise, they say I've got to decide for myself..."

"They're right, of course. It's your life, your future, it must be your decision."

"But it's too big for me. I prayed and prayed but got no sign. I thought you might be able to help. What would you do, in my position?" I twisted the taffeta hanky round and round, turning it into a damp little sausage.

"What I would do is quite irrelevant, child; it's what you are going to do, and what in your heart you feel is right. What does the good Lord want you to do? Suppose I ask you a few questions, would you answer them straight away, without thinking? Answer from your heart with no hesitation?"

I nodded.

"All right then, first question: Do you like Dr Luther?"

"Yes, I do."

"Do you admire him?"

"Yes, I admire him enormously. But I'm also rather scared of him."

"I think we all are. Even the Pope and the Emperor. Next question: have you ever considered him as a possible husband?"

"Yes, as a matter of fact I have. You see, Frau Reichenbach, he proposed to Ave, last year. She turned him down, though, because she and Basilius were already unofficially betrothed; but I realised then that I felt quite jealous – because Dr Luther had chosen her and not me."

"You wished he had proposed to you instead of to your friend?"

"Yes, I suppose so."

"I think that's understandable. After all, it was he who helped you to escape from the convent in the first place. Next question: You like him, admire him, are a bit scared of him. Do you think he is a good man, a godly man?"

"Yes, I do. Children love him. Animals love him. I always think that's a good sign. Godly? Yes, that too, he's very devout. Though he does have quite a temper, I've seen him shaking in rage, red in the face with fury at people, if they've been slow or idle or somehow annoyed him. His tongue can be horribly cutting."

"So you like him, admire him, think he's good and devout, but you're a bit scared of his temper and his razor tongue. Next question: Can you imagine being his wife? Do you think you could handle a man like that? Larger than life, powerful, brave, good but temperamental?"

"I think I could. I think I could help him. I'd run his house, tidy up the garden, get some pigs in the sty and bees for his empty hives. I'd get in two nanny goats too and clean out the dairy."

"And what about the housekeeper, what's her name?"

"Dorothea."

"Yes, Dorothea. Could you work with her? She's a forceful woman and older than you."

"I am a bit scared of her too. I think she might resent some other woman coming in and trying to take over."

"All right, let's pretend you've coped with Dorothea and gone into the Cloister with your new broom and swept and dusted and polished. You've revamped the livestock and the kitchen garden. Now, what about Dr Luther's work? In what way do you think his work would be affected by your presence in his life? Indeed, would your presence as a wife be a help or would you take up his precious time seeking his attention and affection? From your own point of view, don't you think he might lock himself away in his Tower Room and you would never see him? Would that bother you?"

"No it wouldn't. I would never interfere or come between him and his work – it is everything to him. His translations, his lectures, his sermons, his writing – he has to carry on, that is his life's work; I'm sure his name will live on for hundreds of years after he's gone because of what he has done, I feel that very strongly. So I would never get in the way of his work, I would help him, encourage him, keep him well fed, and healthy. So that if anything he would work even better with me at his side to help him."

"Katharina, my dear girl. You don't need my advice. It is quite clear to me what you want to do and I think it's probably fairly clear to you. So go home now and write him a letter, saying you would like to speak to him. When the two of you meet, see what you feel then. You don't have to say yes or no straight away. It is a woman's prerogative to keep a man waiting. But if you want my opinion – nothing to do with what I myself would do, mind you – my opinion is that if you did decide to say yes you would rise to the challenge of being married to such a man; and it would be a challenge, make no bones about that. And I think that you could do the job well. It may be God giving you an important task to do. It's not for me to say this, but of course you need to ask guidance from our Lord. Listen to him in your prayers. I'm sure you have already. But you must be sure. Dear girl, I'm so pleased you came to consult me. I am flattered that you think an old trout like me can give you advice, when you're quite capable of making your own mind up! I look forward to hearing what happens next."

"Thank you, Frau R. You've been such a help."

"I've done nothing. I've listened to you, sorting it out for yourself." We both stood up and she gave me a big hug. Her ample chest felt warm and squidgy and reassuring.

When I stepped out into the street the sun was up and the streets growing warmer; I walked on light feet across the square, which was crowded now with shoppers and traders, the market in full swing; I was not shopping now. Instead I went into the church and fell down on my knees and prayed. I prayed so hard that it hurt. I prayed to Mary, to Saint Anne, to Saint Katharina; I prayed to Jesus and to God the Father himself. I prayed to them all, to give me a sign.

"Dear Lord, is it Your will that I marry this man? Is it a sin, for me, a fallen nun, to marry a man who was a monk? I broke my vows and left the convent; he broke his vows too. He wants to marry me and I think I want to marry him. But Your will be done. You forgave me when I escaped from Nimbschen. You forgave me when I transgressed with the Nürnberger. Now, I ask you to give me a sign. Is it Your will that I break my vow of chastity and marry Your son Martin, who loves You, and understands more than anyone the sacrifice You made for us all, for our redemption?

"Dear Lord, let me know what I should do."

Chapter 13
The Storks' Nest

Wer andere richtet, verurteilt sich selbst.

He who judges others sentences himself.

The next day, Thursday, I wrote the Doctor a short note:

Dear Herr Doktor Luther,
Herr Cranach conveyed to me your proposal of marriage. I am flattered to be the object of your admiration. However, could we meet and talk about it?
Yours respectfully,
Katharina von Bora.

Dear Fräulein von Bora,
Thank you for your letter. Would you be so kind as to visit me at the Black Cloister tomorrow afternoon, after the midday break? I await with anticipation your visit. Dorothea will let you in. Please come up the stairs to my study.
God Bless you, my child.
Martin Luther.

So on Friday morning I washed my face and hands, put on my best dress, braided my hair up neatly and pinched my cheeks. I practised staring boldly at my own image in the mirror, wanting to seem strong and unafraid; nevertheless, my nerves were as taught as harp strings as I walked down the street to the Black Cloister. The small door within the large entrance gate was unlocked. I let myself in, walked through the arched entrance, into the courtyard with the large elm tree, past the water source, which flows all the time into a stone trough, and knocked on the side door leading into the scullery. Why didn't I go to the front door like a respectable visitor? For some reason I felt diffident, not quite worthy, which was stupid, considering the reason for my visit; but this side door had been the one we fugitive nuns had always used during our stay here. Dr Luther's little herrings. How young we were then, and innocent. It seemed more like a decade ago, not just two years. I tugged on the bell-pull and stood waiting, smoothing down my skirt and composing my features. Dorothea opened the door and greeted me with her usual reservation; she led me through the kitchen into the hall.

"The Doctor expects you, Fräulein von Bora. Just go on up, you know where his study is."

I counted the steps as I went up, stopping now and then to catch my breath. Sixty-three. I tip-toed along the corridor carrying my shoes so he wouldn't hear my footsteps. Though he must surely hear my thumping heart! The door to his study was shut. I stood still before it and tried to steady my breathing, to slow down my heart. My bodice was too tight, the laces cutting into my chest. My armpits were damp and prickling. I got a hanky out of my pocket and wiped my sweaty face. 'Come on, you stupid girl, what are you waiting for?' I raised my right fist and rapped on the door.

"Come in."

He stands up as I enter and walks towards me, his hands outstretched. He takes my hands in his and we stand facing each other in silence for what seems like several minutes. Then he leads me to a chair and I sit down. I will my heart to slow down. My breathing is steadier now.

The great man seems rather shy. Can he really be nervous of me, a young woman of no consequence? He sits down behind the desk and runs his fingers through his hair. Then he twists away from me and points out of the window at a heap of sticks on a chimney.

"You see the stork? She's sitting on a clutch. That bodes well, you know, for the coming year."

"Yes, we have a pair at the Cranach House too, though we can't see the nest so close."

"Lovely birds. Where do they disappear to in winter do you suppose?"

"I really wouldn't know, Herr Doktor. Somewhere warmer, I should think."

"Yes, no doubt. They fly south, that much we know."

He turned back to look at me, then looked away again, cleared his throat and shifted some papers about on his desk. Eventually, with averted eyes, he said:

"Fräulein von Bora, you received my message, from Herr Cranach?"

"I did."

"And might I ask if you have had a chance to think about it?"

I looked past him through the window at the birds' nest, and just then the other stork arrived, landing awkwardly on the heap of sticks. It was change of shift for the brooding pair. I thought about my prayers to Jesus, about my asking him for a sign. Was this the sign I had been praying for? A pair of birds, raising their chicks, living and working together, in harmony and mutual affection. Yes, Jesus couldn't have sent a clearer message, a more apt way of telling me that this was the road I should take. That I should indeed accept his proposal and build a nest with him, on our metaphorical chimney, like those long legged birds outside his window.

"I have thought about it. I have prayed too."

"We can make no decision without the help of Our Lord. So let me ask you again, Fräulein, after your thoughts and sleep, after your prayers and supplications, what decision have you come to? Would this young, beautiful one-time nun be prepared to marry this middle-aged ugly, difficult one-time monk?"

"I think so. Yes, I think she might be. Be prepared to, I mean."

"But you're not sure. I'm not an easy man. I think you know that already."

He looks at me with such anxiety and tenderness, I see a yearning in his eyes which I have never seen before. And all of a sudden I hear myself talking with a fluency quite new to me, I hear words spilling out of my mouth almost before they take shape in my head.

"Herr Doktor. I have had reservations, I must admit. I have been wrestling with my conscience. After all, as you know, I took my vows when I was fifteen, I became a Bride of Christ. Then I became disillusioned, partly because of reading your sermons and letters. So with eight other nuns I abandoned my husband, the dear Lord Christ, and we ran away from the convent. I broke my vow of Obedience. I have suffered a heavy conscience about that for two whole years. Now, I find myself weighing up the possibility of yet another betrayal of our Lord, by promising to marry you. That would entail my breaking a second vow made to Christ, the vow of Chastity. And you, Dr Luther, you were a monk and you have broken your vows. Is it not sinful for a monk to marry a nun? I've heard it said that any children born of such a union are evil, cursed, even monsters. You asked me about my reservations. I am doing my best to explain."

"Dear Fräulein von Bora, I understand entirely what you feel and I would worry if you didn't find it necessary to examine your conscience on such a grave matter. But let me explain about celibacy and what I see as God's attitude to our sexuality. God made women in such a way that they are able to bear children and give them milk to suck. He also made men yearn for the comfort and company of women. This is natural. God wants what is natural. As I said, He created men and women to be together in marriage, and what happens in the marriage bed is as natural as eating and drinking. Chastity should only be for those to whom it comes naturally, when it is of their own free will; it should not be imposed upon them. I too have been celibate all my life. But I have preached and written many times about this, and do believe very strongly that every priest should be free to marry if he wants to; because before God and the Holy Scriptures marriage of the clergy is no offence. Clerical celibacy is not God's law but the Pope's; and Christ has set us free from all manmade laws. If he could, the Pope would forbid eating, drinking, the natural movement of the bowels, or growing fat! But he can't.

"No, dear Katharina, it is no sin for an ex-monk and an ex-nun to marry one another. You and I, we both grew up thinking marriage would not be for us; but now you have discarded your veil, and I my cowl. I think we might perhaps suit each other all the better because of that. Jesus would look lovingly upon our union, I feel certain. But do you perhaps have other reservations? Katharina, please ask me, tell me, what is on your mind, I can see you are still hesitant. I want you to be sure. Take your time. I can wait."

At that I feel bolder, and plunge on with my unrehearsed doubts and fears.

"I have wondered, as well, whether you're asking me to be your wife simply as a matter of expedience. You need someone to run your house, to be a hostess to your guests, to help you keep the accounts, care for the animals, prepare the provender. And of course I would be able to run your house, but I don't want simply to be your housekeeper; I want a real husband, a father for my children, a loving companion."

I suppose in a way I want him to tell me he loves me. But why should he? I do not love him and I don't think he loves me. But we respect one another and both feel, instinctively, that we would make a good team. Love can grow later, especially if we are to be blessed with children. I can almost see him now, with a baby in his arms and a toddler at his knee. I have heard him say that his parents in Erfurt long for him to marry and have a family; and I have seen how he enjoys the company of the Cranach children, how he relates to all the little ones in church.

He planted his large hands on the table in front of him and got to his feet. He came round the desk to where I was sitting – a sunbeam was slanting down through the high window with motes of dust swimming about in it. He took my hands in his and with a lightness of touch made as if to lift me to my feet. We stood facing each other, still holding hands, both of us in the sunbeam; then he touched my cheek with the back of his hand and we looked into each others' eyes.

"Katharina. Not a housekeeper. A wife. I want a wife to lie with, to laugh with, to eat with. I want, if God be willing, a mother to my children. I will not say I am in love. But I think we can grow into love. Does that make sense to you? I admire you enormously. You have courage and sometimes a sharp tongue. So have I. You know who you are. You know your God. I like the way you plant your feet on the ground. You will need to keep them there if you are to live with me. And yes, I admit that I do admire the skill with which you manage the dairy and the bees and the vegetable garden at the Cranachs. Of course I need a skilled housekeeper. But above all, Katharina, and I swear this is true, I want you because you are who you are, and I think we can live and work together. So, dear girl, forget about sins and forget about the job of housekeeper. This old professor and priest seeks a loving wife. And he wants, more than anything else, for that wife to be you, Katharina von Bora. If you say 'yes' you will make this old renegade the happiest man in Wittenberg."

"Then I will say Yes, Herr Doctor. Yes, I will marry you and be your wife."

"You will? You really mean that? Oh, dear God, I am quite overwhelmed." He hugs me like a great big bear and lifts me off my feet. "Come, let us drink to this! Let the bells ring out! We shall arrange a date for the betrothal. Soon, soon! There will be rejoicing! Dear Katharina, little did I know when my herrings arrived in the Cloister that one of them would become my wife!"

I refrained from saying, 'maybe not, but your first choice was not me, but Ave.' Nevertheless, the thought lay between us, unspoken, and ultimately, irrelevant.

Then my husband-to-be puts his arms round me again in a clumsy bear hug, and I hug him back. Our first embrace. The first of many. Then he holds my hand and leads me down the spiral staircase to the refectory and we walk arm in arm down Castle Street to the Cranach House.

"Bring wine, bring sack and sherry! The Lady has spoken and she says Yes!" cries the Doctor to anyone who'll hear. "I am to take a wife! Rejoice with me, with us. Here I stand, the luckiest man in Saxony!"

Barbara and Lucas came running towards us grinning; they kissed me and shook the Doctor's hand, amidst laughter and congratulations. The children whooped with pleasure and ran to tell all the staff in the house and the workshops. The lame crane flapped around the courtyard in excitement and the chickens began to cackle. In no time at all tools were laid down, presses put to bed and workshops were closed to make way for a party. The best wine flowed amid laughter, dancing and song.

I have to admit, it was not a love match as it would have been had I become Frau Baumgartner. However, we admired and respected one another and a flame of affection for him burned already in my heart. I knew he was not an easy man and he knew I was strong enough to stand up to him.

My time spent in the stables as a child had prepared me for this. If you tug at a horse he will dig in his toes and grow stubborn, and remind you of his superior strength. Ask him with tact and respect and he will lend you his strength willingly. Men are similar to horses. When I met Martin I recognised in him the same combination of power and timidity, of bravado and hesitation, which I had already come to recognise in those strong, gentle giants.

Of course it is ridiculous to liken Martin to a horse; I only mean to illustrate the way in which I approach him; and if I were to draw a comparison between the Doctor and a horse I would say he is not always reliable in the stable. He has a fierce temper on him. Poor Joachim the garden boy got the rough end of it once. He had stupidly left the gate to the walled garden ajar and the sow and her piglets had wandered in and rootled up all the lazy-beds – rows of young spinach, radish, onions and peas were all ruined. They had even pushed over the beanpoles, and lain down to roll on the soft tilth. It was annoying, because the gardener and Joachim had spent hours over several weeks sowing and planting, and it had all gone to ruin. But to my mind it was pointless yelling at the poor lad and hitting him like that. He was so contrite, and spent the next few days sowing fresh seeds and trying to make amends. Martin pushes himself too hard and never lets himself off easily; at the same time, he is as harsh a judge of others as he is of himself.

His temper is not improved by his poor health. He suffers from boils and constipation and indigestion and gallstones. He also gets headaches. All of this affects his temper and the way he treats others. I was soon to discover just how badly he behaves sometimes; he enjoys making fun of others just to get a cheap laugh. It was during the few short weeks of our betrothal, in early June. I had taken to joining him and his guests now and then for supper at the Black Cloister; we were sitting at table with several erudite guests, engaged in an interesting conversation, about theology and religious practices and how these can affect society at large. I was enjoying myself, taking part in a lively debate, when suddenly, with no warning at all, he turned on me, his eyes flashing, and said: "Fräulein von Bora, kindly oblige us all by talking less and listening more. Our guests did not come all this way to listen to a woman's opinions."

I had taken trouble with my appearance that evening, wanting to make a good impression on the visitors. I was wearing a new dress which Barbara had given me in honour of our engagement. It's made of green taffeta with a black velvet bodice, laced below the bosom. In my vanity I had probably laced it a bit too tight, but when he turned on me like that, saying that I should talk less, my bodice laces began to cut into my chest, I started breathing too hard, and I thought I might faint. I sat quite still, my face burning, my chest heaving, longing to loosen the laces. Then the Doctor heaped coals upon the fire. He leant back in his chair, one fist on the table, the other holding his pewter mug on his paunch, and announced to the table at large: "Men have broad chests and narrow hips, therefore they have wisdom. Women have small breasts, large thighs and broad behinds. On which they should sit quietly." Laughter all round, among the men at least. Even Rörer the secretary chuckled as he wrote it down in his little book; he notes down the Doctor's utterances at table for posterity and calls them *Tischreden* or Table Talk.

I got to my feet, picking up my half-finished mug of beer. I wanted to throw it in his face, but restrained myself and left the room with as much dignity as I could muster. Nobody was laughing now. I stumbled out into the cool dusk of the courtyard and leant against the pear tree gasping for air, loosening my laces, my heart pounding with fury.

After wandering around the grounds for almost an hour, I calmed down and returned to the house. It was dark now. The guests had left or gone up to bed, and Dorothea was closing the shutters and snuffing the lights.

"Dorothea, where is the Doctor?" I asked.

"I reckon he'll have gone to bed, it's late. Should you be going on home?"

"No. Don't trouble yourself, I'm going up to see him."

I stepped through the doorway to the staircase. Dorothea watched me in disbelief. We might be betrothed, but single women are not supposed go upstairs in the Cloister at night, if they want to preserve their good name. But at that moment I did not care about my name, good or otherwise. I was going to have it out with that arrogant, ill-tempered peasant.

I climbed the wide wooden staircase to the first floor, then the stone spiral staircase in the old tower. I knew Martin slept up here somewhere, but as I passed the door to his study I saw a light shining underneath it. I knocked and pushed it open without waiting for him to say come in. He was sitting at his desk, a candle flickering at his elbow. He got to his feet as I entered the room and we stood there in silence staring at each other. The tension in the air was as taut as a long-bow drawn back at full stretch.

"Dr. Luther, if you wish to marry me, you will never speak to me like that again." My voice shook with anger, but I did not allow it to rise. "I am your equal before God, not a foolish chattel to be made fun of in front of callow students and drunken toadies. I want you to apologise and promise not to shame me in public like that again." My whole body trembled, with anger and also fear, for this was not something I could unsay. I knew he was not used to our sex, and that in his eyes women were not equal to men. But it was quite intolerable that my betrothed should belittle me in this way. He had to retract, or we were finished.

Martin dropped his gaze for a moment and stared at the candle, scratching his head. He was wondering what to say. His face was flushed, as much with wine as with anger; or did I see a hint of shame and embarrassment there too? Then he stepped towards me, looking me full in the eyes, thrusting his hands out sideways, palms uppermost; for a moment I thought he might hit me.

"What on earth do you think you're doing, coming up here at this time of night? Can you imagine what people will say? Don't we have enough trouble as it is, without you causing more scandal?" He spoke quietly but his eyes were flashing with fury. I bit my tongue. I was not going to give way. He was wrong, and I think he knew it. Still, I had to keep my temper in check. If this went too far, one or other of us would say or do something unforgivable. Angry as I was, there was inside me a still place, a calm voice, warning me to be careful.

I ignored his gibe about scandal. "I'll say it again, you must promise never again to speak to me like that. I cannot and will not marry a man who does not respect me. I will not be the butt of your witticisms in front of others."

"You are an insufferable woman. What a nerve you have, speaking to me like that! I am a doctor of the church, not some naive youth, like that fair-haired fop from Nürnberg. You forget yourself! If you join us at table, it is to learn, to listen to great minds and not to argue and disagree about things you cannot understand. You women have your area of expertise and we men ours. You must learn to respect the boundaries."

"Do not make my sex a reason for dismissing what I have to say. I can accept criticism, but I will not be humiliated and made fun of in front of your guests; when we are married they will be *our* guests, not just yours. All I am asking for is the respect due to a wife."

"Then I suggest you learn to behave like a grown woman as befits a wife, and not a strident, petulant servant girl!" he growled, his jowl trembling as he pointed a finger at me with little jabs for each insulting word: strident, petulant, argumentative, opinionated, and so it went on.

I was dizzy with rage and had heard enough; so I turned, picked up my candle and made for the heavy oak door, slipping through as it still stood slightly ajar. I wanted to slam the door, but it was too heavy and closed very slowly. But as it closed, I heard a loud crash – Dr Luther must have thrown the pewter candlestick at the door. The light beneath the door had gone out, and I heard him swearing in the dark as he kicked the bottom of the door.

With trembling knees, holding my candle up in front of me, I made my way gingerly down the spiral steps then more easily down the wide staircase, set the candle down on the trestle table, and let myself out into the courtyard; I gasped in the cool fresh air and pushed through the portal in the heavy gate, out into the street. Then I walked unescorted down the street to the Cranachs' house, my footsteps ringing out in the silence of the late night. I was shivering and my legs were weak, but I felt buoyed up with defiance, certain that I had done the right thing: he had to understand, to concede my point. If he would not, could not, then there was no hope of us making a successful marriage.

Then I realised I was not quite alone. At my heels trotted Tölpel, the Doctor's dog. He must have seen me leave the Cloister and decided to accompany me home. I was strangely moved. Despite strict rules about who should enter the town, and all four gates being locked and manned from dusk until dawn, women were not supposed to go about alone after dark. In fact, the Doctor should never have allowed to me to walk back without an escort. But here was the dog, escorting me; it was as if he sensed all was not well between us; it seemed to me that he was pledging his solidarity with me.

I reached the door of the Cranach House and thumped the metal knocker. Shuffling steps inside, the old caretaker unbolted the small port in the oak gate. Before stepping inside I turned to the dog; he was sitting with his head on one side, watching me.

"Go home, Tölpel," I told him, softly. He turned and trotted back towards the Cloister.

Chapter 14
Whitsun Fair

*Himmel und Erde, Leben und Tod sind grosse
Dinge, der Glaube an Christus ist viel grösser.*

Heaven and earth, life and death are great
things, faith in Christ is even greater.

The house was dark and quiet. One lamp always burns in the hallway. I took my own snuffer (marked with a K) and lit the candle. I went up to my room and undid my bodice, slipped out of the green dress and let it fall to the floor. I tried to rub away the sensation of tight laces beneath my breasts by scratching my tummy; I visited the privy, washed my face and hands and crept into bed.

Sleep came instantly, followed by a dream about my father. He's riding through Wittenberg on his favourite horse, Conquest. He sees me and halts. "Käthchen, dear girl. My daughter. Where have you been all this time? Come with me. I'm going to fight in a wonderful war! Come, follow me!" and he waves and trots away without a backward glance.

I want to run after him but he's riding too fast and my legs are heavy; I can't keep up, can't push my way through the crowds. So I just stand there and notice that people are staring at me with open disapproval, even disgust! I look down; oh horror, I had forgotten to put on my blouse and bodice! My breasts are bare to the world for all to see! I wake up in shame, miserable at the loss of my father, guilty at my brazenness, and confused. Very soon, though, I fall asleep again; this time I sleep deeply and sweetly.

But when I woke at dawn a heavy dread took hold of me as I remembered our altercation of the night before. Had I thrown away my chances of a prestigious marriage? Would he reject me now, ask to be released from our betrothal? I knew plenty of his friends would be only too willing to discourage him from the match. On the other hand was I convinced about the match myself? Did I really want to devote my life to a man who respected me so little, who made fun of me in front of other men? I wished Ave were here for me to confide in. I could write to her, but I needed an answer now.

To my surprise, after getting dressed and going downstairs, I felt strong and defiant; I flung myself into work. I sluiced down the dairy, cleaned shelves and washed out all the pans. I shook out fresh straw into the stalls. The cattle festival for Pentecost was in two days' time, so I shampooed both the cows all over, from top to toe, taking particular care with their tails, bottoms and udders; I oiled their hooves and combed out their tail tassels, so that they would look their best for the parade. Barbara came out just as I was finishing.

"Oh well done, Kathe, they look beautiful. We must keep them clean until the parade. I was looking for you, because there's a swarm hanging on the linden tree. We haven't got a spare hive, do you know of anyone who's looking for a swarm?"

"The blacksmith's wife wants one. Shall I take it over to her?"

"Oh yes please. And ask Herr Schmidt, when he has a moment, to come over and measure up for some new shutter flanges for the shop."

I fetched a sack from the back kitchen, and looking through the workshop window asked one of the apprentices to come and help me. Together we approached the swarm. There it was, suspended like an idle dudelsack from a low branch of the linden tree. It hung motionless, more like a single organism than hundreds of individual insects; a dark brown shiny blob with a kind of glisten to it. The only indication of life was a faint hum coming from within. Franz held the sack open and I tapped the branch, loosening it from the tree. It dropped into the sack and we quickly tied it up with string; then I carried the precious bundle across the square to the smithy.

Herr Schmidt was bent double beneath a grey draft horse, pressing a red hot shoe onto his hind hoof; man and horse were swathed in blue smoke giving off the rich smell of scorching hoof; the forge glowed red, and a girl of about eight was pumping the bellows; I knew her as the smith's daughter from his first wife, who had died giving birth to her. Herr Schmidt straightened up when he saw me, and plunged the shoe into a pail of water making it hiss and boil. I showed him the sack.

"Frau Cranach wishes your wife to take this swarm, with her compliments. We heard she was looking for one."

"Fräulein von Bora, how kind, yes indeed, we do have an empty hive just waiting for tenants". He whistled at the girl to fetch her stepmother, who appeared in a moment, a toddler at her feet and a baby in her arms.

"We are honoured indeed, my lady. A swarm from the Cranach House, brought by the Bride of Dr Luther!"

I was quite taken aback that she already knew. How rapidly news travels in this town!

"Many thanks. Can I offer you some beer, or mead perhaps?"

She took the sack from me, and stowed it carefully in the corner.

"Thank you, but I must get back. Frau Cranach did ask me to say they would like some new shutter flanges when your husband is free; the old ones are not secure enough, you know how it is these days."

"Consider it done," she said; her husband was once again crouched beneath the horse, clenches between his teeth, the large hoof cradled on his leather apron between his knees, hammering the new shoe into place.

"When is the happy day, might I ask?" inquired the

blacksmith's wife, shifting the child onto the other hip and swatting away her little boy as he pulled at her apron.

"Oh, we haven't fixed a date yet," I said vaguely, and took my leave. Happy day? It might never happen. Back at the Cranach House I went up to my room and sat alone on my bed.

Barbara sensed something was wrong, but I refrained from confiding in her and she was tactful enough not to enquire. I must negotiate my own way through this thicket of thorns. For two days I heard no word from him. I for my part was determined not to approach him; if he couldn't find the generosity to apologise for his rudeness to me, I would not enter into marriage with him. Our union has to be built on respect: on mutual respect. Without that our marriage would destroy us both. Or this is what I felt.

On the Feast of Pentecost the sun was shining, the sky a cloudless blue, the air sweet with the fragrance of lilac. We all got up early to pick flowers for the cows and calves. They looked so fine with garlands woven in between their horns and head collars, twined hay and red ribbons on their surcingles and ribbons on their tails. Then we dressed up too, in our best frocks and caps, the boys in their breeches and jerkins; and the whole town strolled towards the Church decked out in their Sunday best.

The altar cloth was red for the fire of the Holy Spirit. The opening hymn was:

'Come Holy Ghost, our souls inspire and lighten with celestial fire.'

From the gallery children threw down rose petals onto the congregation, symbolising the coming of the Holy Spirit; then we listened to the reading.

"And suddenly from heaven there came a sound like the rush of a violent wind, and it filled the entire house where they were sitting. Divided tongues, as of fire, appeared among them and a tongue rested on each of them. All of them were filled with the Holy Spirit and began to speak in other languages, as the Spirit gave them ability."

I looked around the crowded church, and couldn't see him anywhere. Bugenhagen was taking the service as usual, but the Doctor often preaches or reads a lesson. Not today.

The reading continued: *'Are not all these who speak Galileans? And how is it that we hear, each of us, in our own native language? Parthians, Medes, Elamites, and residents of Mesopotamia, Judea and Cappadocia, Pontus and Asia, Phrygia and Pamphylia, Egypt and the parts of Libya belonging to Cyrene, and visitors from Rome, both Jews and proselytes, Cretans and Arabs – in our own languages we hear them speaking about God's deeds of power.'* It dawned on me that I had never heard this reading in German before; it came across so vivid and true, and might have happened here, in Wittenberg, in modern times, not fifteen hundred years ago in Palestine. It hit me with a jolt: that is what Dr Luther has done! He has opened our ears to the Holy Scriptures in our own tongue, so we can understand and delight in them. He has spoken with tongues. As this revelation swept over me, trumpets blared out from the ambulatory; they must have been hidden behind the altar and the sound filled the church; they blew to symbolise the coming of the mighty wind.

We sang another hymn but the words of the reading rang on in my ears: *"All were amazed and perplexed, saying to one another, 'What does this mean?' But others sneered and said, 'They are filled with new wine.'"* A lot of people, on hearing the Apostles speaking in tongues, accused them of being drunk; they had their enemies and detractors, just as Dr Luther did.

Bugenhagen preached but I did not listen. My mind was elsewhere, I was filled with doubt and anxiety. At length he announced the final hymn; the second last verse goes like this:

"Hardened scoffers vainly jeered, Listening strangers heard and feared, Knew the prophet's word fulfilled, Owned the work which God had willed."

Bugenhagen gave the final blessing and it was time to leave the church; we shuffled slowly towards the door, the aisles packed, people greeting one another. But where was the

Doctor? As we emerged blinking into the sunlight we came up against a crowd of gypsies gathering in the square, ready for the parade. They must have arrived the day before and set up their tents on the common with their travelling circus; what a mélée! Even as we watched, they began to process down the street; camels ridden by Arabs in long white robes; two elephants walking sedately, being steered by dark-skinned men in turbans; two lions pacing back and forth in a cage on a tumbril; a man dressed like Harlequin leading a dancing bear on a chain; on another cart sat three sad monkeys dressed up like little Turks in silks and satins with gold collars and chains round their necks; gypsy women swathed in exotic flowing skirts and embroidered blouses; flamboyant gold rings swung from their ears and their glossy black hair hung like thick bell-ropes down their backs. They brought with them a whiff of the east, and I thought about the Turks and how easily they could invade and take us over with their heathen practices and alien God.

After a suitable pause the more sedate municipal procession followed on: the town guilds, each one with their particular dressed wagon: the weavers, the basket makers, the printers and papermakers, the masons and carpenters, the smiths and farriers, the cobblers and saddlers; candle makers, bakers, tailors, potters; wainwrights, wheelwrights, woad producers; every guild had a wagon with apprentices and children on board showing the tools of their trade and examples of work; following the guilds came an assortment of local minstrels; dancers, jugglers and itinerant players; and finally in their wake, the ordinary citizens, men, women and children, wanting to join in, some of them leading their livestock.

We fetched our cows and calves and fell in with the crowd as it processed with great noise and commotion towards the fairground. Some families also brought their goats or geese or poultry or caged birds to show off or to sell.

Once through the town gates, we saw the fairground; the field had become a canvas city, with stalls selling all manner of things: grilled fish and sausage; pretzels and doughnuts; waffles with honey; in the beer tent strong-armed women strode about with swinging hips between the tables serving steins of beer to the thirsty crowds. I got separated from the Cranachs and their cows. I'm not very good in crowds; being amongst a throng can make me feel faint and my heart starts beating too fast. So I sat down at a table in a corner of the big tent and ordered a beer. I swallowed it in long cool draughts and felt calmer. All the time, I was looking out for my betrothed, but he was still nowhere to be seen. Was he deliberately avoiding me?

Then I had an idea: I would go and have my fortune told. I had spotted a sign earlier, "Come in and consult the oracle! Learn about your destiny! Madame Oraclieri will gaze into a crystal ball and foretell your future!" I found the tent and was ushered in through the flap. It was dark inside, smelling of something like incense, but different; an old gypsy woman was crouched over a low table, with one candle burning. She had a crystal ball and a piper behind a screen was playing a whining oriental tune. "You want I tell your fortune, dear lady?"

"Yes please," I ventured, poised ready to retreat.

"First let me see the colour of your silver!" she crooned. Her nose was hooked, and her large hoop earrings glinted in the candlelight. I fished in my purse for a small silver coin, and she whipped it away with her heavily ringed hand.

"Sit ye down, good lady. Show me your right hand." She drew a long scarlet fingernail across my palm. Then she looked at my face long and hard; after that she stared into her crystal ball. The pipe played on, and I felt myself being lulled into a sort of trance. "Ah... It is foggy, but I am discerning, gradually. Let me see... You are at a crossroads, my child. One road it is going into desert. That way becomes buried in sand; I am seeing thorn trees, drought, thirst and it is sad. You are lonely and are spending the life searching for oasis. You will die of thirst, not married, an old maid. Now I am looking down the other road. What do we see? This road is bumpy, many holes and bends, but it is coming to meadows and streams. On this road you will marry, my child. You will bear fruit of your loins but will lose some. You will be happy and also sad. Your life will be fulfilled, but you must endure much. Your husband will love you. A great man he will be and you will help him. If you take the right road now."

"Good mother, how should I know which road is which?"

"I cannot tell you that, my child. You alone must make that choice. Your destiny lies within you."

With that she gave me a bow with her hands together, indicating that our interview was at an end; she flicked a square of black samite over the crystal ball and rose stiffly to her feet. I thanked her and bent to leave the tent. I was blinded by the sunlight and felt dazed by what she had said. I no longer wanted to see the freak show or watch the acrobats walking the tightrope or the monkeys riding on circus horses; I didn't even want an elephant ride. I decided to make my way to the show ring where the livestock were being paraded, I might be able to meet up with the Cranachs. But of course above all I wanted to see Martin, to talk to him, make it up with him. I shaded my eyes trying to decide which way to go.

"Fräulein Katharina." I turned, and there he was! He stood staring at me with an almost supplicant air; all the crowds and cheerful hullabaloo fell away as our eyes met. It was as if we two were all alone. He came towards me, hesitantly, and took both my hands in his.

"I've been looking for you everywhere," he said. "I saw you in church but could not get near you, then I got caught up in the procession, so I went to the Cranach House but no one was there. Then I met Barbara by the cattle ring and she said you were here somewhere but still I couldn't find you."

I felt tears welling up but did not want to show him how relieved I was at seeing him. I must maintain my composure. Also, I was hoping he had not seen me emerging from the soothsayer's tent, because he thinks such superstition is wicked, and fortune-tellers have links with the Devil.

"Well, I'm here now," I said, swallowing hard. We stood

still, holding hands shyly, like children. I put my arm through his, smiled up at him and said:

"Have you seen the jugglers?" We wandered together through the fair, like a couple, amongst the sound of drums and singing and tambourines and laughter; the mingled odours of camels and cattle and sweaty bodies and fresh-trodden turf; people shouting: "Roll up, roll up, come and see the counting horse from Seville, the Indian Prince from New Spain, the tumbling Pygmy from Afric's sandy shore! You won't believe your eyes! Worth every penny, the wonders of the world!"

"Are you hungry? How about a grilled zander?" I realised I was, very hungry. We queued up to buy some grilled fish, bought two mugs of beer and carried our meal to the edge of the fairground; we found a tree trunk to sit on in the shade of a maple tree. It was quieter here and we could talk.

Martin blessed the food, said a short grace, then we tucked in. The fish was hot, crackly and greasy, quite delicious, served on a cabbage leaf with a dollop of mustard and a hunk of rye bread. We washed it down with the beer. Then, after wiping his fishy hands on the turf and his greasy chin with a tuft of grass, Dr Luther clasped both my hands in his big fists; as we sat there side by side on the trunk of a felled oak tree he looked at me again and said:

"I'm sorry, Fräulein Kathe. I was wrong. Will you forgive me?"

And I said: "Yes".

Chapter 15
Carp Ponds

Der heilige Geist lobt die Weiber. Die Ehe kann
ohne Weiber nicht sein, noch die Welt bestehen.

The Holy Spirit praises women. There is no such thing
as marriage without women, nor can the world exist.

We were betrothed on June 13th, Saint Margaret's Day, which
was the Name Day of my stepmother and my new mother-in-
law. The Marriage was arranged to take place on June 27th.
It might have seemed hasty, but the Doctor disapproves of
postponing marriage for too long after betrothal, for fear of
gossip and slander.

Much later he said "If I had not held my own wedding
quickly and with the foreknowledge of only a few people, they
would all have tried to hinder me, for my best friends cried:
'Not this one, but another!'"

On the day of our marriage the whole town decided to
celebrate with us. It all began at ten o'clock. Barbara and little
Uschi helped me do my hair; they braided honeysuckle into
it. Then they dressed me. The staff in the printworks saw me
walking into the courtyard, and they all began to clap, their
applause rippling through the yard like a thousand pigeons'
wings. I felt like a queen and smiled at them.

The church bells began to ring and Dr Luther arrived at
the door of the Cranach House, dressed in a fine new jacket

and breeches, with a short cloak over his shoulder. He bowed gravely at me, offered his arm and led me out into the street and across the square to the church. Crowds were already gathered along our way, cheering and shouting good wishes. I was quite overwhelmed. The crowd were excited – some of the children threw flowers before us, or waved flags. When we reached the church the Pastor Bugenhagen was waiting for us in the porch; he married us there, for all the crowd to see, with the bright sun shining onto the flagstones at our feet.

Swifts were shrieking as they swooped overhead but the crowd were hushed, wanting to hear the words of the marriage ceremony. I was in a haze and wondered if this wasn't just a dream? But no, it was real. Then, with my wedding ring on my hand, the two of us linked arms and led the procession back across town to the Black Cloister for the banquet.

I hardly recognised the Cloister as we progressed through the open gate: flowers, wild clematis and vine leaves adorned the doorways and windows; garlands had been strewn over the windowsills, bunches of fragrant flowers were in jugs on all the tables; three minstrels sat under the pear tree, playing cheerfully; a long table was decked out in the courtyard, bright with meadow flowers.

How they had worked, Dorothea, Agnes and Elsa and I don't know who else! What a feast was laid on for us! Fish: an enormous pike in a caper sauce on a bed of wild garlic with a smoked eel in its mouth; jellied lampreys in a nest of watercress; roast guinea fowl, fattened capons and a stuffed goose decorated with sugared rose petals; followed by a bowl of summer berries with goats' cheese and soured cream. The beer and wine flowed in generous measure and we sang songs and danced. I remember that day as if it were yesterday.

We invited only those people closest to me and my Bridegroom. The Cranachs, of course, with the three children, who have become like my own family. Dear Lucas has promised to paint both our portraits as a wedding present, but we haven't found the time to sit for him yet.

Martin's parents, Hans and Margarethe Luther, travelled all the way from Erfurt. Their arrival, two days before, was wonderful. Martin hugged his old mother like a bear, and they both wept. He embraced his father too, and they shook hands warmly, in a blessed moment of reconciliation. The old couple greeted me with polite reserve and curiosity.

His mother soon grew to trust me, however. That evening after they arrived, she and I were sitting alone together; she told me about Martin as a boy. The talent he had shown at a very early age for music, reading, languages; I listened intently, eager to hear more about the man I was soon to marry; then she turned to me, and put her gnarled old hand on mine. "Katharina, my new daughter! At last, our son has seen sense; how long have we waited for this! And what's more, he's chosen a fine woman to take care of him. Every man needs a strong woman to keep him in order." We laughed together, until I realised that her laughter had turned to tears. Martin walked in on us as we were both weeping together.

"What's this, then, two wailing women, on such a happy occasion!"

The estrangement between Martin and his parents had lasted for nineteen years. Now, at last, they are reconciled. Father and son write to each other regularly, and his mother writes to me about women's matters. She sends me recipes, gives advice on running a kitchen, keeping accounts, looking out for bargains in the market.

Leonard Koppe and his wife came from Torgau; the haulier who risked his own life helping us to escape from the convent. I asked them if they had travelled with the same team and wagon he used for that journey. He laughs.

"Oh no, dear lady, for an occasion such as this we travel in style, with our best carriage and a pair of dappled greys. You must see them before we leave tomorrow." So not the heavy old chestnuts I remember pulling us along the potholed road to Torgau on Easter Saturday two years before. Their wedding gift to us, appropriately, was a barrel of salt herrings! Martin laughed at this joke, and I was pleased to think of this good supply of fish for several Fridays to come! Herr Koppe broke the barrel open to show me something special inside: a beautiful, tropical sea-shell packed in with the fish. He demonstrated how, if you hold it to your ear, you can hear the sound of waves on the beach.

From the Town Council we received twenty Gulden and a barrel of the best beer. Prince Johann of Saxony (who has succeeded his good brother Friedrich) gave us a generous 100 Gulden to "to get us started."

And a surprise gift arrived on the morning of the wedding: twenty Gulden from Cardinal Cajetan, Martin's arch-enemy from Worms.

My husband fulminated at his old enemy's gesture of generosity.

"A gift from Cajetan? Never. Send it straight back, I'll take no charity from Papist bullies." But I had other ideas for the money, and it was my first quiet act of duplicity: I hid the coins in a brown jug on a high shelf in the kitchen. Surely it would have been churlish to return it? Instead, I wrote a friendly letter of thanks to the Cardinal. We cannot afford to turn down generous gifts, wherever they come from. Besides, I feel that such a gesture of reconciliation should be welcomed.

Ave and Basilius sent their apologies; Ave is expecting, and the five-day journey from Weimar would have been too risky. But their gift to us remains one of my most treasured possessions: a brand new publication entitled *Otto Brunfels Book of Herbs*; this book contains all one needs to know about herbs: how to grow them and how to use them for medicinal and culinary purposes. Ave gave us something else too, which made me laugh, though the joke was lost on Martin: a large hessian bag of cloves, tied with a blue ribbon. To us ex-nuns from Marienthron it meant the smell of the September Bible, smuggled into our convent, what seemed like a lifetime ago.

One of Martin's former professors from Erfurt was at the wedding too, as well as two friends from his student days and a couple of old family friends from Mansfeld. Herr and Frau Reichenbach were invited, of course; from them we received a beautiful tapestry for the hall, depicting a deer in a forest. She gave me a big kiss, and was delighted to see me settled after what she called, with a complicit wink, my little vicissitudes.

Apart from them I had very few guests of my own; it's not easy after years behind walls to build up a circle of friends. I wrote to my father at our Betrothal, inviting him and my Stepmother to the ceremony. I was hoping for some sort of rapprochement, as had happened with Martin and his parents. His reply was brief, but he did send me a gift: a small book wrapped in brown paper with the following short note: *"Dear Daughter, This little book belonged to your Mother. I regret I cannot come to your Wedding. Good luck. Father."*

It's a small yearbook. It is bound in calf-skin with gold rimmed parchment pages; it fastens with a metal hasp and key. It is about four inches by three inches, and within it are handwritten prayers appropriate for each season. Interspersed in the manuscript text are twelve tiny illustrations of farming in the different months. Ploughing, tilling, sowing, milking, hay making, fishing, reaping, picking fruit, threshing, and, in winter, hunting, skating and sitting by the fire sowing. I cherish this book. On the flyleaf is written in an old-fashioned hand the name of my mother's mother and the date: August 12th 1473. So it belonged to my maternal grandmother, whom I never knew; she died of the plague before I was born.

I should have been grateful to my father, but his apparent indifference towards me still hurts. I know now that he and his wife disapprove of my marriage to the Doctor, because they are against the reforms and blame him for all the unrest and the split in the church. But still, I am his daughter. When I was little, after my mother died, he loved me and needed me. Then his new wife arrived in our home and he no longer noticed me. My mother's little yearbook sits by my bed. I take care not to repeat what happened the first time I unwrapped the parcel and opened it. Smelling the old parchment, imagining my mother and her mother before her reading these pages, my eyes brimmed over and a big salty tear plopped onto one of the pages, smearing the brown ink; the text opposite May, Haymaking, a bright picture of six men and women scything and tossing the green grass, is now smudged and spoilt!

Philip and Catherine Melanchthon attended the wedding, though they had not been invited to our betrothal. Catherine and I do not always see eye to eye, but they are our next-door neighbours and it doesn't pay to bear grudges. Like Philip she has red hair, but unlike Philip, who is mild-mannered and equable, she has a sharp tongue and a quick temper. She most probably says the same about me!

Philip was against our marriage to begin with. He wrote to a mutual friend (and this came back to Martin) saying the Doctor was making an appalling mistake marrying 'the Bora', and that this union, being entered into with such haste, would destroy the great man's concentration, his daily routine, his prodigious output on the Old Testament. However, he has subsequently come to realize that the very opposite is true. I make sure my husband and our numerous guests are fed, his clothes and bed linen kept clean and repaired. I supervise the garden and dairy, the pigs, the poultry, the bees, the brewing. Far from hindering him, it soon became obvious that I helped him apply himself to his work.

I am fond of Philip; he is a kind, soft-spoken man, rather shy and absent-minded, so that he can appear vague, when in fact the opposite is true, as his brain whirrs on a higher plain, much of the time in ancient Greek.

So in the evening we all filed across to the Town Hall to join in more dancing and revelling with the townspeople. How tired I was, but how happy!

That night, Martin and I shared a bed for the first time. Four witnesses sat by our bed all night to confirm the consummation; but of course we did nothing, nor could we sleep, so the next day, when most of the guests were due to leave, we both felt exhausted.

In recognition of our wedding and the new life we were beginning together, Martin decided to take a few days away from his studies and translation work. He wanted to spend time with me and I was grateful for that. It was during these early days of our marriage, when each of us still had so much to learn about the other, that he suggested I go with him to the carp ponds. He is Official-Town-Carp-Pond and Production-Inspector, and so is expected to pay occasional, unannounced visits to the ponds to ensure everything is in order: make sure the sluices are well-greased and maintained, the ponds cleaned out at the appropriate time, the breeding programme being properly managed, fish well fed and so on.

It was a perfect summer afternoon. The sky was a deep blue with a few puffy white clouds, the air clear with a hint of a breeze. We rode through the Elster Gate onto the common. Pale marks from the stalls and tents of the sheep shearing fair the week before still showed on the grass. We greeted Gert the town goatherd sitting on a tree trunk, playing tunelessly on a pipe as he watched his motley flock. The boy raised his hat as we passed, and I recognised our own two nanny goats and even the Cranach nannies, which were of a larger type.

"Martin, I want to ask the Council to allow us one more nanny-goat. Two is simply not enough with the amount of mouths we have to feed. Would they allow us to keep three, as an exception?"

"You can certainly ask them, Kathe. If you want something badly enough, you usually manage to get it."

We laughed and our eyes met. He rode his horse up closer to mine and fondled the mane of my hired bay mare, then we began to trot.

Beyond the fairground strips of land are allocated to different households; we are lucky in having a large vegetable plot within the town walls, while most households have allotments outside the gates. Women, many with babies on their backs, were working the land, hoeing between rows of carrots, tying up beanstalks, weeding lettuces and spinach, transplanting little leeks, watering the onions. Small children played in the culverts, or toddled about near their mothers as they worked. Beside the plots runs a stream, which feeds a series of small conduits in grid lines, providing irrigation for all the strips. The women straightened their backs and shaded their eyes to watch us as we rode by. We raised our hands and they waved back. They all knew who we were, and would gossip about our marriage when they turned back to their work.

We trotted across the causeway, reed beds on either side. New green reed shoots were sprouting up beneath the old ones. The marsh was alive with croaking frogs and rasping crickets; dragonflies glinted like jewels in the bright sun. I caught a glimpse of a beaver's rump as it slipped quietly into the water; a heron flapped slowly up and away from us, an eel writhing in its beak.

After crossing the marsh, you come out into the open meadows. Some of this land is for arable crops: barley, rye, wheat, oats. Most of it, though, is down to grass; the grass had been cut, dried and piled into haycocks, waiting to be brought closer to town and built into larger stacks. The cornfields were already green and lush, and a few cattle were grazing in groups. Between the haycocks flocks of white storks were strolling gracefully about on their long red legs inspecting the grass, occasionally pouncing on a frog or worm. Sometimes they did little hops into the air, or took a short flight up and round, before lowering themselves again gently, vertically, onto the ground.

"Do you think one of those storks is ours?" I asked him as we rode by.

"Could well be. Our chicks are doing well, they'll be ready for flying lessons soon."

We have a pair nesting on our roof; they chose the highest chimney, which is no longer in use. It's supposed to be good luck to have a storks' nest on your house. Does this mean we'll be brought a baby next year? I was glad our pair at the Cloister was doing so well. It's curious, how fond one can get of birds. The way we all love the tame crane which lives with the Cranachs. She is as much a part of the family as the dogs and cats and can no longer migrate in the autumn, so spends the winters here.

At length we reached the carp ponds. They lie about four miles north of the town, half a mile beyond the Leper House, near the ruins of an old monastery. There are three ponds, quite large, but never more than three feet deep. They are on different levels, each connected by a sluice gate to the one below. To one side of them, following the levels, but separate, are three small square ponds for breeding and juvenile fish, with their own dedicated sluice system.

We sat on our horses and watched the surface roiling with black shiny backs as they broke the smooth surface of the water.

"It's beautiful here. So tranquil. And so many fish."

"Yes, it is beautiful. The ponds were built by monks over three hundred years ago."

Martin then explained to me the complexities of carp farming. In spring the breeding process has to be managed carefully. His face lit up with enthusiasm as he explained to me how they trick the breeding stock into spawning, something about a special shallow pond and grass tickling their tummies. I did not listen carefully. I feigned interest but really I just watched him talking, the way he moved his hands and flashed his eyes to illustrate the carp, explaining how they bred and grew. He is a man with boundless energy. Whatever task he takes on, he does it to the hilt. I admire him for that.

As he was telling me all this, we saw an elderly man walking slowly towards us along one of the causeways between the ponds, holding a long pole with a net on the end. He must have come out from a little wooden hut on the other side. Martin said to me:

"Will you be all right if I leave you here for a while? I need to walk around the ponds with the warden."

"I'll be fine. Leave your horse here."

Glad to be alone, I dismounted and tied the horses to a post, leaving them to graze. I gazed across the ponds, churning with fish; the air above them was alive with birds and insects and on the margins of the ponds, reeds, rushes and sedge. Beyond the ponds is an area of alder carr and young willows and beyond that I could see the forest proper.

I imagined getting lost in the dark, wet woods at night, like Little Red Riding Hood. Wolves running silently under the moon, wild boar plunging clumsily through the brush, red deer, brown bears, foxes, lynx; all these animals, and so many more, live in the forest, respect each other, avoid each other, prey on each other; they work out an uneasy but viable alliance and equilibrium. We fear the forest and the wild, but they probably fear us too and with reason.

But out there it was warm and bright. A deep sense of tranquillity came over me, on the edge of this wide smooth pond; the air thrumming with insects, herons standing like sentinels on the banks. Two buzzards were circling overhead, and a flock of cranes fly in a phalanx towards the forest, their long legs stretched out behind, their elegant necks stretched out in front, crowns on their heads. A nightingale pours out his repertoire of rattles, bubbles and long liquid notes of gold. I will cherish this moment. I am happy and I know it. I am young and in good health. I have married a man of rare distinction. I have a task to do, and am determined to do it well. Perhaps, God willing, we shall be blessed with children. I feel like the swallows, flittering above me with such palpable joy, meeting and greeting each other in flight.

The two men are walking back towards me on the spit of land between two ponds. The warden is carrying something, and as he approaches me he makes a little bow, and says:

"Good Lady, God bless you and your husband. This fish is for you."

He holds it up for me to see; its eyes are rolling, its mouth gaping open and shut, its fins quivering. A fine, fat, shiny carp. It must weigh at least eight pounds.

I thank him. He lays it on the grass and from his pocket pulls out a creel, into which he slips the reluctant fish, head first; then he binds it up with sedge, dips it in the stream and says:

"He'll be fine until you get home. Then just put him in your cleansing tank and wait two weeks. I promise he'll make a tasty meal for you and your household."

I laugh and thank the man. Martin tightens his girth and mounts, the warden holding his bridle. Then he hands him up the fish bag, which Martin ties to his saddlebag hook.

The sun is sinking as we ride home, back towards the three towers of Wittenberg: the round tower of Castle Church and the two square towers of the Town Church, silhouetted against a pink and blue streaked sky. The fields are empty now. As we approach the city gates church bells start to ring out across the fields. I am tired and hungry but deeply contented; I feel the warmth of the mare beneath me. We shall eat together, my husband and I. Say that word again: *husband*. And we shall talk, and tell each other stories.

Chapter 16
Martin a Rock

Wie ein Brief ein Siegel braucht, so
braucht der Glaube die Werke.

As a letter needs a seal, so faith needs good deeds.

I soon came to know the pattern of life at the Cloister, the routine and timetables.

On two days a week the *collegium biblicum* convene in the Doctor's study; the translation team consists of Melanchthon, Cruciger, Aurogallus and Dr Luther, who presides and has the final say; his secretary Rörer joins them as recorder and scribe. The four theologians pore over the Hebrew Old Testament, teasing out of it the essence of its meaning, putting it into the simplest and purest vernacular.

Their translations are not the first, so why are they so much more resonant than the previous German Bibles? The *collegium* translate not from the old (and sometimes imprecise) Latin translations but direct from the original Greek New Testament and Hebrew Old Testament. They use as a starting point the *Meissen officialese*, because there are so many dialects in German, and they had to settle for one; but to make it more accessible, Martin weaves in proverbs and folk songs; he employs rhyme and cadence to make it easier for people to learn by heart and make it more musical for singing and reading aloud. My husband is not only a scholar and learned theologian and linguist, he is also a poet, and this shines through in the beauty of the German text. It sounds smooth and natural, as if it had been easy to translate, but he said once: "Dear God, it is such hard work, and so difficult, to make the Hebrew writers speak German!"

He likes to go into the market or sit quietly in the beer tent at a fair so he can listen to ordinary Saxon folk chatting, exchanging news, views, gossip. It brings him back to earth, and reminds him of how ordinary people really do speak. Of course much of what he writes – papers, essays and so forth – is in Latin for the learned, but when translating the Scriptures into German he is doing it for the common people, and so it needs to be close to the vernacular, in language as accessible and acceptable to the ploughman as it is to the learned and the gentry.

You might ask, why did he defy the Church in the first place, thereby putting himself in mortal danger, and bringing turmoil to the people?

He told me about his Tower Experience. It was after our visit to the Carp Ponds. We ate alone that evening; after the table was cleared, he fetched a flagon of wine. We sat at the table, with just one candle burning, making the red wine glow like garnets; and we talked. Did I ask him about it, or did he just choose to describe to me the moment of his enlightenment? I don't remember but this was, in essence, what he said to me.

"It was in the winter of 1516; I call it my Tower Experience because it was a revelation and it happened in the Tower Room, which has been my study since I became Professor of Bible. People laugh about it and say I was sitting in the privy battling with constipation. They can laugh. And yes, I suppose it was a sort of constipation, a spiritual blockage to understanding the nature of God and His love for us. But I was not sitting on the privy, I was in my little study. It was a cold, windy night and the fire was smouldering sulkily. My lamp was flickering in the draught and I drew a woollen rug around my shoulders. I should have given up and gone to bed but I was striving to understand Paul's Epistle to the Romans: *'For therein is the righteousness of God revealed from faith to faith: as it is written, the just shall live by faith.'* I always came to a halt at that expression: 'the righteousness of God'. I understood the word righteousness to mean God punishing the guilty, administering justice. I had been an exemplary monk, but I still felt guilty and unable to win God's love and approval. I came to realise that I did not love Him as one should love a Father, but actually hated and feared Him. As a monk I had tried to appease him with self-denial, hairshirts, physical deprivation; but however hard I tried, I never seemed to win his approval or love.

"All that night and the following day I struggled with the text, trying to make out what Saint Paul really meant. This is an extract from his letter to the Romans:

'Since we are justified by faith, we have peace with God through our Lord Jesus Christ, through whom we have obtained access to this grace in which we stand; and we boast in our hope of sharing the glory of God. And not only that, but we also boast in our sufferings, knowing that suffering produces endurance, and endurance produces character, and character produces hope and hope does not disappoint us, because God's love has been poured into our hearts through the Holy Spirit that has been given to us. For while we were still weak, at the right time Christ died for the ungodly. Indeed, rarely will anyone die for a righteous person – though perhaps for a good person someone might actually dare to die. But God proves his love for us in that while we still were sinners Christ died for us. Much more surely then, now that we have been justified by his blood, will we be saved through him from the wrath of God. For if, while we were enemies, we were reconciled to God through the death of his Son, much more surely, having been reconciled, will we be saved by his life. But more than that, we even boast in God through our Lord Jesus Christ, through whom we have now received reconciliation.'

"I read and re-read the whole letter, trying to unravel it, tease out the real meaning. I daresay I forgot to eat or drink;

I thought and thought and prayed and prayed. At last, in a flash, I was given God's grace; the scales fell from my eyes and I saw the connection between the justice of God and the statement: *'since we are justified by faith'*. By believing in Him we are saved! At that point I felt as if I had been reborn and had gone through open doors into Paradise! The whole of Scripture took on a new meaning and *'the righteousness of God'* was inexpressibly comforting, like a gate into heaven.

"Righteousness is given to the sinner as a gift from God. He meets the conditions and the believer need do nothing other than have complete faith in the promises of Christ. Christ is full of grace, life and salvation. The human soul is full of sin, death and damnation. Now let faith come between them. Sin, death and damnation will then be Christ's, and grace, life and salvation will be the believer's.

"It came to me that we are here to enjoy life as children do; to love each other, to wonder at nature and music and mathematics and art; to marry, experience marital love and have children. Extreme austerity is unnecessary, merely self-restraint; we should allow ourselves freedom, joyfulness, appreciation of being alive; and above all faith. Jesus Christ is our Redeemer, through having died for our sins. To us true Christians it is the greatest comfort to know that God the Father so loved the world that he did not spare his only begotten Son, but gave him up for us all, and that whosoever believes in him should not perish but have everlasting life. That was how I came to an understanding of the Scriptures. My anger at God melted away. My whole being was filled with joy."

"Thank you for telling me that," I said to Martin, and took his hands in mine. "And surely it was God's will that you should give up the Law and enter the Monastery, and go on to study Theology. It was your destiny to shed light on the Holy Scriptures and share your revelation with the People."

We sat quietly together for several minutes, holding hands at the table. The dog snored. An owl hooted in the dark night.

I could feel my love for him growing within my very core.

Before I married him, I saw the public face of this great man. And he is a great man, one cannot deny it. But deep down he is fearful, full of doubt and anxiety. When we were first married and shared a bed he was plagued with recurrent nightmares. He would groan and toss about and break out in a sweat. Then he would cry out and sit up staring about him with wide, unseeing eyes. The first time this happened the hair stood up on my head.

"Dear husband, what is it? Wake up, wake up!" I shook him, embraced him, pulled his hair, but he was oblivious of me. I slapped his face, and squeezed his earlobe with my fingernails and this had the magic effect of waking him! Then I hugged him tight and rocked him in my arms like a child.

"Oh Kathe, I had this dreadful dream. I saw a hare running, jigging to and fro, its ears flat on its back. It looked so scared. Then I saw it was being hunted by a pack of silent hounds – they had red eyes and scaly tails, and suddenly I knew that I was the hare, they were after me, and my legs were growing heavy, I couldn't run any more. It's a sign, Käthchen, it's all my fault. The peasants rampaging about, the bandits and angry hordes. I feel responsible. I never meant, I never thought my words could be so misconstrued. How can we cork up the bottle again, how can we stop it happening? The thugs, they roam about attacking castles and manors, stealing stock, killing farmers and abusing their women. They ransack whole villages, you've seen all the poor refugees arriving in town, with their possessions in one creaky ox-cart, leaving their homes for fear of such brutal attacks. Then I wrote that pamphlet calling on landowners to kill the peasants when they act aggressively, and now so many are dying and they all blame me. The end of the world is near. I am afraid, for you, for all of us."

And so it was, two or three nights a week, for several months, I had to release him from his horrific nightmares. They took on different forms, but usually the same sort of thing – he was the quarry, being hunted down. It was not only his mind which was troubled – he suffered from chronic constipation, headaches, fever and sweats and agony from kidney stones. I have tried all sorts of remedies for these various afflictions: prunes for his constipation, ginger tea for indigestion, feverfew for headaches, melilot for his troubled spirit. Only a few weeks ago he was plagued with stones. "What can I get you?" I asked him in consternation, and he said "Give me a fried herring with cold peas and mustard." I was unsure, but got what he craved, and sure enough, he passed a stone that evening and felt much better. I see that he eats more regularly now; all that fasting in the monastery played havoc with his digestion. His bad dreams have stopped too, thank the Lord. But we are not alone in worrying about Apocalypse.

Albrecht Dürer, the painter from Nürnberg, wrote to Lucas Cranach about a dream he had. He dreamt that a great flood would cover the earth, probably this year; all towns and cities along the valleys would be inundated; in France too, we have heard tell, they have prepared for such an event: an ark has been built and made ready in Villefranche. But in the midst of all this turmoil, the breakdown of law and order, the anticipation of the Second Coming, what can you do? Life must go on. And we in Wittenberg are luckier than many, for this place seems to be comparatively peaceful, thank God. Which is why so many refugees try to settle here, and they have to be strict about who they give residence permits to. Whatever happens in the world, we women have to carry on growing and preparing food, giving birth, looking after our children, our elderly. Anyway, I am happy being married to Martin. Deep down, despite the fear, I am happier than I have ever been before and this is because I know he is too.

Recently at table he said: "Where would we be ourselves if there were no marriage? The world sees only the shortcomings and disadvantages of marriage, she fails to see the great joy and usefulness. We have all crept out of a woman's womb: emperors, kings, princes. Even Christ himself was not ashamed to be born of woman."

We have a beautiful new bed. One of the first things I did when we were betrothed and it was acceptable for me to come into the Black Cloister to make things ready, was to throw out Martin's bed; it was foul and stinking, no more than a sack stuffed with crumbled straw, covered with filthy greasy sheets. I pushed it out of the window into the yard below, ran downstairs and set alight to it with a taper from the kitchen range. It exploded into flames and the bed bugs sizzled and popped! I was reminded of my Stepmother, how she had done the same when she arrived at our own neglected home, and perhaps I forgave her a little.

I spent a whole week scouring and sweeping and throwing things out. I ordered a cartload of sand and strewed all the floors and swept them out, the clean white sand becoming brown with accumulated filth. I wiped down all the shelves and washed the windows; I scrubbed and washed and mopped, then I shut up each room one by one and fumigated it with baldrian to get rid of fleas and bugs and cockroaches. I set mousetraps in the larders and kitchen and rat traps in all the outbuildings. Finally, I polished all the furniture with beeswax and strewed the clean cupboards with freshly dried lavender.

Coming into the house like this was not without its problems. Dorothea had worked for Martin for five years and resented my intrusion; she took my zealous cleaning as an insult. She and I had a stand up row in the kitchen. She stood with her arms on her hips, shaking her jowls at me.

"This is my kitchen, Fräulein. What do you think you're doing coming in here turning everything on its head, tipping sand all over my floors, lighting up fires in the yard? I won't have it."

"Dorothea, I'm sorry to have to say this. But this will be my house shortly. When I am Frau Doktor Luther I will be mistress of this household. You've been in charge here for many years and you've done a fine job, but soon I will be coming in to run the house. If you can't accept me as mistress in this house, I suggest you look for another position. I'm sure the Doctor will give you excellent references."

So to my consternation and guilt, Dorothea packed her bags, called for a cart, and with a defiant flourish drove away, not even saying where she was going. I felt terrible but Martin wasn't worried. "She'll be back. She's done this before." To my huge relief, she did indeed return after two weeks, as Martin had predicted. She and I have been friends ever since; we work well together, though not without the occasional storm; I have to stand my ground with her, and she with me.

As I was saying, our new bed is a fine four-poster, carved in the best oak, with a canopy of blue damask drapes bordered in red brocade. The horsehair mattress is new, our sheets are best Irish linen and our quilt is pure goose down; we also have a soft woollen blanket from England. So on our wedding night we lay side by side, in our new bed decorated with honeysuckle and meadow flowers by Barbara and Frau Reichenbach. Lucas and Barbara Cranach, Nikolaus von Amsdorf and the pastor Bugenhagen acted as our witnesses.

Our real wedding night, however, was the following night, the first time we lay together alone. Usually it is the bride who is shy, the groom who knows what to do. With us, it was the other way round. He was the shy one, awkward, unwilling or unable to show me affection. And though in his head he knows sex within marriage is not sinful, he was nevertheless paralysed with guilt; after all, he had fought for so long against his sexual urges, training himself to resist such temptations, that he found it difficult to put such inhibitions aside. I taught him how to kiss, with open lips and tongue. I stroked him, coaxed him, teased him. At first he sweated, almost as if he were scared of me, so I would leave him in peace and we would turn our backs and sleep.

While I did not come deflowered to our marriage bed, I did know more about such things than he did. I, a woman of twenty-six, a one-time nun, with no property and no dowry; he a man of forty-three and one-time monk; a priest, a thinker and writer, a man whose fame had spread throughout the world. He is my superior, not socially but intellectually. He knows the Bible off by heart and has Hebrew and Greek and Latin; but it was I who taught him the language of the night. Little by little, he thawed, relaxed and began to respond to my attentions.

To start with we slept together chastely. I did my best to cope with his bad dreams. Gradually he grew familiar with the landscape of my body; his hands grew bolder, less clumsy. I embraced him, stroked him, explored him all over, his tummy, his back, even his feet, his knees; I came to love his musky smell. At first his member remained soft as a cow's teat. Little by little, though, the trust between us grew; we would wake together in the darkest hours and his guilt would melt away. One night I woke and he was snoring softly with his back to me. Stroking him gently, I sensed he had woken; with growing excitement I felt, for the first time, his member stirring. I touched him, coaxed him, stroked him and he grew hard for me. And so it was, after three weeks of marriage, that we became man and wife in the true sense.

From then on, his nightmares became less frequent, his dreams less troubled. We made love and slept easy as a couple, our legs entwined. Our love, like a tender seedling, sent out leaves and grew and grew. Before long, another life was growing within me.

Chapter 17
Broad Beans

Ein Schluck Wasser oder Bier vertreibt den Durst, ein Stück Brot den Hunger, Christus vertreibt den Tod.

A draught of water or beer slakes thirst, a slice of bread hunger, but Christ banishes death.

It was July and most of our lodgers had left for the summer recess. Some had gone home to their parents, others had set off on their travels to Italy or France or even to Greece. This world tour was ostensibly to further their understanding of the ancient world, but we suspect their main motives are to have a good time and sample the delights of foreign food, foreign customs, new landscapes and beautiful women.

"Make sure you tell us about everything when you come back to Wittenberg. And I don't mean just the classical ruins." The young men shuffled their feet, blushing; they knew he was teasing them.

Our household was unusually quiet that week. Dorothea had taken a few days away to visit her ailing mother. We had no house guests. I relished the peace and turned my back on all the chores I could be doing; I sat down at my desk and wrote a letter to my father. I wanted to share my good fortune with him, and wondered if I might travel over to Lippendorf to visit him, but Martin was against the idea, saying the roads were too dangerous.

Black Cloister
19th July 1525

Dear Father

The silence from you has become too deafening for me to ignore. I wrote to you a few weeks ago to tell you about our wedding.

My dear Husband Dr Martin Luther is a good man. We are happy together and now that the University is in recess I have some peace and quiet to reflect on my good fortune, and to write some letters. We were sad that you could not make the journey for our wedding, but I do understand that. I would like to visit you and Stepmother, but the roads are too unsafe at present. So let me tell you a little of our life here in the Black Cloister.

I sometimes think of this place as a ship, and I must steer it through the stormy waters, the tidal currents, the doldrums; with my crew I must make sure the sails are trimmed, the tiller well-greased, the food and water in good supply, the course straight and true. Of course I have never even seen the ocean, let alone been to sea, but when I was little you used to tell me stories about sailors and the great wide ocean, and sometimes I imagine what it must be like. Leonard Koppe, who trades in herrings, gave me a seashell from tropical seas; if you hold it to your ear you can hear the sea, and when I do that I pretend I am on a beach watching waves breaking on the sandy shore.

Dear Father, I'm sad that we have met so seldom over the years. I am not angry with you for sending me to the Convent, you thought it was best for me. But I wish you could have visited me more often. Just four times you came over in all the fifteen years I lived there. I am sorry too that you did not write to me as often as other fathers did.

I was touched at your wedding gift of Mother's little book of seasons. I cherish it, and keep it by my bedside. But I sense that you and Stepmother do not approve of my husband, or my marriage to him. Why not? He is probably the most famous commoner in Germany, if not the whole world. From far and wide his admirers travel here to little Wittenberg to meet the great man, to hear him preach, to sit, if they are privileged, at our table and listen to his table talk and ask him questions. What do you have against him? Is it because he is the son of a copper miner? Or is it because you disapprove of his doctrines? Or do you blame me for breaking my monastic vows? If so, please remember the day when I was admitted to the convent of Marienthron to be a professed nun. I was only fifteen, not yet a woman. I had seen so little of the outside world, and knew nothing else. How could I understand what I was promising or renouncing? We girls hardly knew what Chastity meant, and Obedience and Poverty had always been part of our lives in any case. Was I ever offered an alternative to becoming a Bride of Christ? I cried when my head was shaved. You gave away my sisters in marriage at the same age, but for me you chose the habit and veil.

I write to you now in the hope we might meet so that you can meet my husband. Perhaps when the roads are safer he and I can travel over to Lippendorf together? Dr Luther is a good man, and he loves me. I'm sitting now at my desk in our bedroom, looking out of the window at a tall elm tree. Barbara Cranach has just called round and brought me this fine paper from Italy. Martin has given me a bunch of goose quills and a bottle of fresh ink. So dearest Father, please accept this letter as an olive branch, to disperse the cold silence between us. Turn back to your daughter, your eldest child. She wants, more than anything else, your love and recognition. Please give my love to my brother and sisters.

Your affectionate daughter K.

Recess or not, there were plenty of jobs to do, what with the goats, the pigs, the poultry, and the kitchen garden. The broad beans were ripe and overdue for picking; if you leave them too long they become tough-skinned and dry.

"Martin, would you help me pick and pod some beans?"

"Oh Kathe, dear girl, I have work to do." Already he had a foot on the bottom step of the stairs leading up to his study in the tower. Once he disappears up there to his work, the sun courses round to the west before he reappears. This month

I am trying to keep him away from his study, at least in the afternoons.

"The University is in recess. Melanchthon and Aurogallus are both away. Surely you can allow yourself a little time off?"

I put my arm through his and smile at him. I wish he would take more exercise and fresh air. His skin is pale and drawn. All that poring over old Greek and Hebrew manuscripts exhausts his eyes; he must constantly refer to his huge old wordbooks, other translations, earlier versions of the same text. His headaches, though less severe than before, still afflict him.

"You always say you like gardening. Now's your chance. Come on, dearest, I need your help. And I want to talk to you."

"You manipulative woman, how can I say no? I am undone, a serf in my own house!"

He relents with a laugh and puts his arm on my shoulder; together we walk to the kitchen to fetch two bushel baskets. How much easier we are with one another now that we have discovered the delight, the warmth and affection of the marriage bed. He joked the other day to Philip, saying: "I know what being married is like: it's waking up to see pigtails on your pillow." But as he said this he caught my eye and winked. We both know it's a lot more than that.

We go out to the walled vegetable garden; the sun's already hot. The soil in Wittenberg is loamy, black and fertile; it's been worked and tilled for hundreds of years. We have rows of baby carrots, kohlrabi, spinach, beetroot. In another bed are peas supported by birch twigs, runner beans forming green tents along a row of canes and twine; and three rows of broad beans. Rhubarb pushes up in lush clumps in the shade of the north-facing wall, though it's grown too stringy now for anything but wine. In another bed are rows of baby leeks, red cabbages and broccoli coming on for the autumn. Soon the onions will be ready to pull and dry. Along the south-facing wall we have several trained peach and nectarine trees, which will be pruned in the winter; and the central path is shaded by pleached apple and pear trees. This garden and its produce are vital for our large household.

The old caretaker, who worked here with the monks and stayed on, does his best but he's slow and frail. So Martin has put me in charge of the garden and the men now, and I have plans to improve the layout. The herb garden needs to be extended; we'll do that this winter, and sow and plant next spring. Barbara has offered to advise us, they grow such a huge range of herbs for the apothecary.

"The blackfly are bad on these," says Martin as we pick the beans.

"I know, I've shown Joachim how to wash them with soapy water but it doesn't make much difference. But the beans themselves are fine."

We snip and pick and fill the baskets. Above us, fledgling swallows test their wings and twitter for joy. A song thrush sings from the top of a walnut tree. Our baskets are full. They creak as we carry them back to the courtyard and set them down beside the table in the shade of the old pear tree. Tölpel drops down in a pool of shade, panting after the effort of sniffing round the garden in the hot sunshine. I fetch two bowls for the beans and lay a sack on the ground for the pods – the pigs will have them for supper.

The two of us sit, enjoying the unaccustomed quietness, breaking open the leathery pods to reveal soft, white down, and nestling within each pod a row of pale green shiny beans. They plop into our bowls and the soft empty pods drop onto the sack; we talk. My plans for a herb garden; whether I should dry or pickle these beans. Dorothea and her ailing mother; our student lodgers on their journey to Lucca and beyond. Then Martin says:

"I'm going to write to my father this afternoon, I owe him a letter."

"That's funny, because I've just written to my father. I wish you could meet him."

"My parents and I were estranged for far too long. It is a terrible thing. You should try to make it up with your father and his wife. And I want to meet my in-laws. It's ironic really. You disobeyed your parents in running away from a monastic house, whereas I disobeyed mine by going into one."

"Tell me, Martin, what was the true reason why you gave up the law and became a monk?" (Barbara had told me briefly about a thunderstorm and his friend being killed, but I wanted to hear the story first hand.)

So Martin began to tell me about that fateful day, which changed so profoundly the course of his life.

"I was the oldest child and my parents realised from very early on that I was exceptionally gifted. I sang in the church choir in Eisenach. I won prizes for Latin and writing and learning verse by heart. My Father channelled all his hopes and ambitions into me and my future. I think my brothers and sisters resented me, saw me as the favourite and it's true, Father had his plans for me: I would become a rich and powerful lawyer or even Mayor of a large town like Erfurt or Eisenach. I would do all those things he, a copper mine surveyor, had been unable to do. But he was never satisfied. If I came second in a test at school, he would say: 'And why didn't you come top?' If I was not picked to sing a solo in the choir, he wondered why not, and told me I should try harder.

"The parents stood over me as I did my homework or practised music, and beat me if I showed signs of flagging; sometimes I heard them after I was in bed, discussing my progress. I longed to live up to their ambition for me; and yet, however brilliant my marks, however glowing my school report, Father was never quite satisfied.

"One day, my parents' grand plans for me were overturned at a stroke. I was twenty-three, and was studying for my Masters in Law at Erfurt University. We had been studying very hard, with assignments and end of year vivas imminent; I suggested to my friend and fellow student Max that we visit my family for a few days' respite from our books. My brothers and sisters were still living at home then, and the fatted calf was killed for us; we had a jovial and relaxing reunion. Mother cooked, Father opened the best wine; they wanted to hear all about our life in Erfurt; not many miners were able to boast that their son was studying for a Masters in Law. We sang rounds and played cards and sampled the various hostelries of Mansfeld with my brothers until late into the night. All in all, we'd had four amusing and relaxing days."

"And nice to see your family, and have a rest from student life."

"Yes, it was. Straight after church on Sunday 2nd July 1505 – the date is etched on my memory – Max and I set off to walk back to Erfurt. As we reached Stotternheim the sky grew dark and a wind got up. We could hear church bells in the valley ringing to warn of an impending storm. But we needed to cross the hills to get back to Erfurt.

"We did consider staying a night in Stotternheim, but decided to carry on. Dear God, how I regret that decision even to this day!

"Just as we reached the top of the pass the heavens opened. In one minute we were soaked to the skin. There was a flash of lightning, followed at once by a ripping clap of thunder. As we dashed towards some overhanging rocks, our cloaks over our heads, a thunderbolt struck. Like a devil's trident, it hit Max on his head. He fell to the ground, lifeless. I dropped to my knees beside him and shook his shoulder. I turned him over and Kathe, I can't describe it to you, his face was black! Smoke was rising from his coat and his body was hot to the touch. I smelt scorched flesh! What could I do? Where could I hide? I screamed into the driving rain and rolling thunder. I gazed up with dread at the jagged flashes in the sky. God was angry, surely He would take me next! I fell to my knees on the top of that hill, clasped my hands in the pouring rain and prayed as loudly as I could:

"'Saint Anne, Mother of Mary, intercede for me, please! I promise you, I will devote my whole life to God, if only you'll pray to the good Lord to spare me!' The storm raged on and I crouched like a shivering fugitive beneath the rocks, my teeth chattering, staring through my tears and the pouring rain at the corpse of my friend. Barely an hour before, we had been walking along singing and exchanging ribald jokes.

"Then the rain stopped and the clouds rolled away, revealing a clear blue sky. As the sun warmed the sodden ground, steam rose from Max's lifeless body. I scarcely remember how I stumbled down the muddy path, how I reached my lodgings. But my kind landlady must have put me to bed with a hot bottle and sent a message to the Council; a search party went out to bring back Max's body.

"I went down with a fever and the doctor bled me regularly for several days, and put me on a regime of white dittany infusions and beef tea. As I convalesced and began to grasp what had happened I became confused: I was worried about my law assignment, and the impending oral examination; but at the same time I could not banish from my mind the promise I had made to Saint Anne. Was it binding? What, in fact, had I promised her, if I should be spared? What did 'devote my life to God' actually mean? Did it mean I should become a priest? Or a monk? Or simply continue with law and lead an exemplary Christian, if secular, life? No, that was clearly not enough, it meant renunciation of ambition, it meant the taking the cowl, of vows of humility, obedience and chastity. My heart sank at the thought of such a commitment. That had not been my intention and it was certainly not part of my Father's plans for me."

"Didn't you think you could quietly forget all about the promise you made? After all, no one else had witnessed you making it except poor dead Max."

"Ah, you say that. But God was my witness, and Saint Anne."

"Yes, of course. Indeed."

"But yes, I must admit, I was tempted to sweep it all away, try to forget about my pledge. But I knew I would never be able to forgive myself, and doubted whether God would forgive me for such treachery. So the following morning I went to see my Father Confessor and told him everything. Of course he had heard about the storm, and Max's death and my illness; in fact, I gather he had visited me in bed when I was feverish. But could he know about my promise to Saint Anne? As I walked across the town to the cathedral, I hoped and prayed that he would say 'never mind, my son, your best course will be to forget you ever said such a thing and resume your law studies.' But he did not.

"'My son, you pleaded to Saint Anne to intercede on your behalf and save your life. She did intercede for you, the proof is here, you were not struck down by a thunderbolt, you are alive and well; this means that Saint Anne's prayers saved your life. I ask you, should you renege on such a promise? You pledged to devote your life to God, so now, if you continue to pursue earthly ambitions, can you really live the rest of your life with a clear conscience? It is not for me to tell you what to do but simply to offer spiritual guidance. However, if you do decide to honour your promise to Saint Anne, (and it must be a decision made of your own free will, with your whole heart) then I suggest that it be to renounce all worldly pleasures and take the vows of a monk. Pray to our Lord and he will guide you to the right decision at this time. You may go now, my son, and may God be with you.'"

"So did you decide straight away, to ask to become a novice at the Monastery?"

"No, it wasn't that easy. I walked back to my room, lay flat on my bed and tried to sleep. My mind was in turmoil and my stomach churning, my head throbbing. So I got up, went out again, wandered around the town, stumbled into a hostelry and ordered a large beer. I don't know how long I sat there, in the corner of the dark room, or how many beers I put away. I do know that I found myself being helped back to my lodgings late at night by two colleagues; they rang the bell, and my landlady opened the door to us, whereupon I was sick at her feet!

"'Dear oh dear, Mr Luther, what shall we do with you? Let's get you to bed and I'll bring you some gruel to settle the stomach.'

"I lay in my bed and the world was spinning round, with me at its epicentre. 'Oh God, give me a sign. Oh Father, oh Mother, let me go; do not demand so much of me. Oh God, do not ask so much of me. Oh why can't you all just leave me alone?' I wept like a child, then sank into a heavy sleep, almost a coma; shortly before waking I had this vivid dream about Saint Anne. We were up on the hill where Max died, and she was walking towards me, her hand held out to me. She was a fine, mature woman, our Lord's grandmother. Then she spoke to me: 'Martin. The storm is in your own heart. Remember, the still small voice of calm.' That is all she said. Then she smiled at me, turned and walked away down the hill.

"I had a blinding hangover but I knew what I must do. Gingerly I made my way to the University. I asked to see my Professor and told him about my promise to Saint Anne and my decision to abandon Law and apply to enter the cloister. He accepted my resignation from the School of Law with regret but understanding. My next, much harder task, was to tell my parents of my change of career.

"As you can imagine, my father was furious, my mother disappointed, my siblings baffled. In obeying the will of God I set myself at odds with my parents, with my whole family. My father had had such high hopes for me, invested so much money in my schooling, and here I was, planning to lay aside all earthly ambition, shave my head, wear a cowl, a hairshirt and rope sandals and renounce the world. That was when we became estranged."

We had finished shelling the broad beans. We were now just sitting with a large bowl full of pale green beans on the table between us, and a large heap of soft pods at our feet. I was moved by his story, and touched that he had told it to me. I said nothing and we sat together in silence, staring at the beans.

Then Martin got up from the table and went into the kitchen; he came back clasping two pewter mugs brimming with frothy beer.

"So that was the story of how I renounced law and became a monk. All because of a thunderstorm and my promise to Saint Anne!"

"Well, maybe that was exactly what God wanted you to do. If you hadn't given up law and become a monk you wouldn't ever have come to such a deep understanding of the Scriptures. It all turned out for the best, didn't it?"

"Yes, you're right. Like Isaiah in the temple, when God said 'who shall I send and who will go for me?' and Isaiah said: 'Here am I. Send me.'"

He kissed me, and walked back into the house. He looked tired. As I sorted the beans for drying or pickling, I thought about the thunderstorm and the death of his friend Max; Martin could have been struck dead too. I felt sure that Saint Anne had interceded on his behalf. Because of the storm, he became a monk, not a lawyer. Which in turn meant he immersed himself in Theology and the Bible, and that led him to set in motion the huge upheavals in the Church, the reforms. Which in turn led him to write so many wise words about religion, and to translate the word of God for the common people. My husband was simply fulfilling his allotted task on this earth, as planned by God our Father.

Three weeks passed. It was harvest time, so all hands were busy in the fields. Martin disappeared to his study most mornings, but after lunch and a rest we made time to be together, either in the garden, or riding out to see how the mowers and reapers were doing. Dorothea returned from her break and helped me in the kitchen with gathering and preserving fruit.

Then a letter arrived from Lippendorf. I was overjoyed, but on breaking the seal I saw with a stab of disappointment that it was not my Father's hand. It was a letter from my Stepmother.

Lippendorf, July 12th 1525

Dear Katharina,

Your letter to your father arrived by messenger boy from Leipzig
– he had it from a bookbinder there.

I urged your father to write to you himself but he is not very well.
A languor has taken hold of him. He spends much of his time in
the study, trying to reconcile the books, or out in the stable tending
his old horse (which should by now have gone to the knackers), or
riding slowly around the park; he scarcely ever leaves the estate
except occasionally in my company. Why is he suffering like this?
It could be our straitened circumstances, though with thrift and
hard work we get by well enough. It could be due to the turbulent
times we live in, and fear of another attack on our home. Our
physician suspects it is a more deep-rooted disease for which he can
suggest no remedy beyond the usual bleeding. Frankly I attribute
it to his confused faith; I try to persuade him to unburden his soul
to our priest but he is unwilling; like so many unfortunate souls
now, he worries about God, Our Lady, Christ Jesus; whether to go
to confession or not, whether to observe a saint's day or not. I try to
persuade him simply to observe the old customs and not be swayed
by fashion or changing views, but he remains confused.

In this letter I propose to set down for you, now that you are a
married woman, many unsaid things. I want to explain as best I
can the reasons why, apart from your Father's despair, we could
not possibly have attended your wedding in June. It is hard for me
to say this, especially as you and I have had so little contact over
the years; I know we have met only seldom since you left home
for the convent. I feel confident that now, in your maturity, you
do not question the wisdom of our sending you there. You were
not an easy child and your father was foolish about you; the best
course was to allow you to attend the convent school. Believe me,
it was a sacrifice for all of us to send you to Marienthron. And I
do not mean only the dowry. By sending you away we lost a useful
pair of hands. As I say, the decision to send you there was purely
for your own good. You received an outstanding education for a
girl of your class; and as things turned out you were much safer

*within those walls than we have been for the last few years here
at Lippendorf.*

*When your letter arrived out of the blue announcing (no
question, incidentally, of asking your Father's permission) your
betrothal to Dr Martin Luther, we were quite amazed. Of course
we already knew of your escape from Marienthron (a scandal
we both prefer to forget) and your close involvement with the
Protestants at Wittenberg – but to hear that you were so completely
in the pocket of all those people took us aback, to put it mildly. I
have to say, Katharina, by marrying Dr Luther you have placed
yourself at the very centre, in the very eye of the storm, of what we,
your parents, deplore and abjure.*

*Dr Luther should examine his soul and wring his hands in
penitence. He has set ravening wolves loose in the sheepfold. He
has broken down the hurdles of the fold which kept them safe and
the flock are wandering loose and unshepherded; indeed, some of
those sheep have turned into wolves themselves. Allow me, if you
will, to spell out some of the horrors which have unfolded before
our eyes as a direct result of your rebellious monk's incitements.*

*Firstly, on the 15th August, Feast of the Assumption of the
Virgin two years ago, a once sacred and beautiful ritual was turned
into a desecration. It happened in our village church, which has
taken on the new form of worship. As you well know, for longer
than anyone can remember, the common folk have celebrated the
Assumption by gathering flowers and herbs, and strewing them
all around the church, especially at the feet of the statue of Our
Lady. During the service they are blessed and then taken away to
be strewn in barns, stalls, fields and meadows. They are believed
to be a potent protection against illness in humans and animals,
and a precaution against bad weather. Well, last year, when all
the women and children had gathered flowers from the roadsides
and meadows and the church was sweet with their fragrance, the
pastor with his new ideas said "This is ignorant superstition! Those
flowers have no magic properties, they're nothing but common
weeds. Just take them out into the street after the service and
destroy them." So the flowers were swept up by youths looking*

for a fight, and chucked onto the street; there they were trodden and danced upon with profane singing and ugly rhymes, thrown beneath the wheels of carts and into the filthy gutters. I saw the small children who had picked them and lovingly laid them around the church crying at this senseless destruction.

The following August, the pastor decided to forbid the bringing of any flowers into the church, to avoid a similar fracas. Women and children, arriving at the church with their arms full of flowers were told to leave them in the porch and not to decorate the church. You can imagine the disappointment this caused.

In another village, not far from here, worse things have happened. Statues of Mary and the Saints were torn down from their plinths, taken outside and smashed. The Virgin's head was sawn off, and Joseph was broken up and defiled, even the blessed infant Jesus smashed, then they were all heaped up into a pyre and burned. Other atrocities took place, which I will not shock you with.

Thirdly, just after Epiphany, a horde of angry peasants attacked our house. They forced open the park gates, pushed past old Herr and Frau Blankenagel, and marched up the drive waving pitchforks and pikes. The stable boy warned us and we managed to raise the drawbridge just in time so that they were unable to break into the house. But they hurled stones across the moat, breaking some windows, and yelled obscenities. One of them shot an incendiary arrow onto the roof but thank the Lord it began to rain just at that moment, so the fire never took hold. They slunk off home, gesticulating and cursing. Since then we have kept the drawbridge well-greased and oiled, and closed most of the time.

Your husband has made a dreadful mistake inciting the peasants to this insurgency. Hans says it's hardly to be wondered at. They are confused. They hear the gospel story in their own tongue, which seems to question the established social order. This makes them envious and greedy. At the same time they are told the saints they learnt to venerate are worthless, the statues 'graven images', their old customs and beliefs superstitious. Worst of all, Our Lady has been dethroned. Is it any wonder the people are in turmoil and confusion? I should say that most of the trouble-makers are the younger ones; the older people like Cook and poor old Magdalena Blankenagel just want things to stay the same, they don't want to make trouble. But the young are insolent, unruly, uncouth. They seem to have lost the fear of God's wrath and have no respect for their elders and betters. Children are learning to read as well, which gives them ideas above their station.

I have written enough now. I am glad you liked the little year book. It belonged, so I understand, to your maternal grandmother. I hope it might remind you of more peaceful, devout times, when people knew where they stood in this world and how they might prepare themselves for the next.

Your affectionate Stepmother,
Margarethe

So they do not approve of the reforms. Or at least Stepmother does not, and Father, by the sound of it, isn't very sure about anything. Such unrest, all because of religion! Adherents of Rome moving south, protestants moving north, in wagons, carts, on foot, in boats. Intolerance, uncertainty, distrust. The Wittenberg Council have sent out a decree forbidding housemaids or any servants from discussing religion at the wells and pumps or any public place; it's a sensible law because all too often such talk leads to scuffles and fights.

But I am sorry they think so ill of Martin. Wouldn't they change their minds if they met him? He's a good man. His work is changing the world for the better. He has exposed the rottenness within the Church of Rome. He has brought light into the darkness, and swept away fear and ignorance; he has shown sinners that Jesus loves them and that God the Father is not angry and vindictive, but loving and generous.

Chapter 18
Tante Lena's Letter

Viel tun und wohl tun schickt sich nicht zusammen.

Doing a lot and doing good are not necessarily compatible..

We were sitting alone, enjoying the privacy of a Sunday evening. Sundays after church are a day of rest for us all: the servants, the animals, the students and my husband; everyone knows to leave the doctor and me in peace at this time. This particular November day we were both dog-tired; added to that, I was feeling nauseous because of my pregnancy. My first attack of morning sickness took me quite by surprise. I was in the brewhouse, and the smell of fermenting hops, usually a delicious, sweet aroma, was rich and overpowering. I brought my breakfast up all over the floor in one great gush. I was hastily trying to mop it up, not wanting Agnes to see, when the world about me went dark and I fainted. Agnes found me prostrate on the cold tiles; she helped me to my feet, and led me into the kitchen. The next morning I was sick again, this time as soon as I got out of bed. Dorothea nodded wisely at me. "You're in the family way, ma'am, no doubt about it."

"She may be right, dear wife, but let's not rely on her opinion. I'll send for Frau Wischnau, she's the best midwife in town, and she'll know for sure whether you are indeed with child."

The midwife arrived within the hour. We climbed up to

my bedroom together and she examined me. She looked in my mouth and my eyes, told me to lie on the bed and looked at me down there; she pressed my abdomen, felt my breasts and nipples and listened to my chest through a cow's horn ear trumpet; she took my pulse and smelt my breath and fingered the texture of my hair.

"You can get dressed now, good lady." She turned her back on me, packing away her instruments in her leather bag. Then she turned round to look at me with satisfaction as I sat on my bed, tying up my bodice, and said:

"Yes, Frau Doctor. You are with child, I would guess in your third week. The nausea is quite normal and will go on for ten weeks. I'll give you an infusion to settle the stomach, peppermint for the morning and motherwort at night. I'll pop by and see you once a week until your condition has settled down. After that once a fortnight will be ample."

Together we consulted the calendar which she keeps in her bag and she worked out when the birth was likely to be. Early June. It was hard to imagine midsummer, when we were now descending into winter with the nights drawing in and the coldest weather still before us.

The prospect of motherhood filled me with a mixture of trepidation and joy. But wasn't that one of the main reasons why my sisters and I had escaped from Nimbschen? Martin was delighted, he hugged me like a great big bear and grinned from ear to ear. I know that if it should please God to give us a healthy child, he will be a most devoted and caring father.

I welcomed the shortening days, the retreat into winter. How busy we have been, filling up the larder with provender! It all falls on me, as mistress of this house, to make sure we have enough food to see us through the winter. At Nimbschen it was the senior nuns who saw to it, and at the Cranachs it was Barbara. So my first autumn in charge of a household I was doubly anxious to do it well. The surplus pigs and billy-goats had been slaughtered, the meat soaking in brine, or already cured and smoked.

In the summer we had picked soft fruits and preserved them or put them into the rum pot for Christmas. We made cider, apple cheese and dried apple rings and made strap out of pears, medlars and quince. The larder was stocked with pungent cheeses. Two sides of bacon hung from hooks, wrapped in muslin, alongside cervelat sausage, hams and liverwurst. We filled a barrel with sauerkraut and jars of gherkins in dill vinegar stand in rows on the cool stone shelves. Agnes and her little brothers went out mushrooming in September and we dried and packed up a bushel of them, always such a welcome addition to winter stews.

Outside, the barn loft is packed to the eaves with sweet hay, and more haystacks stand in the yard. In the cellar the firkins of wheat, barley, oats and rye are stacked up on pallets to keep dry. With the blacksmith's wife's help we collected, separated and potted ninety pounds of honey. In short, despite the unrest and universal food shortages, Dorothea, Agnes and I have provided this household, with so many hungry young men to feed, for the winter and spring ahead.

Every woman in charge of a household welcomes the long nights with a sigh of relief, if – and I must emphasise if – the putting by has gone well. Supposing it has not gone well, for whatever reason, if the larders are only poorly stocked, then her heart will be cold with dread, thinking, how soon should we begin rationing, how soon before our stores run down? As it is, this year I think we may well have a surplus to sell or give to the poor when necessary.

At any rate, we can feel free to sit with our feet up by the fire in the parlour, a candle burning; we can talk or read aloud, or simply snooze.

I am fiercely jealous of our Sundays. All the rest of the week Martin is so busy. If he's not preparing or delivering a lecture at the University or tutoring his students, then he'll be writing a sermon or preaching in church. As Vicar General of the diocese he has to chair meetings about schools and churches in the rural parishes. Or he is closeted in his study in the tower, either on his own, writing essays or letters, or in discussion with his colleagues on matters of faith and doctrine. Our weeks run to a timetable, so I usually know where he is, and with whom. In the vacations he has more free time and this is when he rides out to the villages to see how the country pastors are getting on.

Now and then he helps with haymaking, gardening or harvest and I try to encourage him in this, because he needs the fresh air and exercise. What remains constant, like a beacon of tranquillity, is the peace of our Sundays. Martin and I have had our differences. We've had several fiery fights – but we have never yet quarrelled on a Sunday afternoon. Martin calls it close season. We both, instinctively, avoid touchy topics on that day.

He's not an easy man to live with but I'm learning. When you put a stockpot on the range it can boil over, the lid pushes up and boiling liquid spills out onto the hot metal – which hisses and gives off steam and a scorching smell. So what do you do? You move the pot to a cooler place where it can simmer gently. Herr Doktor and I have been looking for a good spot for simmering, avoiding contentious areas which can lead to boiling over; on the whole I think we have found it, a good *modus vivendi*. I am mistress of the household. Himself is master of the table, of conversation and being a genial host to our guests. And of course it stands to reason I never interfere with his academic and pastoral work.

Sometimes our visitors have important matters to discuss, for which they travel far on perilous roads to see Martin: theology, the liturgy, the art of translation; or the rebellious peasants, politics, the future of the Church in Rome; on these occasions I tend to leave them to it. I eat quietly in the kitchen with Dorothea and Agnes and we women take it in turns to make sure they have enough to eat and drink. A sisterly warmth has developed between us women. Working together under pressure makes for a feeling of closeness, as we used to find in the convent.

He can be master of the table and I can be mistress of the rest. I support him in his work and he appreciates that. But at night, when the house sleeps, the candles are snuffed and bedroom doors are shut, he becomes mine, and mine alone. That is when we remind ourselves that getting married to each other was the best thing we have ever done. Admittedly, I sometimes have to count to ten before responding to some of his outbursts or patronising remarks. But Sundays are special; he is always more equable on the Lord's Day.

This particular Sunday was windy but not cold; a strong south-westerly was snatching the last leaves off the elms behind the cloister. The inclement weather outside made us feel all the more snug in our little parlour. The fire crackled and hissed, the logs sometimes shifting and settling. We sat together on the oak settle with red velvet cushions, our feet on stools, staring into the flames. Tölpel slept by the hearth. I took his hand in mine and stroked it.

"I had a letter yesterday."

"Oh yes, who from?"

"From my aunt. Tante Lena, my father's sister. She was a nun with me at Marienthron. They've closed down the convent."

"So where is she now?"

"She's at Lippendorf, with my parents. But she's not happy there. Martin, could she come and stay here with us, at least for a little while?"

"Of course she can, dear girl. She can stay for as long as she likes. This house is your house. Our families are one. She'll be a friend for you. Besides, you could do with another pair of hands about the house now with the baby on the way."

"Shall I read to you what she writes?"

"Yes, do."

Lippendorf, 4th November 1525

Dearest Niece Katharina

I hope you are well and that married life agrees with you. I was so pleased for you, and proud too, when you wrote and told me of your marriage to the famous Dr Luther. Who would have believed it, eleven years ago, when you first took your vows?

You will have heard by now, Marienthron Convent has been closed down. I had no choice but to throw myself on the mercy of your Father and Stepmother. They were kind and took me in, and I do my best to help in the garden and the kitchen. However, they have difficulties of their own and I don't want to outstay my welcome. I am writing to ask you and your husband whether I might be able to come and stay with you in Wittenberg, at least for a little while. I have no money and no friends. The outside world is not as I remember it; I find it hostile and frightening. Single women are suspect and no one seems to value quiet prayer. I hope you do not mind my asking you for help.

Please commend me to your husband.

Your affectionate Aunt Magdalena.

"You must write back to her at once. With any luck she can get here before Christmas. I'll apply to the Council for her residency tomorrow."

"Oh thank you, Martin. I'm so excited, it'll be lovely to have her here!"

I wrote back to her that evening.

Wittenberg, November 17th 1525

Dearest Tante Lena,

Our home is your home. We've already decided which room you shall have. Martin was delighted when I suggested to him that you come and live with us. He said: 'Another pair of hands, Käthchen, and a kinswoman, just when you need more help. What good fortune.' He is referring to the fact that I am with child! You can help me in the garden, particularly with the herbs; we have bees too, and you are skilled at managing hives. Then I have to oversee the linen cupboard, the dairy (though we only have three goats as yet, no cows) and brewing. Not to mention simply getting food onto the table day after day, for our lodgers or visitors. The men sit at the refectory table, the one the monks used to eat at, listening to Martin, learning from him. They discuss religion and politics and the meaning of life and the life hereafter. They tell stories and jokes and as the evening wears on their speech grows bawdy and maudlin and Latin gets mixed up with German, often in strong dialect!

Meanwhile, they absently shovel away any food and drink we women put before them. I think talking and arguing must make men hungry. All that food and beer, and they never seem to wonder where it comes from, or who has produced and prepared it. Though I can tell you, dear aunt, if one evening the table were bare, then they would notice soon enough! I'm always a bit annoyed by the story about Mary and Martha – Mary gets all the praise for sitting at our Lord's feet, listening to Him, while poor old Martha slaves away in the kitchen and scullery getting the meal ready and gets no thanks or appreciation. Nothing changes!

I was in such a temper a few days ago (feeling like Martha, no doubt!), and I banged a pitcher of beer down on the table so hard it tipped over and splashed several guests. They were silenced for a minute, then they all got up in a flurry of mopping up and tut-tutting. I just stood and watched them in their confusion, but as I stomped back out to the kitchen I heard Martin say: "If I can withstand the rage of the devil and sins and a bad conscience, then I can withstand the rage of Katharina von Bora." They all laughed heartily at that, and the conversation resumed as if nothing had happened.

I'm painting a picture of such toil and strife and you probably won't want to come and join us in Wittenberg. I must admit, I do get quite tired, I have two women to help me in the house, apart from two little maids who come in by the day; and you know what the autumn is like, you just have to keep on putting by, or suddenly it's too late. But I'm glad to say our larder and cellar are full and we've enough fodder too. Food is not easy to come by; these are troubled times, even here in Wittenberg, though many *people flock here as refugees, thinking it's a haven of peace and security. Which means you need all the more food, for all the extra residents.*

Then there's the small matter of money: My husband hates to ask our guests for payment, he prefers to dish out hospitality for free, but who is to pay for all this food, the laundry, the fuel, the labour? So it falls to me to ask them; I usually write out a little bill, and hand it to them with a smile, saying sweetly: 'It's been so nice having you with us'. Usually they pay up. Only twice have guests left without paying; then I make a mental note to take payment in advance if they should ever turn up here again!

But enough of our domestic worries. I cannot think of anything nicer than to have your company. You can help us just by being here, to bring your calmness and wisdom and prayers to a rather stormy household. And when my time comes, you will be here for me. Also, you can advise us on Martin's stomach cramps, I have tried a great many remedies but he still suffers and our physician is running out of ideas.

I've been going on about us, but what about you? You must have had a difficult time, being thrown out into the wide world; it must have been worse for you than for me; I ran away of my own free will, but you had no choice but to go; I was behind convent walls for only fifteen years, whereas you must have been there almost thirty. The world must have changed a great deal since you were last outside its confines.

So dear Aunt, please do come to Wittenberg, as soon as you can arrange your journey; if you have difficulty paying the fare, the Doctor says we can send you a permit to travel. He also says, avoid travelling alone, try to find a trustworthy man to travel with, someone who is going at least part of the way. We are applying to the Council for you to become a resident, a member of this household. We are sending you under separate cover a letter of recommendation to ease your passage here from Leipzig.

Please give my love to Father.

I remain your affectionate niece,

Katharina von Bora.

My aunt's reply arrived in under three weeks; the postal service is remarkably good, considering everything.

Lippendorf December 2ⁿᵈ 1525

Dear Kate

I was overjoyed to receive your letter, which arrived safely via the bookbinder in Leipzig. The messenger boy is staying the night, so I write to you by return. I am excited at the prospect of living with you and Dr Luther.

Yes, the shock of being outside the walls of Marienthron is only just beginning to wear off. I want to cover my face from the gaze of men, they look at me with hatred in their eyes. Only last week I was shopping in the market and a man selling pots spat at my feet. Men smell so strong, it almost nauseates me, I need to hold a pomander to my face. They seem to know instinctively that I was a nun, even though I do my best to cover my cropped head. Society is so unsettled! Before I took the veil, the peasants and trades people were prosperous but they were respectful too. Growing up at Lippendorf, the peasants would doff their caps to us as we drove in our carriage, and they called me Miss Magdalena. Now they look at us direct in the eye, with insolence and hostility. Then there's the highways – they used to be properly maintained, the trees and scrub cut back along them, to keep them safe. They're now full of pot-holes, they've become dark, spooky tunnels in many places and you never know who might leap out at you. And the houses! So many farms and cottages dilapidated, abandoned; the cattle are thin, fields lie fallow, rank with thistles. And for all their insolence, the people look anxious and hungry too.

I am fearful of going out on my own. Last week I drove with your father to the village, we were taking a pig to the butcher. A great crowd was assembled in the square; what do you think it was for? They were milling around a pyre, watching a public burning! The victim was already dead, blackened and curling up, it was horrible, the stench of roasting flesh, like pork but sweeter. Your father knew all about it.

"Oh yes, that'll be old Mother Rappolt. She lived on her own in a thatched hovel down there by the river. She's said to have had sixteen children by sixteen different men. She was a well-known witch. She grows – sorry, used to grow – herbs and concocted elixirs and infusions, and the poor called her in as a midwife. She used to sing songs in the street, about how the plants spoke to her in dreams. The authorities tolerated her as being a trifle touched as well as immoral. But last year, she was spotted flying on her broom across the river at dusk for an assignation with the devil. It wasn't just once, either, she was seen by several different witnesses on different nights, so it must have been true. I understand she was tried in the usual way and convicted of witchcraft."

Hans picked up the whip to tickle the pony's back and hummed a little tune to himself. What shocked me, even more than the sight of the pyre and the gawping crowd, was Hans's indifference to the old woman's plight. He does not seem to make the connection between her and me! I grow herbs and make remedies, though I have not yet been called upon to deliver a baby. I am a single woman too. Supposing they suddenly suspected that I was a witch? If accusing fingers were to start pointing in my direction, who would stand up for me? I suspect not even my own brother.

I ought not to be ungrateful, your Father and Margarethe have taken me in and been very kind, but I should not impose on them much longer. So I look forward so much to joining you in Wittenberg and meeting your husband. I hope I may be a help to you and all those who you live with.

Your devoted Tante Lena.

So my father's sister came to live with us three weeks later, and has settled in to our routine. She helps me in more ways than I can say.

Chapter 19
The Good Book

Ich möchte alle meine Bücher ausgetilgt haben, damit über
die heiligen Dinge nur noch in der Bibel gelesen würde.

I should like to have all my books eradicated
so that on matters of divinity people would
look no further than the Bible.

The great bell in the church tower was just striking one – the midday meal had been served and cleared away and I had climbed up slowly to our room for my rest. My body was growing heavy and I felt very tired. March had been cold and this winter seemed to have gone on far too long; I felt like hibernating. But we women have to keep going, whether or not we are pregnant or with small children to care for. I was just settling into bed when the door creaked open; my husband came in sideways, pushing it with his shoulder, holding a rectangular parcel wrapped up in blue linen. With an almost reverential gesture he laid it before me on the bed. He was grinning like a small boy.

"Go on. Open it," he said.

"Is it what I think it is?"

"Probably. Unwrap it. It's for you."

Gingerly I untied the blue cloth tape and folded back the linen. It lay before me, glowing; the most beautiful book you could imagine, bound in brown vellum; on its spine, in gold letters, PENTATEUCH and HISTORICAL BOOKS. I opened the frontispiece, and saw the elaborated title, scrolled about with pictures:

Herein in the German Language are compiled the following Books from the Old Testament, translated from the Hebrew by Dr Martin Luther.

Illustrated by Lucas Cranach. Printed by Melchior Lotther and Published by Lucas Cranach, Wittenberg 1525.

I turned the pages one by one, marvelling at their beauty and precision. I saw woodcuts of animals, birds, trees, Adam and Eve. I saw the bold clear print, on the fine paper from Milan; I smelt the odour of well-cured calfskin.

"Well? What do you think?"

"It's wonderful, Husband. Quite wonderful."

"And the binding? How do you like the binding?"

"It's very fine. How many have been bound like this?"

"Only four. One for you and me; one for the Town Church; one for the Elector and one for my Father and Mother. The other volumes will be shipped without binding."

"And it's just in time for the Frankfurt Book Fair. They must be so relieved to have got it out in time!"

"They are. The whole team are taking the afternoon off to celebrate, having completed the stitching. The boys are packing them up for shipment. Barbara's arranging a feast for Thursday night, they've already killed a fat weaner and the butcher's preparing it."

The book filled me with awe. New books always do, especially when it's one of Martin's. With the printing press it is possible for my husband to write an essay, a sermon, a pamphlet, or even to say something at mealtimes – his words are always noted down by Rörer – and within a few days it can be printed and distributed throughout the civilised world. He said once at supper "I fart today and they smell it in Rome tomorrow!" (He can be very vulgar, my husband.)

Most of what he writes is in Latin, intended for academics, clerics, philosophers, theologians; his readers are all over the world: Avignon, Rome or Lucca, Seville or Toledo, Oxford, Paris, Ghent or Elsinore. Whatever he writes is pounced on, printed, published and distributed within a few weeks. For this reason, more and more printers are setting up shop here in Wittenberg. They recognise a good market and want to take advantage of a famous name and a famous place.

I had in fact seen the five books already, published separately, but now they were beautifully bound together in one edition, called the PENTATEUCH. Genesis, Exodus, Leviticus, Numbers and Deuteronomy.

"Surely the power of the word will win over the power of the sword," said Martin. "Pray God the peasants will not misconstrue the message again, and use it as an excuse to go on the rampage. They heard Saint Paul's letter to the Galatians: *'For freedom Christ has set us free. Stand firm therefore, and do not submit again to a yoke of slavery.'* But they were deaf to the next part, where he warns them to use the freedom wisely: *'Only do not use your freedom as an opportunity for self-indulgence, but through love become slaves to one another... If you bite and devour one another, take care that you are not consumed by one another'.*

"I feel bad, Kathe, because they did and it was because of what I said. Never before has the power of the word sent such shockwaves round the world; we thinkers have to weigh our words with care, now that they can be broadcast so far and so fast! I heard today that there's been a revolt in Nördlingen; the peasants and the poorer townspeople, the weavers, basket makers and butchers banded together to overthrow the Council; the Council wanted to bring in the League to suppress them, but in the end they reached some sort of compromise. Not before some bloodshed, though, and battles in the streets and outside the city gates. The ringleaders have been hanged, I'm glad to say."

"Nördlingen, of all places. I thought it was a peaceful, well-run town."

"It was peaceful and well-run. That's what is so alarming.

Once these peasants are roused out of their torpor, they'll stop at nothing. To think that Thomas Müntzer was one of my pupils, here in Wittenberg! He incited them, encouraged them to read rebellion into the words of the Gospel. They seem to think I was in favour of their rebelliousness. They're nothing but a band of uncouth thugs."

"Oh dear. Our poor baby, what a world he's coming into!"

"What a world, indeed. I don't want to scare you, dearest Wife, but the signs are there: revolutions, tempests, the plague. The stars are not propitious. Last Thursday the full moon rose huge and blood red. Crowds gathered in the town square, transfixed by the sight, and they were afraid. I did not want you to see it. They took it as a sign that Apocalypse is coming and I think they may be right. God is angry with us."

"But don't you think He might forgive us, just as an angry father forgives his children when they're sorry? You always say we should love and trust the Lord, because he is kind and loving towards us and not angry or vindictive. Didn't Jesus take the burden of our sins on his own shoulders?"

"Yes, we must pray that Jesus will intercede for us. I sometimes wonder whether mankind have gone too far, learnt too much, overstepped the mark. That we humans have gone beyond what God intended for us. The Spanish, for instance, have discovered a vast new country south of America called Mexico. A Spaniard called Cortez and a few men with horses conquered it five years ago; I've just read an account of it. The natives are a brown-skinned people called Aztec, they have an emperor and live in cities with elaborate buildings and streets and gardens. They're skilled craftsmen too with vast amounts of gold and jewels but they have no horses, imagine that, Katharina! No horses! So when they saw the Spaniards mounted on horses they took them for supernatural beings. Also, these people are heathens. They have not yet heard the Word of the Lord, and are innocent of any Christian understanding. The Spanish are already building a great cathedral on the site of their pagan temple, called Tenochtitlan, in fact they're replacing the existing temples with churches all over the country. So the Church will be gaining many thousands of souls."

"The Church of Rome that is."

"Yes, but still, it's our God, the true God, and Jesus Christ the Saviour."

"We missed you at lunch. Did you eat with the Cranachs?"

"Yes, we wet the baby's head, so to speak. Anyway, now and then I need a rest from Rörer and the others hanging on my every word."

"But you enjoy it, you love sitting at the end of the table pontificating."

"I do not pontificate, you insolent woman! Pearls of wisdom fall from my lips. But that Rörer! I've never met a man who could write so fast, he uses a special set of symbols and only he can transcribe what he has scribbled."

Georg Rörer is my husband's amanuensis. He's a thoughtful man, very modest and so quiet, you scarcely notice his presence; however, you notice when he is *not* there, and I am grateful to him for keeping my husband's study and affairs in order. During meals he writes down many of the remarks Martin makes at table, which have come to be known as Table Talk. You may have noticed that I have written one of these remarks at the beginning of each chapter of this book. Rörer eats in the kitchen before the main meals are served; Dorothea grumbled about it at first, until I pointed out that he is secretary to the Doctor and spends all mealtimes writing in his notebook, and we mustn't let him go hungry! Now I think she's come to enjoy his company as she bangs about with her enormous saucepans or tells Agnes to turn the spit above the range or kneads dough, her arms dusty with flour.

"Thank you for that book, it's marvellous. How hard you've all worked to get it done. And I love the illustrations. Dearest, would you read me a passage, before I have my nap?"

"What shall I read?"

I leafed through the book and chose a passage from the Book of Exodus.

"Here. This page, please."

I snuggled down under the feather quilt and listened to Martin's deep voice as he read to me from his own translation of the Old Testament.

A man from the house of Levi went and married a Levite woman. The woman conceived and bore a son; and when she saw that he was a fine baby, she hid him for three months. When she could hide him no longer she got a papyrus basket for him and plastered it with bitumen and pitch; she put the child in it and placed it among the reeds on the banks of the river. His sister stood at a distance to see what would happen to him. The daughter of Pharaoh came down to bathe at the river, while her attendants walked beside the river. She saw the basket among the reeds and sent her maid to bring it. When she opened it she saw the child. He was crying, and she took pity on him. 'This must be one of the Hebrews' children,' she said. Then the child's sister said to Pharaoh's daughter, 'Shall I go and fetch you a nurse from the Hebrew women to nurse him for you?' Pharaoh's daughter said 'Yes.' So the girl went and called the child's mother. Pharaoh's daughter said to her, 'Take this child and nurse it for me, and I will give you wages.' So the woman took the child and nursed it. When the child was weaned, she brought him to Pharoah's daughter and she took him as her son. She named him Moses, 'because,' she said 'I drew him out of the water'.

Even when he speaks quietly in the intimacy of our bedroom, Martin's voice booms with power. He intones and enunciates with unusual clarity and force. I wonder whether his magnetic power, which attracts the people in such droves, is not partly due to the sound of his voice and the way he commands the attention of a crowd. Here in Wittenberg church, for instance, where every Sunday he delivers his sermon, this large church can be packed from wall to wall; but they don't shuffle about, whisper, sneeze, scratch or shift their feet as is usual in a church service. They stand quite still with their eyes on him, and Martin's voice reaches into the farthest corner of the church. So while I get annoyed with him, especially with his lack of financial sense, I feel proud and privileged to have time alone with him; scholars, students and noblemen travel miles to hear him speak, to be in the same room with him and, if they are lucky, to speak personally to him. I and I alone share his bedchamber, and his bed!

And it is not only the learned and high-born who seek him out. Simple people too – peasants, labourers, cobblers, fishwives, widows, sweepers, beggars – flock to hear him preach and gather in the streets to watch him pass by.

In 1521, when he was summoned by Emperor Charles to the Diet of Worms, he was promised safe conduct for his journey. His progress turned into a triumphal procession. Supporters decided to travel along with him, and the train grew as it progressed, until it must have resembled an Arab caravan. Wherever he went he was welcomed and given hospitality. In Leipzig the Magistrate greeted him publicly in the square with a ceremonial cup of wine.

In Erfurt, where of course he had lived, both as a student and a monk, the Rector of the University received his 'entourage' at the city gate, as if he were a prince. He got down from his covered wagon and the crowds cheered him along the streets as he walked across the famous Krämer Bridge to the church. They ushered him into the church and he went straight to the pulpit and began to speak. The building was packed, every aisle, every little corner. As always, the crowd were quiet and attentive. But then panic nearly broke out when a creaking sound followed by a loud crack rang out from the wooden gallery above; the structure was groaning under the weight of too many people. There might have been a stampede but Martin kept his head; he held up his hand with all the authority at his command and said: "Please, good people, stand quite still. Nothing evil will happen. The devil is trying to frighten us." The crowd calmed down and sat very still; the gallery stopped creaking and Martin finished his address.

Then he told them to leave quietly and in good order, one row at a time, and all was well.

Philip told me this story; Martin tends not to tell me stories in his own favour. He may be stubborn and overbearing and maddening; he can have a filthy temper. He worries too much about his health. But Martin is not a boastful man. So the stories I hear from him tend to be about those occasions when he might have been seen as weak or vulnerable or fearful or failing in some way, as when he was so fearful in the thunderstorm when his friend Max was killed.

I slipped away into delicious sleep as his voice intoned from the Old Testament. The old Hebrew, rendered into my own mother-tongue, a tale of ancient Egypt transported into modern Saxony. Moses was a Wittenberg baby, left in a basket in the reed beds beside the Elbe. But who was Pharaoh's daughter? And who was Moses?

Chapter 20
A New Life

My time is drawing near. Frau Wischnau the midwife is awaiting our call and Barbara and Tante Lena are to take it in turns to attend me. Tante is an herbalist but has no experience in childbirth. Barbara has had four confinements herself, all attended by Frau Wischnau; the midwife is over fifty, and has been delivering babies since she was eighteen, having learnt the calling from her own mother – in fact, most young people of some standing who were born here were delivered by her. She's highly thought of among the women of Wittenberg.

She has been calling in to see me since I've been confined to my bedchamber; she listens to my abdomen with a cow's horn ear trumpet, to hear the child's heartbeat. She feels my tummy all over, to find out how the baby sits; she looks in my mouth and eyes, and down there. She asks me how I feel, and if she has time she gives me a massage with soothing oils, especially around the neck and shoulders, my feet and ankles. Her hands are strong and kind, her manner gentle but matter of fact. Babies are being born all the time, all over the world, she says, it's completely normal, and this one will be the first of many fine babies for you, good lady. You're a strong, healthy woman, not yet too old. I see no reason to worry. With her skilled hands and quiet voice, she smooths my anxiety away. She's just left, but thinks it will be tonight or tomorrow morning.

I've been praying to Saint Margaret, the patron saint of childbirth. But when I asked Martin to join me, he said it was better to pray directly to Our Lord. He doesn't believe in praying to saints to intercede. But what does Jesus, an unmarried man, know about such things? Can he understand about the heaving struggles in my abdomen, the darting pains in my lower back? My breathlessness, the need to urinate, the swollen ankles? The sense of being prematurely old while still in my prime? The sudden eruption of tears at the unlikeliest events or remarks? Did Jesus know about such things? So in Martin's absence, Tante Lena joins me in asking Saint Margaret to intercede on my behalf. She was a woman and several times a mother; she understands.

I may die and leave a motherless child. I may survive but my baby be born blue or die as an infant. Or, much worse, it might be an evil thing, the Antichrist, our punishment for a sinful union, as our enemies have predicted. Their taunts and mutterings eventually drove Martin to keep me confined for my safety, for the safety of the child. I turn the pages of my book. When he gave it to me only eight weeks ago the pages were creamy white and quite blank, except for his own dedication on the flyleaf. Now I have only three blank pages left; what a lot I have written! Page after page is filled with my writing, the product of how many goose quills, of how many pots of ink? Yesterday I numbered the pages with great care, and it comes to one hundred and ninety-six. I have written densely too, as neatly as I could, but occasionally I have had to cross things out.

When I was trimming my first quill I planned to write my story, but it has become entwined with Martin's, as my life has. A memory comes to me, clear as crystal. I was very small, four or five years old. I was standing on a stone bridge over a river in some very old town, I don't know where it was. I was with my parents, but my brother and sister were not there. My mother lifted me up onto the parapet so that I could look down to the river below. "What do you see, Käthchen?" I saw a river, but it was two different colours. Two rivers, flowing side by side in the same channel, on the left murky and brown but on the right clear and translucent, fish and frondy weeds visible. My Mother said: "It's a confluence, that means the place where two rivers flow together and become one. You can see the difference in the water, one of them is flowing from low country, from the plains; that's the muddy water. The other river has come down from the mountains, and the water is clear and clean." I watched it flow beneath us, the clear and the murky, side by side, and felt my mother's breath as she kissed the top of my head. I think that the rivers kept their separate identity for so long because of the different temperature; the mountain river must have been cooler; gradually, further downstream, with eddies and swirls, they would have blended and became one.

My story is a bit like that. Living most of my life in a convent, I learnt to put myself and my own wishes last. I was part of a community and that community was dedicated to the service of God. However, after three years of life outside, I have discovered a sense of 'me', of Katharina von Bora; I am a separate, distinct person. I have learnt this about myself: I have strength, I am attractive to men. I have the range of skills required for a woman in my position. I am me, a married woman, and as worthy of respect and of God's love as any man.

When I became '*die Lutherin*' the Lutheress – as some people choose to call me – Martin suggested I retain my maiden name. I think he likes the fact that I come from patrician stock. But I have married a giant. His personality, his voice, his presence, his fame, fill up a room, a house, a church. No, they fill the whole of our little town – so that when he goes off on his travels the town seems in a sense diminished. Inevitably, my life has been subsumed in his. I don't mind. I am proud to be part of his life. I think of our two rivers as our two stories so far. Rising from very different sources, but flowing towards each other. Now, we have reached confluence. For a few months our waters flowed side by side, discrete, the colours still distinguishable; but now our waters have coalesced and we are as one. My story is his and his is mine. The birth of our first child, if I am spared, will be the living manifestation of our union.

The pains began at dusk yesterday. Joachim was sent to fetch the midwife. The preparations are made: jugs and bowls filled with boiled water; clean sheets and towels folded neatly on the chest; and in the corner, the Cranach's crib of carved oak with new stitched linen awaits its new occupant. Barbara came over and conferred with Tante Lena. My husband was banished from his own bedchamber, for this is women's work.

The pains wash over me like waves. The tropical shell which Herr Koppe gave us holds within it the song of the sea. Occasionally, when I want to calm down, I sit very still in a quiet place and hold it to my ear; then I pretend to myself that I'm on a sandy shore, the wide horizon stretching before me, the waves washing at my feet. But these waves of pain are not the gentle murmuring kind which you hear in the shell. This wave is ten feet high; it rolls in with a roar, and tumbles over me, engulfing my whole being, crashing in white spume on the beach. Then it recedes and I'm left gasping like a stranded fish, my eyes staring at the wall of our bedchamber. With intense clarity I see the edge of my bed, its damask drapes hanging down. I see, and smell, a bunch of yellow roses – for steadfastness – in a vase on the mantelpiece. On the book shelf I read the titles: my grandmother's yearbook, our September Bible, the Pentateuch. Where is my husband now, is he keeping watch? Is he praying somewhere for his wife and unborn child? Or is he trying to concentrate on his work in his tower room?

Another wave. I groan, my brow is damp with sweat and Barbara's cool hand soothes me with a fresh linen cloth. Then again sweet respite. My own dear Mother, who handed me over to be fed by another; was she ill following my birth? I see her now as she was in my dream, running on a cloud with two angels, learning how to fly. But the image is chased away as another wave engulfs me in pain and I bite onto a towel. How small my hand looks, lying on the pillow in front of me. I think of Father, and the time when I showed him a fairy garden I made in the roots of the oak tree; he said it was beautiful. It was our secret, his and mine.

And so, for several hours, I withstand as best I can the waves of pain, then surface and notice again my attendants, their kindness, their affection; in my mind's eye I recall people and places I have known. Sister Clara, consoling me when I was forced to wear the red felt tongue; my pet owl Eule, flying silently out of the dark to land on my windowsill when I called his name; I had to leave him behind when I went to school. My father's horse Conquest, breathing sweet hay-breath into my neck as I reached up and stroked him behind his ear. My sense of betrayal, of treachery in my little sister, as she wheedled and simpered with our Stepmother. Stepmother's cold grey eyes turned on me.

The pains are worse now and more frequent. Frau Wischnau tells me to get up and walk about, and helps me to my feet. My past life recedes into mist. I can do nothing but concentrate on this, on atoning, as Martin would have it, for Eve's transgressions. I have watched cows calving and mares foaling and goats giving birth; they all suffer, as we must. Forget about Eve, this is what happens to any mothers to be. I must labour with all my might to bring a new life into the world.

It is June 7th. I am alone in my bed. They have left me to sleep. But I am not alone. A little bundle lies beside me in the carved oak crib, wrapped up like a sausage in white cloth. Swaddled. I lean down and grab it inexpertly, pull it up onto the bed in front of me. The swaddling has come loose; the whole bundle is unravelling. I try to wrap it up again, but I'm clumsy and ham-fisted. So I pick it up anyway and clasp this creature awkwardly to my breast. Oh yes, untie your nightgown first. Try again. He's no fool, he knows exactly what to do. He latches onto my nipple and my breasts swell up, brimming over in response to him. The baby clamps on with primeval power and sucks and sucks. My milk flows. And I weep. Warm sweet milk, hot salt tears. I am the centre of the world. I am my mother, my grandmother, my great grandmother, in a chain of mother–child–mother–child stretching back into a time when our language was quite other. Only two words: *Mother and Milk*. When people did not read or write.

I am a mother. A joy such as I have never felt flows through my veins, from the top of my head to the tips of my toes. Never have I been so happy. No, more than happy, I am triumphant. My son lies in my arms, his perfect little nose and mouth and tiny hands, with nails already a little too long. I look into his eyes, a milky blue, and they already have something knowing about them. But when he cries his face screws up and he looks tragic, as if he knew all the misery of the world; I cradle him and put him to my breast as once Our Lady did to Jesus, and he sucks. I still his crying. My power is absolute.

Martin baptised him within an hour of his birth; we have called him Johannes, or Hans, after Martin's father, and after mine too. Dr Luther is overjoyed. I have made him a father. He wanted a son and I have given him one.

My husband has achieved so much; he has instigated a Reformation, as he puts it, that will make the Pope's ears ring and many hearts burst. But he can never, as I have done, bring a child into the light. He once called his September Bible his first-born. Now he has a real first-born, little Johannes Luther.

My book is complete; I will write no more now. My son lies swaddled in my arms. His lusty cries fill our bed-room. Surely the whole of Wittenberg must hear him! The church bells are ringing joyfully, is it because Martin Luther has a healthy son?

But in my heart two simple words ring out their own sweet refrain: Mother and Milk. *Mutter und Milch.*

Acknowledgements

I have to thank a great many people for their encouragement in not only researching and writing the book in the first place, but persuading me to follow through to publication in time for the 2017 Reformation Anniversary.

In particular I must mention the following: David Simpson, who read each chapter as it emerged and advised me on theological matters. My daughters Elly and Laura Clarke for their on-going support; my son-in-law Toby Fisher for suggesting where to inject more drama into the story. Three German friends, Marianne Ufer, Paul Kremmel and Sibby Ruschmeier for their feedback and cultural tips; Dick and Janet Lewis of the Anglican Lutheran Society. Celia Catchpole, for her advice about the publishing world; Ronald Blythe for his interest, and for writing the Foreword; Sister Angela Morris for her advice on life in a convent; Michael Hughes for his careful edit and suggestions; my publishers at Clink Street. And finally, all those friends who listened to me going on about the Reformation in Germany, and urged me to pursue publication when I was losing heart: Meriel Baker, Rosemary Morris, Sarah Crofton, Emily Jones, Kate Knowles, Charles and Sophie Campbell and others. Without them Katharina would never have come to print.